WESTFIELD MEMORIAL LIBRARY
WESTFIELD, NEW

W9-DFM-365

WESTFIELD MEMORIAL LIBRARY
WESTFIELD, NEW JERSEY

AND

OTHER STORIES

WESTFIELD MEMORIAL LIBRARY
WESTFIELD, NEW JERSEY

TERRY BISSON

BEARS DISCOVER FIRE

AND
OTHER STORIES

TOR®

A TOM DOHERTY ASSOCIATES BOOK
NEW YORK

SF
Bis

This is a work of fiction. All the characters and events portrayed in this book are fictitious, and any resemblance to real people or events is purely coincidental.

BEARS DISCOVER FIRE

Copyright © 1993 by Terry Bisson

All rights reserved, including the right to reproduce this book, or portions thereof, in any form.

This book is printed on acid-free paper.

A Tor Book
Published by Tom Doherty Associates, Inc.
175 Fifth Avenue
New York, N.Y. 10010

Tor® is a registered trademark of Tom Doherty Associates, Inc.

Edited by David G. Hartwell
Design by Lynn Newmark

Library of Congress Cataloging-in-Publication Data

Bisson, Terry.
      Bears discover fire / Terry Bisson.
            p. cm.
      "A Tom Doherty Associates book."
      ISBN 0-312-85411-0
      I. Title.
  PS3552.I7736B4   1993
  813'.54—dc20   93-26550
                                    CIP

First edition: November 1993

Printed in the United States of America

0 9 8 7 6 5 4 3 2 1

WESTFIELD MEMORIAL LIBRARY
WESTFIELD, NEW JERSEY

For my children:
Nathaniel, Peter, Zoë, Kristen,
Gabriel, Welcome

WESTFIELD MEMORIAL LIBRARY
WESTFIELD, NEW JERSEY

✦ PERMISSIONS ✦

All stories are reprinted by permission of the author and the author's agent, Susan Ann Protter.

"Bears Discover Fire," copyright © 1990 by Davis Publications. First published in *Isaac Asimov's Science Fiction Magazine,* August 1990.

"The Two Janets," copyright © 1990 by Davis Publications. First published in *Isaac Asimov's Science Fiction Magazine,* November 1990.

"They're Made Out of Meat," copyright © 1991 by Omni Publication International, Ltd. First published in *Omni,* April 1991.

"Over Flat Mountain," copyright © 1990 by Omni Publication International, Ltd. First published in *Omni,* June 1990.

"Press Ann," copyright © 1991 by Davis Publications. First published in *Isaac Asimov's Science Fiction Magazine,* August 1991.

"The Coon Suit," copyright © 1991 by Mercury Press, Inc. First published in *The Magazine of Fantasy and Science Fiction,* May 1991.

"George," copyright © 1993 by Terry Bisson. First published in *Pulphouse,* October 1993.

"Next," copyright © 1992 by Mercury Press, Inc. First published in *The Magazine of Fantasy and Science Fiction,* May 1992.

"Necronauts," copyright © 1993 by Playboy. First published in *Playboy,* July 1993.

"Are There Any Questions?" copyright © 1992 by *Interzone,* August 1992.

"Two Guys from the Future," copyright © 1992 by Omni Publication International, Ltd. First published in *Omni,* August 1992.

"The Toxic Donut," copyright © 1993 by Terry Bisson. First published in *Science Fiction Age,* June 1993.

8 ✧ PERMISSIONS ✧

"Canción Auténtica de Old Earth," copyright © 1992 by Mercury Press, Inc. First published in *The Magazine of Fantasy and Science Fiction*, October/November 1992.

"Partial People," copyright © 1993 by Terry Bisson, Inc. First published in *The Magazine of Fantasy and Science Fiction*, December 1993.

"Carl's Lawn & Garden," copyright © 1992 by Omni Publication International, Ltd. First published in *Omni*, January 1992.

"The Message," copyright © 1993 by Bantam Doubleday Dell Magazines. First published in *Isaac Asimov's Science Fiction Magazine*, October 1993.

"England Underway," copyright © 1993 by Omni Publication International, Ltd. First published in *Omni*, July 1993.

"By Permit Only," copyright © 1992 by *Interzone*. First published in *Interzone*, July 1993.

"The Shadow Knows," copyright © 1993 by Bantam Doubleday Dell Magazines. First published in *Isaac Asimov's Science Fiction Magazine*, September 1993.

WESTFIELD MEMORIAL LIBRARY
WESTFIELD, NEW JERSEY

✦ Contents ✦

Bears Discover Fire	11
The Two Janets	24
They're Made Out of Meat	34
Over Flat Mountain	38
Press Ann	55
The Coon Suit	64
George	68
Next	78
Necronauts	88
Are There Any Questions?	121
Two Guys from the Future	127
The Toxic Donut	142
Canción Auténtica de Old Earth	147
Partial People	152
Carl's Lawn & Garden	155
The Message	167
England Underway	172
By Permit Only	199
The Shadow Knows	206
Afterword	251

❦ BEARS DISCOVER FIRE ❦

I WAS DRIVING with my brother, the preacher, and my nephew, the preacher's son, on I-65 just north of Bowling Green when we got a flat. It was Sunday night and we had been to visit Mother at the Home. We were in my car. The flat caused what you might call knowing groans since, as the old-fashioned one in my family (so they tell me), I fix my own tires, and my brother is always telling me to get radials and quit buying old tires.

But if you know how to mount and fix tires yourself, you can pick them up for almost nothing.

Since it was a left rear tire, I pulled over to the left, onto the median grass. The way my Caddy stumbled to a stop, I figured the tire was ruined. "I guess there's no need asking if you have any of that FlatFix in the trunk," said Wallace.

"Here, son, hold the light," I said to Wallace Jr. He's old enough to want to help and not old enough (yet) to think he knows it all. If I'd married and had kids, he's the kind I'd have wanted.

An old Caddy has a big trunk that tends to fill up like a shed. Mine's a '56. Wallace was wearing his Sunday shirt, so he didn't offer to help while I pulled magazines, fishing tackle, a wooden tool box, some old clothes, a comealong wrapped in a grass sack, and a tobacco sprayer out of the way, looking for my jack. The spare looked a little soft.

The light went out. "Shake it, son," I said.

It went back on. The bumper jack was long gone, but I carry a little quarter-ton hydraulic. I found it under Mother's old *Southern Living*s, 1978–1986. I had been meaning to drop them at the dump. If Wallace hadn't been along, I'd have let Wallace Jr. position the jack under the axle, but I got on my knees and did it myself. There's nothing wrong with a boy learning to change a tire. Even if you're not going to fix and mount them, you're still going to have to change a few in this life. The light went off again before I had the wheel off the ground. I was surprised at how dark the night was already. It was late October and beginning to get cool. "Shake it again, son," I said.

It went back on but it was weak. Flickery.

"With radials you just don't *have* flats," Wallace explained in that voice he uses when he's talking to a number of people at once; in this case, Wallace Jr. and myself. "And even when you *do*, you just squirt them with this stuff called FlatFix and you just drive on. Three ninety-five the can."

"Uncle Bobby can fix a tire hisself," said Wallace Jr., out of loyalty, I presume.

"*Him*self," I said from halfway under the car. If it was up to Wallace, the boy would talk like what Mother used to call "a helot from the gorges of the mountains." But drive on radials.

"Shake that light again," I said. It was about gone. I spun the lugs off into the hubcap and pulled the wheel. The tire had blown out along the sidewall. "Won't be fixing this one," I said. Not that I cared. I have a pile as tall as a man out by the barn.

The light went out again, then came back better than ever as I was fitting the spare over the lugs. "Much better," I said. There was a flood of dim orange flickery light. But when I turned to find the lug nuts, I was surprised to see that the flashlight the boy was holding was dead. The light was coming from two bears at the edge of the trees, holding torches. They were big, three-hundred-pounders, standing about five feet tall. Wallace Jr. and his father had seen them and were standing perfectly still. It's best not to alarm bears.

I fished the lug nuts out of the hubcap and spun them on. I usually like to put a little oil on them, but this time I let it go. I reached under the car and let the jack down and pulled it out. I was relieved to see that the spare was high enough to drive on. I put the jack and the lug wrench and the flat into the trunk. Instead of replacing the hubcap, I put it in there too. All this time, the bears never made a move. They just held the torches, whether out of curiosity or helpfulness, there was no way of knowing. It looked like there may have been more bears behind them, in the trees.

Opening three doors at once, we got into the car and drove off. Wallace was the first to speak. "Looks like bears have discovered fire," he said.

When we first took Mother to the Home almost four years (forty-seven months) ago, she told Wallace and me she was ready to die. "Don't worry about me, boys," she whispered, pulling us both down so the nurse wouldn't hear. "I've drove a million miles and I'm ready to pass over to the other shore. I won't have long to linger here." She drove a consolidated school bus for thirty-nine years. Later, after Wallace left, she told me about her dream. A bunch of doctors were sitting around in a circle discussing her case. One said, "We've done all we can for her, boys, let's let her go." They all turned their hands up and smiled. When she didn't die that fall she seemed disappointed, though as spring came she forgot about it, as old people will.

In addition to taking Wallace and Wallace Jr. to see Mother on Sunday nights, I go myself on Tuesdays and

Thursdays. I usually find her sitting in front of the TV, even though she doesn't watch it. The nurses keep it on all the time. They say the old folks like the flickering. It soothes them down.

"What's this I hear about bears discovering fire?" she said on Tuesday. "It's true," I told her as I combed her long white hair with the shell comb Wallace had brought her from Florida. Monday there had been a story in the Louisville *Courier-Journal,* and Tuesday one on NBC or CBS *Nightly News.* People were seeing bears all over the state, and in Virginia as well. They had quit hibernating, and were apparently planning to spend the winter in the medians of the interstates. There have always been bears in the mountains of Virginia, but not here in western Kentucky, not for almost a hundred years. The last one was killed when Mother was a girl. The theory in the *Courier-Journal* was that they were following 1-65 down from the forests of Michigan and Canada, but one old man from Allen County (interviewed on nationwide TV) said that there had always been a few bears left back in the hills, and they had come out to join the others now that they had discovered fire.

"They don't hibernate anymore," I said. "They make a fire and keep it going all winter."

"I declare," Mother said. "What'll they think of next!" The nurse came to take her tobacco away, which is the signal for bedtime.

Every October, Wallace Jr. stays with me while his parents go to camp. I realize how backward that sounds, but there it is. My brother is a Minister (House of the Righteous Way, Reformed) but he makes two thirds of his living in real estate. He and Elizabeth go to a Christian Success Retreat in South Carolina, where people from all over the country practice selling things to one another. I know what it's like not because they've ever bothered to tell me, but because I've seen the Revolving Equity Success Plan ads late at night on TV.

The school bus let Wallace Jr. off at my house on Wednesday, the day they left. The boy doesn't have to pack much of a bag when he stays with me. He has his own room here. As the eldest of our family, I hung on to the old home place near Smiths Grove. It's getting run-down, but Wallace Jr. and I don't mind. He has his own room in Bowling Green, too, but since Wallace and Elizabeth move to a different house every three months (part of the Plan), he keeps his .22 and his comics, the stuff that's important to a boy his age, in his room here at the home place. It's the room his dad and I used to share.

Wallace Jr. is twelve. I found him sitting on the back porch that overlooks the interstate when I got home from work. I sell crop insurance.

After I changed clothes I showed him how to break the bead on a tire two ways, with a hammer, and by backing a car over it. Like making sorghum, fixing tires by hand is a dying art. The boy caught on fast, though. "Tomorrow I'll show you how to mount your tire with the hammer and a tire iron," I said.

"What I wish is I could see the bears," he said. He was looking across the field to I-65, where the northbound lanes cut off the corner of our field. From the house at night, sometimes the traffic sounds like a waterfall.

"Can't see their fire in the daytime," I said. "But wait till tonight." That night CBS or NBC (I forget which is which) did a special on the bears, which were becoming a story of nationwide interest. They were seen in Kentucky, West Virginia, Missouri, Illinois (southern), and, of course, Virginia. There have always been bears in Virginia. Some characters there were even talking about hunting them. A scientist said they were heading into the states where there is some snow but not too much, and where there is enough timber in the medians for firewood. He had gone in with a video camera, but his shots were just blurry figures sitting around a fire. Another scientist said the bears were attracted by the berries on a new bush that grew only in the medians of the interstates. He claimed this berry was the first new species in recent history, brought about by the mixing of seeds along the highway. He ate one on TV, making a face, and called it a "newberry." A climatic ecologist said that the warm winters (there was no snow last winter in Nashville, and only one flurry in Louisville) had changed the bears' hibernation cycle, and now they were able to remember things from year to year. "Bears may have discovered fire centuries ago," he said, "but forgot it." Another theory was that they had discovered (or remembered) fire when Yellowstone burned, several years ago.

The TV showed more guys talking about bears than it showed bears, and Wallace Jr. and I lost interest. After the supper dishes were done I took the boy out behind the house and down to our fence. Across the interstate and through the trees, we could see the light of the bears' fire. Wallace Jr. wanted to go back to the house and get his .22 and go shoot one, and I explained why that would be wrong. "Besides," I said, "a twenty-two wouldn't do much more to a bear than make it mad.

"Besides," I added, "it's illegal to hunt in the medians."

The only trick to mounting a tire by hand, once you have beaten or pried it onto the rim, is setting the bead. You do this by setting the tire upright, sitting on it, and bouncing it up and down between your legs while the air goes in. When the bead sets on the rim, it makes a satisfying "pop." On Thursday, I kept Wallace Jr. home from school and showed him how to do this until he got it right. Then we climbed our fence and crossed the field to get a look at the bears.

In northern Virginia, according to *Good Morning Amer-*

ica, the bears were keeping their fires going all day long. Here in western Kentucky, though, it was still warm for late October and they only stayed around the fires at night. Where they went and what they did in the daytime, I don't know. Maybe they were watching from the newberry bushes as Wallace Jr. and I climbed the government fence and crossed the northbound lanes. I carried an axe and Wallace Jr. brought his .22, not because he wanted to kill a bear but because a boy likes to carry some kind of a gun. The median was all tangled with brush and vines under the maples, oaks, and sycamores. Even though we were only a hundred yards from the house, I had never been there, and neither had anyone else that I knew of. It was like a created country. We found a path in the center and followed it down across a slow, short stream that flowed out of one grate and into another. The tracks in the gray mud were the first bear signs we saw. There was a musty, but not really unpleasant smell. In a clearing under a big hollow beech, where the fire had been, we found nothing but ashes. Logs were drawn up in a rough circle and the smell was stronger. I stirred the ashes and found enough coals to start a new flame, so I banked them back the way they had been left.

I cut a little firewood and stacked it to one side, just to be neighborly.

Maybe the bears were watching us from the bushes even then. There's no way to know. I tasted one of the newberries and spit it out. It was so sweet it was sour, just the sort of thing you would imagine a bear would like.

That evening after supper I asked Wallace Jr. if he might want to go with me to visit Mother. I wasn't surprised when he said yes. Kids have more consideration than folks give them credit for. We found her sitting on the concrete front porch of the Home, watching the cars go by on I-65. The nurse said she had been agitated all day. I wasn't surprised by that, either. Every fall as the leaves change, she gets restless, maybe the word is "hopeful," again. I brought her into the dayroom and combed her long white hair. "Nothing but bears on TV anymore," the nurse complained, flipping the channels. Wallace Jr. picked up the remote after the nurse left, and we watched a CBS or NBC Special Report about some hunters in Virginia who had gotten their houses torched. The TV interviewed a hunter and his wife whose $117,500 Shenandoah Valley home had burned. She blamed the bears. He didn't blame the bears, but he was suing for compensation from the state since he had a valid hunting license. The state hunting commissioner came on and said that possession of a hunting license didn't prohibit ("enjoin," I think, was the word he used) *the hunted* from striking back. I thought that was a pretty liberal view for a state commissioner. Of course, he had a vested interest in not paying off. I'm not a hunter myself.

"Don't bother coming on Sunday," Mother told Wallace Jr. with a wink. "I've drove a million miles and I've got one hand on the gate." I'm used to her saying stuff like that, especially in the fall, but I was afraid it would upset the boy. In fact, he looked worried after we left and I asked him what was wrong.

"How could she have drove a million miles?" he asked. She had told him forty-eight miles a day for thirty-nine years, and he had worked it out on his calculator to be 336,960 miles.

"Have *driven,*" I said. "And it's forty-eight in the morning and forty-eight in the afternoon. Plus there were the football trips. Plus, old folks exaggerate a little." Mother was the first woman school-bus driver in the state. She did it every day and raised a family, too. Dad just farmed.

I usually get off the interstate at Smiths Grove, but that night I drove north all the way to Horse Cave and doubled back so

Wallace Jr. and I could see the bears' fires. There were not as many as you would think from the TV—one every six or seven miles, hidden back in a clump of trees or under a rocky ledge. Probably they look for water as well as wood. Wallace Jr. wanted to stop, but it's against the law to stop on the interstate and I was afraid the state police would run us off.

There was a card from Wallace in the mailbox. He and Elizabeth were doing fine and having a wonderful time. Not a word about Wallace Jr., but the boy didn't seem to mind. Like most kids his age, he doesn't really enjoy going places with his parents.

On Saturday afternoon the Home called my office (Burley Belt Drought & Hail) and left word that Mother was gone. I was on the road. I work Saturdays. It's the only day a lot of part-time farmers are home. My heart literally missed a beat when I called in and got the message, but only a beat. I had long been prepared. "It's a blessing," I said when I got the nurse on the phone.

"You don't understand," the nurse said. "Not *passed* away, gone. *Ran* away, gone. Your mother has escaped." Mother had gone through the door at the end of the corridor when no one was looking, wedging the door with her comb and taking a bedspread which belonged to the Home. What about her tobacco? I asked. It was gone. That was a sure sign she was planning to stay away. I was in Franklin, and it took me less than an hour to get to the Home on I-65. The nurse told me that Mother had been acting more and more confused lately. Of course they are going to say that. We looked around the grounds, which is only a half acre with no trees between the interstate and a soybean field. Then they had me leave a message at the sheriff's office. I would have to keep paying for her care until she was officially listed as Missing, which would be Monday.

It was dark by the time I got back to the house, and Wallace Jr. was fixing supper. This just involves opening a few cans, already selected and grouped together with a rubber band. I told him his grandmother had gone, and he nodded, saying, "She told us she would be." I called Florida and left a message. There was nothing more to be done. I sat down and tried to watch TV, but there was nothing on. Then, I looked out the back door, and saw the firelight twinkling through the trees across the northbound lane of I-65, and realized I just might know where to find her.

It was definitely getting colder, so I got my jacket. I told the boy to wait by the phone in case the sheriff called, but when I looked back, halfway across the field, there he was behind me. He didn't have a jacket. I let him catch up. He was carrying his .22 and I made him leave it leaning against our fence. It was harder climbing the government fence in the dark, at my age, than it had been in the daylight. I am sixty-one. The highway was busy with cars heading south and trucks heading north.

Crossing the shoulder, I got my pants cuffs wet on the long grass, already wet with dew. It is actually bluegrass.

The first few feet into the trees it was pitch-black and the boy grabbed my hand. Then it got lighter. At first I thought it was the moon, but it was the high beams shining like moonlight into the treetops, allowing Wallace Jr. and me to pick our way through the brush. We soon found the path and its familiar bear smell.

I was wary of approaching the bears at night. If we stayed on the path we might run into one in the dark, but if we went through the bushes we might be seen as intruders. I wondered if maybe we shouldn't have brought the gun.

We stayed on the path. The light seemed to drip down from the canopy of the woods like rain. The going was easy, especially if we didn't try to look at the path but let our feet find their own way.

Then through the trees I saw their fire.

* * *

The fire was mostly of sycamore and beech branches, the kind that puts out very little heat or light and lots of smoke. The bears hadn't learned the ins and outs of wood yet. They did okay at tending it, though. A large cinnamon-brown northern-looking bear was poking the fire with a stick, adding a branch now and then from a pile at his side. The others sat around in a loose circle on the logs. Most were smaller black or honey bears, one was a mother with cubs. Some were eating berries from a hubcap. Not eating, but just watching the fire, my mother sat among them with the bedspread from the Home around her shoulders.

If the bears noticed us, they didn't let on. Mother patted a spot right next to her on the log and I sat down. A bear moved over to let Wallace Jr. sit on her other side.

The bear smell is rank but not unpleasant, once you get used to it. It's not like a barn smell, but wilder. I leaned over to whisper something to Mother and she shook her head. *It would be rude to whisper around these creatures that don't possess the power of speech,* she let me know without speaking. Wallace Jr. was silent too. Mother shared the bedspread with us and we sat for what seemed hours, looking into the fire.

The big bear tended the fire, breaking up the dry branches by holding one end and stepping on them, like people do. He was good at keeping it going at the same level. Another bear poked the fire from time to time but the others left it alone. It looked like only a few of the bears knew how to use fire, and were carrying the others along. But isn't that how it is with everything? Every once in a while, a smaller bear walked into the circle of firelight with an armload of wood and dropped it onto the pile. Median wood has a silvery cast, like driftwood.

Wallace Jr. isn't fidgety like a lot of kids. I found it pleasant to sit and stare into the fire. I took a little piece of Mother's Red Man, though I don't generally chew. It was no different from visiting her at the Home, only more interesting, because of the bears. There were about eight or ten of them. Inside the fire itself, things weren't so dull, either: little dramas were being played out as fiery chambers were created and then destroyed in a crashing of sparks. My imagination ran wild. I looked around the circle at the bears and wondered what *they* saw. Some had their eyes closed. Though they were gathered together, their spirits still seemed solitary, as if each bear was sitting alone in front of its own fire.

The hubcap came around and we all took some newberries. I don't know about Mother, but I just pretended to eat mine. Wallace Jr. made a face and spit his out. When he went to sleep, I wrapped the bedspread around all three of us. It was getting colder and we were not provided, like the bears, with fur. I was ready to go home, but not Mother. She pointed up toward the canopy of trees, where a light was spreading, and then pointed to herself. Did she think it was angels approaching from on high? It was only the high beams of some southbound truck, but she seemed mighty pleased. Holding her hand, I felt it grow colder and colder in mine.

Wallace Jr. woke me up by tapping on my knee. It was past dawn, and his grandmother had died sitting on the log between us. The fire was banked up and the bears were gone and someone was crashing straight through the woods, ignoring the path. It was Wallace. Two state troopers were right behind him. He was wearing a white shirt, and I realized it was Sunday morning. Underneath his sadness on learning of Mother's death, he looked peeved.

The troopers were sniffing the air and nodding. The bear smell was still strong. Wallace and I wrapped Mother in the bedspread and started with her body back out to the highway. The troopers stayed behind and scattered the bears' fire ashes and flung their firewood away into the bushes. It seemed a petty thing to do. They were like bears themselves, each one solitary in his own uniform.

There was Wallace's Olds 98 on the median, with its radial tires looking squashed on the grass. In front of it there was a police car with a trooper standing beside it, and behind it a funeral home hearse, also an Olds 98.

"First report we've had of them bothering old folks," the trooper said to Wallace. "That's not hardly what happened at all," I said, but nobody asked me to explain. They have their own procedures. Two men in suits got out of the hearse and opened the rear door. That to me was the point at which Mother departed this life. After we put her in, I put my arms around the boy. He was shivering even though it wasn't that cold. Sometimes death will do that, especially at dawn, with the police around and the grass wet, even when it comes as a friend.

We stood for a minute watching the cars and trucks pass. "It's a blessing," Wallace said. It's surprising how much traffic there is at 6:22 A.M.

That afternoon, I went back to the median and cut a little firewood to replace what the troopers had flung away. I could see the fire through the trees that night.

I went back two nights later, after the funeral. The fire was going and it was the same bunch of bears, as far as I could tell. I sat around with them a while but it seemed to make them nervous, so I went home. I had taken a handful of newberries from the hubcap, and on Sunday I went with the boy and arranged them on Mother's grave. I tried again, but it's no use, you can't eat them.

Unless you're a bear.

❧ THE TWO JANETS ❧

I'M NOT ONE of those people who thinks you have to read a book to get something out of it. You can learn a lot about a book by picking it up, turning it over, rubbing the cover, riffling the pages open and shut. Especially if it's been read enough times before, it'll speak to you.

This is why I like to hang around used-book stores on my lunch hour. I was at the outdoor bookstall on the west side of Union Square, the one that opens out of huge crates, when my mother called. It is tempting here to claim to remember that I was looking at an old paperback of, say, *Rabbit Run*, but actually it was Henry Gregor Felsen's *Hot Rod*, the cover telling the whole story through the hairdos.

The pay phone on the corner nearest Sixteenth Street was ringing and wouldn't stop. Finally, I picked it up and said, "Hello? Mother?"

"Janet? Is that you?" My mother has this uncanny, really, ability to call on pay phones and get me. She does it about once a month.

Well, of course it was me: otherwise, would I have answered "Mother"? "Did you have trouble finding me?" I asked.

"If you only knew. I called three phones, and the last two you wouldn't believe." It doesn't always work.

"So how's everything?" I asked. It came out "everthang." My accent, which I have managed to moderate, always reemerges when I talk with anybody from home.

"Fine." She told me about Alan, my ex-fiancé, and Janet, my best friend. They used to call us the Two Janets. Mother keeps up with my old high school friends, most of whom are of course still in Owensboro. Then she said: "Guess what. John Updike just moved to Owensboro."

"John Updike?"

"The writer. *Rabbit Run?* It was about a week ago. He bought a house out on Maple Drive, across from the hospital there."

"This was in the paper?"

"No, of course not. I'm sure he wants his privacy. I heard it from Elizabeth Dorsey, your old music teacher. Her oldest daughter, Mary Beth, is married to Sweeney Kost Junior who sells real estate with that new group out on Leitchfield Road. She called to tell me because she thought you might be interested."

It is well-known that I have an interest in literature. I came to New York to get a job in publishing. My roommate already has one at S&S (Simon and Schuster) and I called her before I went back to work. She doesn't go to lunch until two. She hadn't heard anything about John Updike moving to Owensboro, but she checked *PW (Publishers Weekly)* and found an item saying that John Updike had sold his house in Massachusetts and moved to a small Midwestern city.

That bothered me. Owensboro sits right across the river from Indiana, but it's still the South, not the Midwest. The northernmost statue to Confederate heroes sits on the courthouse lawn. I'm not touchy about that stuff but some people are. Then I thought that if you just looked at a map, as they might have done fact-checking at the *PW* office, or as Updike himself might have done, looking for a new place to live, you might think Owensboro was in the Midwest since it's much closer to St. Louis than to Atlanta. Then I thought, maybe Updike was just saying "Midwest" to throw people off. Maybe he was, like Salinger, trying to get away from the world. Then I thought, maybe he didn't move to Owensboro at all, and the whole thing was just a mistake, a coincidence, a wild flight of fancy. The more I thought about this theory, the better I liked it. "Small city in the Midwest" could mean Iowa City, where a well-known writer's workshop is held; or any one of a hundred college towns like Crawfordsville, Indiana (Wabash); Gambier, Ohio (Kenyon); or Yellow Springs, Ohio (Antioch). Or even Indianapolis or Cincinnati. To a New Yorker, and all writers, even when they live in Massachusetts, they are New Yorkers (in a way); Indianapolis and Cincinnati are small cities. Or if you wanted to get really close to home there is Evansville, Indiana, at 130,500 definitely a "small city" (Owensboro at 52,000 is only barely a city) and one that might even attract a writer like John Updike.

With all this, I was eleven minutes late getting back to work. But what are they going to do, fire a temp?

That was on Thursday, May 18. I had the usual weekend, and on Monday night, right after the rates changed, Alan, my ex-fiancé, made his weekly call. "Found a job yet?" he asked (knowing he would have heard from my mother if I had). Then he added, "Did you hear Saul Bellow moved to Owensboro?"

"You mean John Updike," I said.

"No, that was last week. Saul Bellow moved here just yesterday." Alan runs two of his father's four liquor stores. He and I still share an interest in books and literature.

"How could that be?" I said. I would have thought he was making it up but Alan, to his credit (I guess), never makes things up.

I thought about calling Janet but I am always calling her,

so the next morning I called Mother from work. I was temping for an insurance adjuster with a WATS line. "Mother, did Saul Bellow move to Owensboro?" I asked, getting right to the point.

"Well, yes, dear, he did. He's living out in those apartments on Scherm Road. The ones where Wallace Carter Cox and Loreena Dyson lived right after he got his divorce."

"Why didn't you tell me?"

"Well, you didn't seem very excited when John Updike moved here, dear, so I thought you didn't much care. You have made a new life for yourself in New York, after all."

I let that go. "It sure is mighty nice of you to keep up with where everybody lives," I joked.

"When a famous person moves to a town like this," she said, "everybody notices."

I wondered about that. I didn't think people in Owensboro, outside of Alan, even knew who Saul Bellow was. I'll bet not twenty people there have read his books. I have only read one, the most recent one. The other Janet reads only nonfiction.

The next week Philip Roth moved to Owensboro. I found out from Janet, who called me, a new thing for her since it's usually me who puts out the effort, not to mention the money, to stay in touch.

"Guess who we saw in the mall today," she said. "Philip Roth."

"Are you sure? How did you know?" I asked. I couldn't imagine her recognizing Philip Roth.

"Your mother pointed him out. She recognized his face from a story in *People* magazine. I'm not sure he would be considered handsome if he wasn't a famous writer."

"Wait a minute," I said. "Was he just visiting or has he moved to Owensboro too? And what mall are you talking about?"

"What mall!" Janet said. "There's only one, out Livermore Road. It's so far out of town that hardly anybody ever goes out there. I couldn't believe it when we saw Philip Roth out there.''

"What were you doing out at the mall with my mother?'' I asked. "Is she bothering you again?''

"She gets a little lonesome. I go by and see her, and maybe we go shopping or something. Is that a crime?''

"Of course not,'' I said. I'm glad my mother has friends. I just wish they weren't my best friends, with the same name as me.

Mother called me at work the next day. I have asked her not to do this when I am temping, but sometimes she can't make the pay-phone thing work. Most companies don't like for temps to get calls, even from family. E. L. Doctorow had moved to Owensboro and was staying in Dr. Crippen's house on Wildwood Drive, only two blocks away.

"He has a little beard,'' Mother said, "He has a little dog and walks it regularly every day. He's renting the house while Dr. Crippen and his wife are in Michigan.''

"So he hasn't exactly *moved* to Owensboro,'' I said, somehow relieved.

"Well, he's out here every morning,'' she said, "walking his dog. Call it whatever you want to.''

I know the house very well. The Crippens are not ostentatiously tacky the way some (indeed, most) doctors are. It was the Crippens who had encouraged me to go ahead and move to New York if that was what I wanted, when everybody else in my class was getting married. It's not an older home, of the kind I prefer, but if you had to live in a suburban-style house, theirs would do.

All day I imagined E. L. Doctorow watering the plants and looking through Dr. and Dr. (they are both doctors) Crippen's books. They have the most books of anybody in Owensboro. The next day at lunch I went to Barnes and Noble and looked through Doctorow's novels in paperback. All together they made a neat little stack the size of a shoebox.

I decided I was glad he had moved to Owensboro.

It's hard to make friends in New York. I wondered what it was like in Owensboro for famous writers. Did they ever meet? Did they know one another? Did they pay visits, talk shop, drink together? I asked Alan when he called Monday night (right after the rates changed) but he seemed embarrassed by the question.

"Apparently, they have all moved here independently," he said. "They're never seen together. I wouldn't want to speculate."

When William Styron moved to Owensboro the last day in May, I wasn't so surprised. At least he was from the South, although two more different regions than the lower Ohio Valley and the Tidewater of Virginia could hardly be imagined. May and even June are nice in Owensboro, but July and August were coming, and when I thought of Styron blinking in the fierce muggy heat, he seemed even more out of place than the urban Jewish writers like Roth, Doctorow, and Bellow. And Updike, a New Englander! I felt sorry for them all. But that was silly. Every place now has air-conditioning.

When I called Janet, she reminded me that Mother's birthday was coming up. I knew I was expected to fly home. Janet told me all about how she and Alan were planning to take her out to dinner. This was to make me feel guilty. I wasn't planning to fall for it like I did last year, at the last minute.

It is very hard to make friends in New York. My roommate and her ex-roommate had shares in a house in the Hamptons (well, almost the Hamptons) and I had been invited out for the weekend. "You can't go home for your mother's birthday every year," I tell myself.

Mother called me a few days later—a pay phone again, this one near a deli on Thirty-ninth Street where she had gotten me once before—to announce that J. D. Salinger had moved to Owensboro.

"Wait a minute," I said. This was getting out of hand. "How come no women writers ever move to Owensboro? What about Ann Tyler? Or Alice Walker? Or Bobbie Ann Mason, who is actually from Mayfield (not that far away)? How come they're all men, and all these old guys?"

"I suppose you expect me to ask them that!" Mother said. "I only found out the author of *Catcher in the Rye* moved here because Mr. Roth told Reverend Curtis."

"Mr. Roth?" So now it was "Mr." Roth.

"Philip Roth, *Goodbye, Columbus?* He's renting Reverend Curtis's son Wallace's house out on Livermore Road, and you know how Reverend Curtis won't take checks, and they saw this strange-looking man at the cash machine, and Mr. Roth whispers, 'That's J. D. Salinger. *Catcher in the Rye?*' Alan said he looked like some hillbilly in town from Ohio County."

"How did Alan get into this?"

"He was standing in line behind them at the cash machine," Mother said. "He just happened to overhear."

On Monday night, Alan told me Philip Roth had seemed as surprised as the rest of them to see J. D. Salinger in Owensboro.

"Maybe they had all moved to Owensboro trying to get away from him," I said, trying to be funny.

"I doubt that," Alan said. "Anyway, it's hardly the kind of question you can ask."

It's Mother who should marry Alan, not me. They think exactly alike.

As Mother's birthday approached, I tried to concentrate on my upcoming weekend in the Hamptons. I knew what I had to guard against was the last-minute temptation to fly home.

When I called Janet later in the week from a lawyer's office—they never watch their phone bills—she said, "Do you know the movie *Bright Lights Big City?*"

"Michael J. Fox has moved to Owensboro," I said, astonished in spite of myself.

"Not him, the other one, the author. I forget his name."

"McInerney," I said. "Jay McInerney. Are you sure?" I didn't want to say it because it sounded so snobbish, but Jay McInerney didn't exactly seem Owensboro caliber.

"Of course I'm sure. He looks just like Michael J. Fox. I saw him walking down at that little park by the river. You know, the one where Norman Mailer hangs out."

"Norman Mailer. I didn't even know he lived in Owensboro," I said.

"Why not?" Janet said. "A lot of famous writers make Owensboro their home."

Make Owensboro Their Home. That was the first time I'd heard it said like that. It seemed to make it official.

Janet's call made me think, and for the first time since I broke up with him, I called Alan. At least he knew who Jay McInerney was, although he had never read the book. "The other Janet said she saw McInerney and Mailer down there at the park," I said. "Does that mean the famous writers are starting to meet one another and hang out together?"

"You always want to jump to conclusions," Alan said. "They might have been in the same park at totally different times of the day. Even when they do meet, they don't talk. The other day at the K Mart, Joe Billy Survant saw E. L. Doctorow and John Irving both in Housewares, and they sort of nodded, but that was all."

John Irving? But I let it go. "Housewares," I said instead. "Sounds like folks are really settling in."

"We're taking your mother to dinner at the Executive Inn for her fifty-first birthday Friday night," Alan said.

"I've been invited for a weekend in the Hamptons," I said. "Well, almost the Hamptons."

"Oh, I understand," he said. Alan likes to imagine he understands me. "But if you change your mind I'll pick you up at the airport in Evansville."

Evansville, Indiana, is thirty miles from Owensboro. It used to seem like a big city to me, but after eighteen months in New York, it seemed pathetic and insignificant: all trees from the air, and hardly any traffic. The one-story terminal looks like a shopping-center bank branch. You climb down out of the plane on a ladder.

There was Alan in his sensible-with-a-flair Olds Cutlass Supreme. I felt the usual mixture of warmth and dismay on seeing him. I guess you might call it warm dismay.

"Who's that?" I asked, gesturing toward a bearlike figure at the USAir ticket counter.

Alan whispered, "That's Thomas M. Disch. Science fiction. But quality stuff."

"Science fiction?" But the name was familiar, at least sort of. Although Disch isn't exactly famous, he seemed more the Owensboro type than McInerney. "He's moving to Owensboro, too?"

"How should I know? He may have just been here in Evansville for the speedboat races. Anyway, he's leaving. Let's talk about you."

We drove back home on the Kentucky side of the river, through Henderson.

That whole weekend in Owensboro, I only saw three famous writers, not counting Disch, who is not really famous and who was in Evansville, not Owensboro, anyway. Tom Pynchon was at the take-out counter at the Moonlight, buying barbecued mutton. He bought three liters of Diet Coke, so it looked like he might be having a party, but on the way home from the Executive Inn we drove past his house on Littlewood Drive and it was dark.

For dinner, we had steak and salad. Mother was a hoot. Alan insisted on paying as usual. We were home by ten, and by ten-thirty Mother was asleep in front of the TV. I got two cans of Falls City out of the refrigerator and sneaked her Buick out of the garage. I picked up the other Janet, just like in the old days, by scratching on her screen. "The Two Janets," she whispered melodramatically. She said the cops were rough on DWI (Driving While under the Influence) these days, but I wasn't worried. This was still the South; we were still girls. We cruised down Griffith, out Frederica, down Fourth, down by the river. There was hardly any traffic.

"Has Alan asked you to marry him again?" I asked.

"Not yet."

"Well, if he does, I think you should."

"You mean you wish I would."

The streets were still and dark and empty.

"Sure isn't New York," I sighed.

"Well, nobody can say you haven't given it a shot," the other Janet said.

At midnight we went to the all-night Convenience Mart at Eighteenth and Triplett for two more cans of beer. John Updike was looking through the magazines (even though the little sign says not to). At 12:12 A.M. Joyce Carol Oates came in for a pack of cigarettes, and surprising us both, they left together.

✦ THEY'RE MADE OUT OF MEAT ✦

"THEY'RE MADE OUT of meat."

"Meat?"

"Meat. They're made out of meat."

"Meat?"

"There's no doubt about it. We picked up several from different parts of the planet, took them aboard our recon vessels, and probed them all the way through. They're completely meat."

"That's impossible. What about the radio signals? The messages to the stars?"

"They use the radio waves to talk, but the signals don't come from them. The signals come from machines."

"So who made the machines? That's who we want to contact."

"They made the machines. That's what I'm trying to tell you. Meat made the machines."

"That's ridiculous. How can meat make a machine? You're asking me to believe in sentient meat."

"I'm not asking you, I'm telling you. These creatures are the only sentient race in that sector and they're made out of meat."

"Maybe they're like the orfolei. You know, a carbon-based intelligence that goes through a meat stage."

"Nope. They're born meat and they die meat. We studied them for several of their life spans, which didn't take long. Do you have any idea what's the life span of meat?"

"Spare me. Okay, maybe they're only part meat. You know, like the weddilei. A meat head with an electron plasma brain inside."

"Nope. We thought of that, since they do have meat heads, like the weddilei. But I told you, we probed them. They're meat all the way through."

"No brain?"

"Oh, there's a brain all right. It's just that the brain is *made out of meat!* That's what I've been trying to tell you."

"So . . . what does the thinking?"

"You're not understanding, are you? You're refusing to deal with what I'm telling you. The brain does the thinking. The meat."

"Thinking meat! You're asking me to believe in thinking meat!"

"Yes, thinking meat! Conscious meat! Loving meat. Dreaming meat. The meat is the whole deal! Are you beginning to get the picture or do I have to start all over?"

"Omigod. You're serious, then. They're made out of meat."

"Thank you. Finally. Yes. They are indeed made out of meat. And they've been trying to get in touch with us for almost a hundred of their years."

"Omigod. So what does this meat have in mind?"

"First it wants to talk to us. Then I imagine it wants to explore the Universe, contact other sentiences, swap ideas and information. The usual."

"We're supposed to talk to meat."

"That's the idea. That's the message they're sending out

by radio. 'Hello. Anyone out there. Anybody home.' That sort of thing."

"They actually do talk, then. They use words, ideas, concepts?"

"Oh, yes. Except they do it with meat."

"I thought you just told me they used radio."

"They do, but what do you think is *on* the radio? Meat sounds. You know how when you slap or flap meat, it makes a noise? They talk by flapping their meat at each other. They can even sing by squirting air through their meat."

"Omigod. Singing meat. This is altogether too much. So what do you advise?"

"Officially or unofficially?"

"Both."

"Officially, we are required to contact, welcome, and log in any and all sentient races or multibeings in this quadrant of the Universe, without prejudice, fear, or favor. Unofficially, I advise that we erase the records and forget the whole thing."

"I was hoping you would say that."

"It seems harsh, but there is a limit. Do we really want to make contact with meat?"

"I agree one hundred percent. What's there to say? 'Hello, meat. How's it going?' But will this work? How many planets are we dealing with here?"

"Just one. They can travel to other planets in special meat containers, but they can't live on them. And being meat, they can only travel through C space. Which limits them to the speed of light and makes the possibility of their ever making contact pretty slim. Infinitesimal, in fact."

"So we just pretend there's no one home in the Universe."

"That's it."

"Cruel. But you said it yourself, who wants to meet meat?

And the ones who have been aboard our vessels, the ones you probed? You're sure they won't remember?"

"They'll be considered crackpots if they do. We went into their heads and smoothed out their meat so that we're just a dream to them."

"A dream to meat! How strangely appropriate, that we should be meat's dream."

"And we marked the entire sector *unoccupied.*"

"Good. Agreed, officially and unofficially. Case closed. Any others? Anyone interesting on that side of the galaxy?"

"Yes, a rather shy but sweet hydrogen-core cluster intelligence in a class-nine star in G445 zone. Was in contact two galactic rotations ago, wants to be friendly again."

"They always come around."

"And why not? Imagine how unbearably, how unutterably cold the Universe would be if one were all alone . . ."

✤ OVER FLAT MOUNTAIN ✤

THEY DIDN'T USED to call Louisville the Mile High City. I know because I was raised there, in the old West End, when the Falls of the Ohio were just dry limestone flats bypassed by a canal, and the river was slow and muddy, and the summer nights were warm.

Not anymore, though.

It was chilly for August when I rolled into Louisville from Indianapolis, heading south and east for Charlotte. The icy mist was rising off the falls where they plunge into the gorge. It was too much trouble to dig a flannel shirt out of the back so I bought a sweatshirt in the truck-stop annex, figuring I would give it to Janet or one of the girls later—they wear them like nightgowns—and rolled on out of there without a second piece of pie.

The shirt said "Louisville—Mile High City of the South."

I bought a CD, *50 Truckin' Classics*, forty-nine of which I already had. I have a library of eleven hundred CDs in my cab. Imagine how much space that would have taken in the old days when they were as big as cookies.

I don't generally pick up hitchhikers but I must have felt sorry for this kid. I was an hour south and east of Louisville, just under the cloud shadow, when I saw him standing in the rain by the CRAB ORCHARD COGWAY 40M/64K sign, wearing a black garbage bag for a raincoat, and I figured, what the hell. He looked more than a little wet. It rains six days out of five south of Louisville since the Uplift.

When we Flat Toppers run, we run. I just barely pulled over and was back in low-two before he was up the ladder and through the inside airlock lens, peeling off his garbage bag like a landlobster molting. He couldn't have been more than sixteen. He had greasy blond hair tied back with a rubber band under a Delco cap, and under his garbage bag a windbreaker over a T-shirt. Glad to see he had a coat at least. Boots had "hand-me-down" written all over them. Carried his things in a K Mart plastic bag.

He combed the rain off the bill of his cap with one finger and perched on the edge of the seat until I swept the CDs off the seat into my own hat and dumped them into the glove compartment.

"Nice gun," he said. I had a Brazilian 9 mm in the glove compartment. I closed it.

"Wet out there," he said.

I nodded and popped Ricky Skaggs into the player. I hadn't picked him up for conversation. I picked him up because I'd done some hitchhiking myself at his age. Sixteen going on twenty-one.

"Appreciate your stopping," he said.

"Nice rig," he said.

I was pulling a two-piece articulated, with a Kobo-Jonni. The KJ is an eight-liter steel diesel with that mighty ring that engines used to have before they went to plastic. A lot of guys fall all over the new plastic mills cause they don't need oil, but I like oil. I had built the KJ three times, and was just through breaking in the third set of sleeves. Plastic, you just throw away.

The kid told me his name but I forgot it. "They call me

CD,'' I said. I popped out Ricky and popped in the Hag to show him why.

He had those narrow eyes and sallow skin, like he'd never seen the sun, and if he was from south and east of Louisville he probably hadn't. And I could tell by his accent he was. Listen, I knew this kid. He was me thirty years ago. You narrow up your shoulders and narrow up your eyes, and since everything in the world is new to you, try to look and act like nothing is.

"I'm going up to Hazard," he said.

I had figured that from his being by the cogway sign.

"My pa works up there at the robot train," he said.

"Guess you're going on over Flat Mountain," he said.

Anybody could tell that from my airlocks. He said it as if it was the most natural thing in the world, but it wasn't. Not many trucks go over Flat Mountain. Most just go up the cogway to Hazard and offload for the robot train, and come right back down.

"Well, there it is," he said.

The bottom part of Flat Mountain is the only part most folks ever see. Since it's almost always raining under the cloud shadow, you can almost never see it from more than ten miles away. We were rounding the old Winchester bypass just east of where Lexington used to be, and from there it looks like a wall of logs and trash and rock, running almost straight up into the clouds that are always there at 11,500.

I turned off onto the Crab Orchard feeder road, which follows the front twenty miles south and west, then turns in at a ghost town, Berea, where the wall eases off to a little less than 45 degrees. There were about six trucks ahead of me at the cogway, none of them Flat Toppers. I got in line next to a stream choked with old cars and house pieces. It didn't have a name. Lots of these new rivers don't have names.

While we were in line for the cogway I called Janet and the girls from my cab phone and the kid got out. Maybe he was embarrassed by all the family stuff. I watched him walking up and down under the long board shed trying all the candy bar machines. I moved the truck up ten feet at a time and other trucks pulled in behind me. Gravy Pugh came by in his yellow slicker to clip my ticket. "Going up top?" he asked. "Watch out, CD, lobsters got Sanders yesterday."

This is his standard joke. I don't lobster anymore and he knows it.

"Snapped his pecker off," he said, and clipped another corner off my violet Crab Orchard Cogway pass.

The kid climbed back into the truck just as I was flagged to the approach grade. He was shivering. He had left his garbage bag in the truck and it rains about as hard under the board shed as outside of it. When I was his age I had hitchhiked a thousand miles, but this was out west where it never rained in those days. I let the flagman wait while I leaned up over the seat and fished a dry flannel shirt out from under the tools and spare parts. The kid pulled off his T-shirt and wrapped my flannel shirt around him. He could have fit in it twice.

"I hope your pa's expecting you," I said. "You know, you can't go around outside up at Hazard."

"I been up there," was all he said.

The guy behind me was honking but Gravy didn't let him around. The cogway never stops, and there is a certain trick to magging on. The ramp is concrete but it's cracked and crazy tilted, and there's only one stretch where you can make enough speed for a hitch. If you miss, you have to turn down the cutoff and get back in line. I always make it, but I've been doing this run for twelve years.

"Piece of candy?" The kid held out a Collie Bar but since it looked like his entire supper I turned him down. It was getting dark. Magged on, I let the big old KJ idle. With the truck tipped almost straight up, it's better to have the pumps running to keep the air out of the lines.

It's a long ride up the western front. The Crab Orchard Cogway is slow and noisy, fourteen miles of squeaking, rattling chain. It's powered by steam generated from the coal and trash that rolled off the lower slopes when the mountain uplifted, helped by the weight of the trucks coming down. Even in the dark I could see them through the rain twenty yards away. I know most of the drivers, even the up-and-backs, or yoyos as we Flat Toppers call them. The mountainside looked junky in the headlights. The lower slopes, from 7,200 to the clouds at 11,500 are overgrown with weeds and weird new ferns and what's left of the trees—plus whatever else rolled down when the land rolled up. Some say they see giant volunteer tomatoes back in the weeds but I never see them.

The first hundred trips or so, it's a scary ride. The kid tried to act cool but I knew exactly how he felt. Your truck is tipped back at 45 degrees, you're wondering if the mag and the safety under it will hold, and even if it does, what about that clattery old chain? Then every once in a while the chain hauls up short—maybe a truck had trouble unhooking at the Hazard end, or maybe the world is coming apart—and the boards under your tires creak and the leaf springs sway, and the wind howls across the splinters of the trees, because we're still low enough on Flat Mountain for there to be wind, and you realize you're just hanging there like a wet pair of jeans on a line.

I popped in some Carl Perkins, the early stuff where he sings like George Jones, and managed to mostly close my eyes.

Then here come the clouds, above 11,500. The clouds make it easier. Thinking I wasn't looking, the kid unfolded a ten-dollar bill from his watch pocket, folded it up again, and put it away. I remembered hitchhiking and feeling the same way: checking it every hour or so to make sure it hadn't turned into a five.

At Hazard, you're still in the clouds but they loosen up as the mountain levels off a little and the cogway ends. All of a sudden there's noise and lights all around. For most of the trucks, the robot train roundabout is the end of the line. It's a big semicircular modular building—hauled up since the Uplift, naturally, since nothing of the old town survived. The yoyos unhitch and snake in and unload, load up whatever's contracted down, and get back in line for the cogway down. No deadheads in this business. Of course there are some loads that can't wait three weeks for a backed-up robot train, and that's where me and the other Flat Toppers come in— trucks that go all the way over Flat Mountain.

I figured the roundabout was where the kid's dad worked, since there's a lot of hand labor involved loading and unloading, not to mention the guys who jockey the trucks through the line for a few bucks while the drivers are sitting in the Bellew Belle. This is barely a living. They sleep in a pressure shed behind the roundabout.

"This must be the place," I said.

"Appreciate the ride, mister."

"CD," I said. He started to open the airlock and I said, "Whoa. Aren't you forgetting something?"

He looked back at me, scared, and started to unbutton the shirt.

I had to laugh. "Keep the shirt, kid," I said. "But you can't go around up here without breath spray. You're a mile higher than Everest. Open your mouth." I sprayed his throat with C-Level and told him to run before it wore off.

Carrying his plastic bag, he hurried out the airlock and into the roundabout.

I drove across the lot to the Bellew Belle. It's the only diner in Hazard and the drivers call it the Blue Balls. It isn't airlocked and the revolving door spins on its own from the pressure inside, easing out a continual little cloud of coffee and hamburger steam. Hazard can use it. It's a cold, dark, nasty place where nobody would live unless they worked there, or work unless they couldn't work anywhere else.

I wondered if the kid's dad knew he was coming. Or if he even existed. When I was his age I told folks I was hitching to Dallas to see my dad, who was a police officer. If you don't lie people will figure you're a runaway.

Flat Toppers tend to sit together. "How's the weather down under, CD?" they ask. "How's the weather up top?" I ask back. That's our standard joke, because the weather below the western front is always the same—always raining. And of course there's no weather on top of Flat Mountain. You can't have weather without atmosphere.

I used the lobby phone to call Janet and the girls again. I was already too high for the cab phone and this would be my last chance until I got back from Charlotte, since satellite calls over the mountain are so expensive. One of the guys at the table told me claws were bringing $100 in Charlotte, but they had to be unmarked because nobody eats road kill. I told him I didn't lobster anymore anyway.

It was just after midnight and I was getting up to go when the kid came in the revolving door, nursing a bloody nose with the sleeve of my shirt. He had run across the lot without any breath spray.

"Find your dad?" I asked, and he shook his head. He sat down, looking at the french fries the other guys had left on their plates. I bought two hamburgers out of the machine, even though I had already eaten, and acted like I didn't want one of them. That's the way you have to do it with a kid like that.

But I had to get going. "I guess you better head back to the roundabout and catch a ride back down the mountain," I said.

The kid shook his head. He said his mother had got married and moved out of Louisville. He claimed his dad had left ten dollars for him back at the roundabout, to catch a ride across to Charlotte where his grandma lived. I didn't believe that for a minute. He showed me the same folded-up ten I'd seen him looking at on the cogway.

I said, "Insurance won't allow me to carry you over Flat Mountain." This was a lie. The fact is, no Flat Topper's insured. Not because it's dangerous, although it can be, but because it's not a part of any state anymore. It's not *actuarily* part of the world anymore, my insurance man says.

"I know exactly where she lives," the kid says, acting like he hadn't heard me. He took a yellow piece of paper from his watch pocket and started unfolding it. He was doing good at not crying.

When I was his age, and I was hitchhiking, I had a ten-dollar bill in my watch pocket. That was it. This Mexican guy from St. Louis picked me up. He kept a pearl-handled revolver under the car seat. First time we stopped to eat, I tried to unfold my ten so he wouldn't see what it was, figuring I knew about Mexicans. And he told me to put it in my shoe because everybody knows to look in your watch pocket. He bought my meals all the way across Missouri and Oklahoma.

"One twenty-one Magnolia Street," the kid read off the paper, but he pronounced it "mangolia" like an aircraft metal. I could tell he'd never been to Charlotte. I wasn't surprised. Too high to fly over, too thick to tunnel through, Flat Mountain has split up a lot of families. It's not like an ocean that took a million years to form. They say it's even making the days longer, at almost an hour a year, because the bulge makes the Earth turn slower, like a skater throwing her arms out.

Slower days, that's all we need.

The other Flat Toppers had all left, heading down the Crab Orchard to Louisville and points beyond.

What the hell, I figured. "Let's go," I said. "And don't keep your money in your watch pocket. Everybody knows to look there."

At 34,500, Hazard would be snowy if the vents off the mountain didn't keep the clouds half steam. Cold steam. I was half frozen by the time I had finished letting all but eight pounds out of my tires and topping off the oxy and fuel in the injection system. You don't need an oversuit down so low, but you do need to keep a can of breath spray handy. C-Level gives the cells enough oxygen to get by, and fools your nerves into thinking you're breathing. I keep a can in my pocket.

"I could have helped," the kid said when I got into the truck. "I know pretty much about trucks." I handed him an oversuit and made him slip it on, even if he didn't want to zip it up. My rig is pressurized at fifty-five hundred and I've never had an accident, but you never know. Stuffed with fries, he went to sleep. I popped in old Lyle Lovett and hit the road, the only road east.

For the first two hours out of Hazard it's nothing but clouds. Flat Mountain's not flat yet and you're riding an 8-percent switchback patched together out of old highways.

If you ever saw the original Appalachians from the air, they looked like a rug somebody had kicked, with the ridges like long folds running parallel. The theory was that Africa had bumped into the USA a million years ago and folded them up. The Uplift killed that theory. Now they say that the Appalachians were the wrinkles left when the Cumberland Dome collapsed a million years ago—unwrinkled when it rose up again twenty years ago. They say it's not stable, and it's true: if you get out of your truck you can still feel the ground humming through your shoes. Cold fusion, twenty miles down.

It's funny, the Appalachians are gone but their ghost is in the roads. The route over Flat Mountain is patched together out of the old highways which followed the valleys, running close enough to parallel to make a natural switchback. You back-and-forth your way up what used to be Pine Mountain,

Crab Orchard Mountain, Black Mountain, Clinch Mountain—all humped together now into one gravelly slope, invisible in the permanent fog. Low-range fourth or high-range second gear all the way.

Twenty miles up and east of Hazard there's a little snow belt, which in the winter extends all the way down to the roundabout and the town. This time of the year, though, it's no sooner noticed than gone. Then it gets too high to snow and too high to breathe all at the same time. I came out of the clouds at 2:10 A.M. and it was almost dawn. "Dawn's dawn," Janet used to call it, back when she used to ride with me, before the girls were born. Above one hundred thousand feet the days are nineteen hours long in the summer.

I was tempted to wake up the kid. Behind me and below, in the big mirrors, a sea of clouds stretched two hundred miles. Ninety percent of the atmosphere was below us. You never actually see Kentucky and Tennessee from up here, only their permanent cloud roof. The clouds are pushed in from the west by the jet stream and they pile up like foam along the west front of Flat Mountain for two thousand miles, from Maine to Alabama. It's as beautiful from the top as it is gloomy from the bottom. The clouds ate the whole city of Lexington, not to mention Pittsburgh, and Huntsville, and a hundred little country towns that nobody remembers anymore, north and south.

I let the kid sleep and popped in Loretta Lynn. For some reason I like girl singers better up on top.

A few more hours of driving and the clouds are hidden under the bulk of the mountain. There's nothing in any direction but stone and sky, bone-white and blue-black. The stars look like chips of ice, too cold to twinkle. It's a hundred below outside and you're at 122,500. This is where if you're looking for landlobsters you start finding them.

The kid woke and sat up, rubbing his eyes. He didn't say anything for forty miles and I appreciated that, because when you're looking at the high top of Flat Mountain there is truly nothing to say. It's my favorite part of the route. It gets flatter and emptier the higher you go. I always imagine it's like Creation must have looked before they got to the plants and animals, and how it'll look when it's all over.

Toward the very middle of the high top I always play Patsy Cline, and if you don't know why, don't ask.

There's no longer a sign of Knoxville. No longer a sign of Asheville. During the eight years of the Uplift, the constant high-frequency vibration from the dome expanding turned the soil to jelly, and most of it ran into the cracks opening in the ground or ran off the mountain in sheets like slow-motion water taking the trees and what was left of the towns with it. All the way in Nashville, you could hear the mountain groan. The high top looks scoured, with every once in a while a long shallow ditch filled with logs and leftover trash. These ditches are all that's left of mighty forests and cities and it can't help but put your pride into perspective to look upon them.

The road across the top of Flat Mountain is straight and the slope is gentle, less than 3 percent, up for forty miles, then down for another forty. The road jogs between old 23 and Interstate 40. This is where Flat Toppers can gear up and roll out, to gain back the time they spent sniffing steam at the Blue Balls.

The log ditches are where you look for landlobsters.

"My dad sold one once," the kid said. He was looking hard for one, maybe thinking I would stop to kill it. He didn't know how hard they were to kill.

Your dad must have swapped or stole it off a Flat Topper, I thought to myself, since they never wander down as far as Hazard, though I didn't say this.

"He got a hundred dollars. Said they were descended from other planets."

Actually, the real truth is better. When the Appalachians uplifted, it either proved or disproved evolution, depending on who you're talking to. One thing it proved was that it doesn't take millions of years for a new species to evolve. The first landlobsters showed up less than six years after the Uplift started, although they weren't nearly as big as the ones today.

"Do you sell them?" the kid asked.

"Used to."

"Wonder what they eat," the kid said.

"Wood and glass." At least they say they eat glass. I've seen them eat logs. They won't eat anything alive but if they get hold of a man they'll drag him off until he dies and then gnaw him like a dog with a bone.

It's not often you see one on the road. The kid was watching the log ditches off to the side so he didn't see it. I was listening to Dolly sing "Blue Ridge Mountain Boy," a song they don't play much anymore, and I almost didn't swerve in time to hit it.

"What was that?" the kid says as I throw on the brakes. He started zipping up his oversuit and got two zippers jammed. It was the first time I'd seen him get excited and I had to laugh. He thought we were having a wreck. I had my oversuit zipped up and my mask on—it protects your face and eardrums—before he looked in the rear-view mirror and saw what we had hit.

"You don't want to be getting out," I said. I sprayed my throat with C-Level and stuffed the can in my pocket. "Hand me that Boy Scout hatchet from under the seat," I said.

He was watching it in the mirror, gray-white, the color of gravestones, and at least thirteen feet across the claws. I doubted he'd seen one before, alive. Not many people have. "You going to kill it?" he asked. "It's still flopping."

Once you crack the shell, they're dead from decompression, but dying can take all day. I hadn't gone looking for it, but since it came to me—I flipped down my mask and climbed across the kid, since the airlock is on his side. I crossed under the truck and approached it carefully. It was still venting steam out of the cracks in the shell where my truck had passed over it. I had missed all but one claw. There's about sixty pounds of meat under the back but High Top Meat won't buy lob out of the shell. With the hatchet, jumping in, I cut off the one big and four smaller claws I hadn't marked, tossing them under the truck. Since the lobster was dragging itself away from me, toward the shoulder, I turned my back on it. After all that activity, I needed another shot of C-Level, which means lifting your mask for a second. I gathered up the claws and I was about to strap them onto the spare tire rack with a bungee cord when, next thing I knew, the thing had pulled my leg out from under me and was dragging me toward the side of the road.

It was the tire-marked claw. I should have cut it off and tossed it away. I shouldn't ever have turned my back on it. It had me by the boot and was starting that slow sideways cut even while it pulled, and I knew I was in trouble. He still had six legs, each as big as a fencepost, and he was taking me home with him.

I reached for but missed the tire rack. I reached for but missed the hatchet. I reached for the big, soft rear trailer tire, even though there's no place to grab it—then I saw two shots crack the lobster's shell. You don't hear shots in a near vacuum. I looked back and saw the kid ducking under the truck from the other side, shooting. Even with the big gloves on he hit it twice more, but you can shoot those things all day long. They're like snapping turtles. I pointed at the Boy Scout hatchet, waving my arms, but the kid was falling. I hadn't left any breath spray for him. He was sealed in his suit and turning blue. But just as he fell he pushed the hatchet close enough for me to reach it.

Thank God for the Boy Scouts. I chopped my foot free, and wearing the claw like a clamp on my leg, dragged the kid under the truck, up the ladder and into the cab. Even inside in the air, he could barely breathe. The fall had knocked his mask loose, and his tongue and throat had swelled up from decompression. Luckily they make a spray for that, too, and I had some in my first-aid kit under the seat. I've had it used on me and it's bad. It puckers you up like eating a green persimmon but it works. It's called GAZP.

I pried the claw off my boot and stuck it up under the seat. When I was sure the kid was breathing, I went back out and got the 9 mm where he had dropped it. The lobster was gone and the claws I had cut off were gone, too, so the whole thing was a waste. I wasn't surprised. They say he eats them.

"Well, kid," I said when we were in gear again. "You saved old CD's butt back there."

"Weren't nothing. You get the claws?"

"Just the one he had me with. It's under the seat. That's that smell." Landlobsters smell like piss on coals until they're decompressed, and then it's gone.

The claw wasn't worth anything because it was tire-marked, but I didn't mention that.

All that talking wore me out, and the kid too, I guess. I looked over and saw he was asleep. I was in high third. On either side of the highway, nothing but miles and miles of stone. It's amazing to me that so many people could live for so long in those little mountains and leave so little sign. Twenty miles further and the road got steeper, going down. I had to gear down to low fifth. I popped in Hank Senior and the kid whimpered a little from a dream. At that minute I might have been driving past his great-grandaddy's grave. I could tell from the way he talked it was up here somewhere—somewhere between eastern Kentucky and western North Carolina, northern Virginia, and east Alabama. Somewhere in those endless wrinkled little hills that got unwrinkled and raised up, and rolled their children out into the world, rubbing their eyes and wondering when they get to go home.

Maybe someday. I read in *Popular Science* that Flat Mountain is sinking again, at about a foot and a half a year. At that rate it'll only be one hundred thousand years.

From the edge of the western slope you see a snow-white roof of clouds, but from the eastern slope you see what looks like the edge of a giant blue-green ball. You first see it just as the switchbacks start, at about ninety thousand, when there is just enough air to leave a little vapor trail back over the road. Far ahead the sky is not black anymore but dark blue. Then you see it's really the sea. And not just a few miles of it: you are looking halfway to Bermuda from eighteen miles high. From here you can see that the water and the air are two versions of the same stuff.

The roads down the eastern slope are better, probably because the highways were newer, mostly four lanes. The switchbacks are long—forty, fifty miles a swoop. Morgantown, Hendersonville, Bat Cave, just names given to turns anymore, since the towns are long since gone. At Bat Cave (no bats, no cave) the kid woke up, and this time he didn't try not to look impressed. We were far enough east and far enough down Flat Mountain to see the Atlantic Coast all the way from Morehead City to Savannah. The Carolina Desert is the color of October woods, red and orange and yellow and brown. It's a fast trip down, with no cogway needed. Here on the eastern slope, the yoyos are muscle trucks, and the robot train roundabout is set in a cold, dry cloudless perch called Shelby, which looks down fifty miles onto Charlotte. There's a good diner there but I just rolled on past and hit the hard switchbacks below 21,500 with my KJ barking like a hundred-dollar hound.

It gets dark early in Charlotte, but it felt good to be down in the air. I unsealed the locks and let the dry night wind run through the cab. There used to be magnolia trees in Charlotte but that was before the Uplift. Now they were just street names, like the towns on Flat Mountain. We found Magnolia on my map, but first I took the kid and bought him supper.

The reason I bought his supper was, I kept remembering the Mexican who bought my meals all the way across Missouri and Oklahoma when I was just a kid. He said he used to hitch, and he even tried to give me a five when he dropped me off, but I shook my head and wouldn't take it. The thing is, when he looked under his car seat later on, his pearl-handled revolver was gone. I sold it in Fort Worth for twenty dollars. I have always felt ashamed of that ever since.

The kid had two black eyes from the decompression but his throat was better, good enough for him to eat. He didn't complain when I paid for his supper. Then I stopped at High Top Meat. I told the kid to wait in the truck. The night broker shook his head when I unwrapped the claw and he saw the tire marks. "Too bad, CD," he said. "I can't buy road kill unless it don't look like road kill."

"How about for dog food?" I said, and he gave me a five.

The kid looked nervous and asked how I'd done, and I lied. "Good," I said. I gave him a twenty and told him it was half the money. He folded it and put it in his watch pocket with the ten.

Magnolia was one of those dirt streets with no sidewalks and little modular houses, all alike. Any one of them could have been his grandma's house, or any one not. "Don't turn in, I'll get out here," he said at the end of the street, gathering up his stuff in a hurry.

"Vaya con Dios," I said.

"What's that mean?"

"Means good luck finding your pa." I never did find mine.

I slept eleven hours while my rig was serviced and loaded.

I was halfway up Flat Mountain the next day before it occurred to me to look in the glove compartment for my 9 mm. Of course it was gone. I popped in Crystal Gayle and had to laugh.

↓ Press Ann ↓

WELCOME TO CASH-IN-A-FLASH
1324 LOCATIONS
TO SERVE YOU CITYWIDE
PLEASE INSERT YOUR CASH-IN-A-FLASH CARD

THANK YOU
NOW ENTER YOUR CASH-IN-A-FLASH NUMBER

THANK YOU
PLEASE SELECT DESIRED SERVICE—
    DEPOSIT
    WITHDRAWAL
    BALANCE
    WEATHER

"Weather?"

"What's the problem, Em?"

"Since when do these things give the weather?"

"Maybe it's some new thing. Just get the cash, it's 6:22 and we're going to be late."

WITHDRAWAL
THANK YOU
WITHDRAWAL FROM—
    SAVINGS
    CHECKING
    CREDIT LINE
    OTHER

    CHECKING
THANK YOU
PLEASE ENTER DESIRED AMOUNT—
    $20
    $60
    $100
    $200

    $60
$60 FOR A MOVIE?

"Bruce, come over here and look at this."

"Emily, it's 6:26. The movie starts at 6:41."

"How does the cash machine know we're going to the movie?"

"What are you talking about? Are you mad because you have to get the money, Em? Can I help it if a machine ate my card?"

"Never mind. I'll try it again."

$60
$60 FOR A MOVIE?

"It just did it again."

"Did what?"

"Bruce, come over here and look at this."

"Sixty dollars for a movie?"

"I'm getting money for dinner, too. It is my birthday after all, even if I have to plan the entire party. Not to mention get the money to pay for it."

"I can't believe this. You're mad at me because a machine ate my card."

"Forget it. The point is, how does the cash machine know we're going to a movie?"

"Emily, it's 6:29. Just press *Enter* and let's go."

"Okay, okay."

WHO IS THE GUY WITH THE WATCH?

    BOYFRIEND

    HUSBAND

    RELATIVE

    OTHER

"Bruce!"

"Emily, it's 6:30. Just get the money and let's go."

"Now it's asking me about you."

"It's 6:31!"

"Okay!"

OTHER

"Excuse me, do you two mind if I—"

"Look, pal, there's a problem with this machine. There's another cash machine right down the street if you're in such a goddamn hurry."

"Bruce! Why be rude?"

"Forget it, he's gone."

HAPPY BIRTHDAY EMILY

WOULD YOU LIKE—

    DEPOSIT

    WITHDRAWAL

BALANCE
WEATHER

"How does it know it's my birthday?"

"Jesus, Em, it's probably coded in your card or something. It is now 6:34 and in exactly seven minutes . . . What the hell is this? Weather?"

"That's what I've been trying to tell you."

"You're not going to press it!"

"Why not?"

WEATHER
THANK YOU
SELECT DESIRED CONDITIONS—
    COOL AND CLOUDY
    FAIR AND MILD
    LIGHT SNOW
    LIGHT RAIN

"Em, will you quit playing around!"

LIGHT RAIN

"Rain? On your birthday?"

"Just a light rain. I just want to see if it works. We're going to the movie anyway."

"Not if we don't get out of here."

PERFECT MOVIE WEATHER
WOULD YOU LIKE—
    DEPOSIT
    WITHDRAWAL
    BALANCE
    POPCORN

"Em, this machine is seriously fucked up."

"I know. I wonder if you get butter."

"It's 6:36. Just press *Withdrawal* and let's get the hell out of here. We have five minutes until the movie starts."

WITHDRAWAL

THANK YOU

WITHDRAWAL FROM—

    SAVINGS

    CHECKING

    CREDIT LINE

    OTHER

"Excuse me. Are you two going to see *Gilded Palace of Sin?*"

"Shit. Look who's back."

"I was just at the theater and the newspaper had the times listed wrong. According to the box office, the movie starts at 6:45. So you have nine minutes."

"I thought you were at the other machine."

"There's a line and I didn't want to stand outside in the rain."

"Rain? Bruce, look!"

"It's just a light rain. But I'm wearing my good suit."

OTHER

"Emily, it's 6:37 and you're pressing *Other?*"

"Don't you want to see what else this machine can do?"

"No!"

THANK YOU

CHOOSE OTHER ACCOUNT—

    ANDREW

    ANN

    BRUCE

"Who the hell are Andrew and Ann? And how the hell did my name get in there?"

"You told me the machine ate your card."

"That was . . . another machine."

"Excuse me. Ann is my fiancée. Well, was. Sort of. I thought."

"Are you butting in again?"

"Wait! You must be—"

"Andrew. Andrew P. Claiborne the Third. You must be Emily. And he must be—"

"He's Bruce. Don't mind him if he's a little uncouth."

"Uncouth!"

BRUCE

"Hey, that's my account, Emily. You don't have any right to press *Bruce*!"

"Why not? You say you wanted to pay for dinner and the movie, but the machine ate your card. So let's go for it."

GO FOR IT, EMILY
PLEASE ENTER DESIRED AMOUNT—

$20
$60
$100
$200

$60
SORRY. INSUFFICIENT FUNDS. WANT TO TRY FOR $20?

$20
SORRY. INSUFFICIENT FUNDS.
WOULD YOU LIKE A BALANCE CHECK?

"No!"

<u>YES</u>
BRUCE'S BALANCE: $11.78
SURPRISED?

"Surprised? I'm furious! Some birthday celebration! You didn't even have enough to pay for a movie, much less dinner! And you lied!"

"Excuse me, it's your birthday? It's my birthday too!"

"You stay out of this, Andrew, or whatever the fuck your name is."

"Don't be vulgar, Bruce. He has an absolutely perfect right to wish me a happy birthday."

"He's not wishing you a happy birthday, he's butting into my life."

"Allow me to wish you a very happy birthday, Emily."

"And to you, Andrew, the very same."

"Plus he's an asshole!"

NO NAME CALLING PLEASE
WOULD YOU LIKE ANOTHER BALANCE CHECK?
    BRUCE
    EMILY
    ANDREW
    ANN

"I still don't understand who Ann is."

"My girlfriend. Sort of. She was supposed to meet me at the movie but she stood me up for the last time."

"How terrible! On your birthday! Andrew, I know exactly how you feel."

"As a matter of fact, you're both a couple of assholes!"

NO NAME CALLING PLEASE
EMILY AND ANDREW,

PLEASE ALLOW ME TO TREAT YOU
TO A BIRTHDAY DINNER AND A FILM

"A hundred dollars!"

"It says it's treating us. Take it, Emily."

"You take it, Andrew; I think the man should handle the money. And you can call me Em."

"I can't fucking believe this!"

"We'd better hurry. Excuse me, Bruce, old pal, do you have the time?"

"It's 6:42. Asshole."

"If we run we can catch the 6:45. Then, how about Sneeky Pete's?"

"I love Tex-Mex!"

PLEASE REMOVE YOUR CARD
DON'T FORGET TO TRY
THE BLACKENED FAJITAS

"You're all three assholes! I can't fucking believe this. She left with him!"

WELCOME TO CASH-IN-A-FLASH
1324 LOCATIONS
TO SERVE YOU CITYWIDE
PLEASE DON'T KICK THE MACHINE

"Go to hell!"

PLEASE INSERT YOUR CASH-IN-A-FLASH CARD

"Fuck you."

GO AHEAD, BRUCE
WHAT HAVE YOU GOT TO LOSE?

THANK YOU
IT WASN'T 'EATEN' AFTER ALL, WAS IT?

"You know it wasn't. Asshole."

NO NAME CALLING PLEASE
WOULD YOU LIKE—
    SYMPATHY
    REVENGE
    WEATHER
    ANN

"Excuse me."
"Jesus, lady, quit banging on the door. I know it's raining. Tough shit. I'm not going to let you in. This is a cash machine, not a homeless shelter. You're supposed to have a card or something. What?"
"I said, shut up and press *Ann.*"

↯ THE COON SUIT ↯

I'M NOT MUCH of a hunter and I don't care for dogs. I was driving out Taylorsville Road in Oldham County one Sunday, when I saw this bunch of pickups down in a hollow by a pond. My own old yellow and white '77 Ford half-ton was bought from a coon hunter, and it could have been the truck as much as me that slowed down to take a look. Men were standing around the pickups, most of which had dog boxes in the beds. I saw a Xeroxed sign stapled to a telephone pole, and realized I had been seeing the same sign for a couple of miles along the road.

COON RUN, SUNDAY, CARPENTERS LAKE.

If this was Carpenters Lake, it was not much more than a pond. I could hear dogs barking. I pulled over to watch.

There was a cable running across the water. It ran from a pole where the trucks were parked into the trees on the other side of the pond. Hanging under it, like a cable car, was a wire cage. While I watched, two men took six or eight hounds out of the back of a half-ton Ford and down to the bank. The dogs were going wild and I could see why.

There was a coon in the cage. From where I was parked, up on the road, it was just a little black shape. It looked like a skunk or a big house cat. It was probably just my imagination, but I thought I could see the black eyes, panicky under the white mask, and the handlike feet plucking at the wire mesh.

A rope ran from the cage, through a pulley on a tree at the far end of the cable and back. A man pulled at the rope and the cage started across the cable, only three or four feet off the water. The men on the bank let the dogs go and they threw themselves into the pond. They were barking louder than ever, swimming under the cage as it was pulled in long slow jerks toward the woods on the other side.

My wife Katie tells me I'm a watcher, and it's true I'd generally rather watch than do. I wasn't even tempted to join the men by the pond, even though I probably knew one or two of them from the plant. I had a better view from up on the road. There was something fascinating and terrifying at the same time about the dogs splashing clumsily through the water (they don't call it dog-paddling for nothing), looking up hungrily at the dark shape in the wire cage.

Once the cage was moving, the coon sat dead-still. He probably figured he had the situation under control. I could almost see the smirk on his face as he looked down at the dogs in the water, a sort of aviator look.

On the bank the men leaned against their trucks drinking beer and watching. They all wore versions of the same hat, drove versions of the same truck, and looked like versions of the same guy. Not that I think I'm better than them; I'm just not much of a hunter and don't care for dogs. From the boxes in the truck beds, the other hounds waiting their turn set up a howl, a background harmony to the wild barking from the pond.

The situation wasn't fair, though, because whenever the dogs fell behind, the man pulling the rope would stop pulling and let them catch up. While the cage was moving the coon was okay, but as soon as it stopped he would go crazy. He would jump from side to side, trying to get it going again, while the hounds paddled closer and closer. Dogs when they're swimming are all jaws. Then the man would pull on the rope and the cage would take off again toward the trees on the other side, and I could almost see the coon get that smirk on his face again. That aviator look.

The second act of the drama began when the cage reached the tree at the end of the cable. The tree tripped the door and the coon dove out and hit the ground. In a flash he was gone, into the woods that ran up over the hill alongside the road. A few seconds later and the dogs were out of the water after him, the whole pack running like a yellow blur up the bank, shaking themselves as they ran, the water rising off their backs like a cloud of steam. Then they were gone into the trees too.

One of the pickups was already on its way up the road, presumably to follow. The guys in it looked at me kind of funny as they drove by, but I ignored them. Down by the pond the cage was being pulled back, six more dogs were being taken out of the trucks, and a man held a squirming gunnysack at arm's length.

Another coon.

They put him into the cage and I should have left, since I was expected somewhere. But there was something interesting, or I guess fascinating is the word, about the whole business, and I had to see more. I drove a hundred yards up the road and stopped by the edge of the woods.

I got out of the truck.

The brush by the roadside was thick, but after I got into the woods things opened up a little. It was mostly oak, gum, and hickory. I made my way down the slope toward the pond, walking quietly so I could listen. I could tell by the barking when the dogs hit the water. I could tell when the cage stopped, and when it started up again. It was all in the dogs' voices. Through them, I could almost feel the coon's terror when the cage stopped and his foolish arrogance when it started moving again.

Halfway down the hill I stopped in a little clearing at the foot of a big hollow beech. All around me were thick bushes, tangles of fallen limbs, and brush. The barking got louder and wilder and I knew the cage was reaching the cable's end. There was a howl of rage, and I knew the coon was in the woods. I stood perfectly still. Soon I heard a sharp slithering sound and, without a warning, without stirring a leaf, the coon ran out of the bushes and straight at me. I was too startled to move. He ran almost right across my feet—a black and white blur—and was gone up the hill, into the bushes again. For a second I almost felt sorry for the dogs: how could they ever hope to catch such a creature?

Then I heard the dogs again. Pitiless is the word for them. If they had looked all jaws in the water, they sounded all claws and slobber in the woods. Their barking got louder and wilder as they got closer, at least six of them, hot on the coon's trail. Then I heard a crashing in the brush down the hill. Then I saw the bushes shaking, like a storm coming up low to the ground. Then I heard the rattle of claws on dry leaves, getting closer and closer. Then I saw a yellow blur as the dogs bolted from the bushes and across the clearing straight at me. I stepped back in horror.

That's when I realized, or I guess remembered is the word, that I had my coon suit on.

⚐ GEORGE ⚐

THE SUMMER BEFORE George was born, Katie and I lived in a house on a high hill. The hill sloped up gently on three sides, covered with thick grass kept short by the wind; but in the back, behind the house, it fell off sharply, down a high, rocky cliff, to the sea. The house was right at the top, about thirty yards from the edge of the cliff, and all we could see of the ocean from there was its top edge, where it tilted up against the sky. The cliff was so high and the wind from the sea was so noisy that usually we couldn't hear the surf, even from the edge of the cliff. I would go there sometimes and peer down; there was no sound except the wind; and the surf moved in and out like great wings, beating against the wind and rock that pinned them down.

On the other side of the house, at the bottom of the hill, there was a highway, and the house was turned inland toward it, away from the wind. Often Katie and I would sit here, on the porch steps, and watch the cars passing and the gulls riding over on the wind. It was nicest in the evening right before dark. Sometimes, just as the sun went down, the wind would quit all of a sudden; the gulls would catch and tremble in the air and wait; Katie and I would almost hold our breaths; and then, finally, the noise of the sea would come in, low, to fill the air.

It was at such a time that the baby first moved—the quickening, they call it. The noise of the surf was just breaking in on the quiet; the wings of the gulls began to stir, ever so slightly; Katie started, caught herself, and then turned to me. She said that the baby had moved—just a quick flutter, like a tiny bird beating against her womb.

Then the summer was gone, and it was too cold for the house on the hill. We moved to a small town about thirty miles inland where I got a job and we settled down to wait. Katie had never made friends easily before, but now she had something in common with all of the ladies in the neighborhood; we were heaped with baby clothes, good wishes, and advice. The minister called on us several times and we joined the church. We were sure that the baby would be a boy; we decided to call him George.

Finally, in December, the time came. I couldn't stay in Katie's room at the hospital, so I sat out in the waiting room. It was a nice waiting room, with new leather chairs and lots of ashtrays and a gaily colored picture on the wall of bathers at Donaldson Beach.

In the picture, it was summer again. The surf was gentle, and it must have been warm, for there were children playing in it. Their mothers were gathered in little groups up on the beach, talking and sunbathing. Far off in the distance you could see the cliffs where the high land broke out into the sea, where we had lived during the summer. Here, though, in the picture, the land sloped down gently, and the beach was broad and even and covered with people.

I studied the picture for hours: everyone was having a great time at the beach. I began to enjoy myself too. The nurse came in every so often and interrupted me, telling me that it would only be another three hours, or two, and that the pains were coming at such and such intervals. I hoped that it wasn't hurting Katie too much, but the nurse said she was doing very well. The pains, she told me, were sort of like waves—it was only a matter of relaxing and rolling with them.

After that, I began to see the pains as waves, each one bigger than the last. Where was Katie, though? I searched the beach, trying to complete this curious image. My son was in the water, struggling to reach the shore—or struggling against it? Or were the waves of pain the child himself, beating against his mother like the sea against the earth, like the mile-long wings of surf against the rock and air. I began to get seasick. The whole room was rocking and swaying. Then suddenly it stopped, and the nurse came in to congratulate me.

I was the father of a boy, she said—George. He was perfectly healthy, and he weighed eleven pounds four ounces. Most of the weight was in his wings. "Yes," she said, "he has wings! But he's beautiful!"

Katie was back in her room, exhausted but still awake, when I ran in. "Oh yes!" she said. "He has little white wings, like an angel. When they held him up, he looked like an angel!"

I was surprised at this, and the doctor was too. "I've examined the boy," he said, "and he's strong and healthy. His arms and legs are perfectly formed—but these wings are very strange. Frankly, I've never seen anything like it."

Fathers aren't usually allowed in the nursery, but the doctor decided that this was a special case, so he took me with him. There was only one other baby in the nursery, and it was crying. George was very still. He was lying on his stomach, and the first thing I saw were his wings, folded carefully along his back. They weren't very big, but they were very bright. When we shut the door they trembled.

* * *

When the word got around, the whole town was in an uproar. Everybody congratulated Katie and me and had a look at George. Reporters and doctors came from all over, and we were famous for a little while. The doctor wrote a report for a medical journal, and I got two weeks off from work. We all answered a lot of questions, but there wasn't really very much that anyone could say. There weren't any explanations or theories, it was just a curious fact; George had wings.

So things quieted down pretty quickly, especially after I took Katie and George home. A baby was born soon afterward in Kansas which could whistle—no tunes or anything; it just whistled instead of crying. This became the big story, and we were quickly forgotten. A few more reporters and doctors came by; I told them I would call when George learned to fly.

As might be expected, we had a few peculiar problems. One was with the down: after George had been home for a few days and had shed whatever coating had protected him in the womb, small bits of down began to come off his wings. We were afraid that he might choke on them at night, so Katie began brushing his wings with her hands after each feeding so that they wouldn't shed in his crib. It was also difficult to bathe him, because once his wings were wet it took them hours to dry. Soon, however, both these problems were solved as his wings became coated with a kind of oil. We kept them brushed and smoothed, and they became bright and water-repellent. We were also afraid of fire, so I reluctantly pulled one of his feathers and tried to light it. It didn't burn.

His big problem was sleeping. At first we were afraid to lay him on his back for fear that he might injure his wings. He grew tired of sleeping on his stomach, though, and we found that his wings were very tough. He began to prefer sleeping on his back with his wings folded under him like a pillow; I believe he could have slept on a stone floor. Perhaps this was what the wings were for; he never unfolded them, but kept them tight against his back as if they warmed and comforted him.

The doctor told me one afternoon, in the most matter-of-fact way, that he wanted to cut off George's wings. He thought that in a few months George would be strong enough for the operation. I was shocked; I had never even thought of it. The doctor said, "Of course! We can't leave them on—the boy would be a freak. We must wait, however, until he is a little older before operating."

I began to look at my son with a more critical eye. He did look strange, unusual—but what father's first child doesn't? As for the wings, he seemed perfectly at home with them. They trembled slightly with pleasure, as toes curl up, when he was at his mother's breast; but otherwise, they just remained folded at his back, as though for decoration only. I tried to visualize how he would look without his shining wings: with nothing between his arms and his behind except a naked, fatty back.

I was reluctant to tell Katie about the doctor's proposal. I knew that she would be against it for the same reason that I was—we both liked George just as he was. But on the other hand, his whole future was at stake; we couldn't get emotional about it. So I decided to talk to the doctor again. "Doctor," I said, "I like the boy just as he is."

"Of course," said the doctor, "but you must think of his future—of the way he *will* be. Right now he's just a baby; the wings are small and unobtrusive. But consider: if the wings are functional—as I'm sure they are—they will become much larger in proportion to his body. He will no longer look like a cherub, but like a bird; he will be a freak.

"He won't be a baby all his life," the doctor continued. "He will grow up, and what then? He won't be able to run or jump, dragging those ponderous wings like an albatross. He'll barely be able to walk. He won't be able to swim or take part in any sports; he'll hardly even be able to sit down. I tell you, we must cut off those wings!''

The doctor was right. I had visions of George standing on the sidelines, watching the others play football, his wings waving heavily in the breeze. Or I could see him walking slowly along the beach, past the children playing in the surf, past the curious groups of mothers, bent forward like a hunchback to counterbalance the weight of his wings dragging in the sand.

How could I be sure, though? The wings might be a handicap, but what if there were worse consequences in cutting them off? What if George had the soul of a bird? Perhaps, I thought, he was spiritually and emotionally formed for wings, and would be unhappy walking around anyway. Still, I couldn't talk to Katie; she would just get emotional about it. So I took my doubts to the minister.

"Absurd!" said the minister. "No one has the soul of a bird, except perhaps, a bird. But boys—boys are not born, but made. If George is brought up as a normal, healthy boy, he will be happy as a normal, healthy boy. What alternative do you have—to raise him as a bird in a family of people? A seagull in a city of men? If those wings are not removed he will be an outcast; everywhere he goes he will be stared at and tormented. He will not only be physically handicapped, but emotionally crippled as well. What kind of life could he have? Consider: all the normal courses of human life will be cut off from him. The most ordinary activity, like riding the bus, will become for him a nightmare of stares and whispers. If he goes to school, the other children will pull his wings and set them on fire . . ."

"They don't burn," I said.

"He will be unable to wear a suit or drive a car. How can he get married, make friends, or run for office? I plead with you, sir, for the child's sake, deliver him from those wings!''

"George is over a month old," I said. "If we remove his

wings, won't he remember them? Even a normal, healthy boy sometimes longs for strange powers."

"Never," said the minister. "Does the child remember the womb or the kingdom of Heaven? Better yet: tell him about them. Save the clippings and photographs from his birth and show them to him when he is older. Let him have the pleasure and amusement of a famous birth, but not the bitterness of an estranged life."

All this made sense. I could make George's birth only a curious incident in a happy, normal life. I had only one more hesitation—the operation itself. Would it be difficult or dangerous?

"Nothing to it," said the doctor. "Nothing to it. The wings can be removed as simply as any other growth. We must only wait another month until the child is old enough to take anesthesia."

"It may take me longer than that to convince Katie," I said.

"We can't wait too long. The wings must be removed as soon as possible, before the cartilage and muscle begin to harden. As it is now, the boy will be barely scarred. He will be left with only two small stumps, like handles, for a remembrance."

"Okay!" I thought. "Fine!" All that was left now was to persuade Katie; I must be firm. I went home decided, full of resolution, but it was soon gone. Katie was quiet and surly; she seemed to know that I was up to something. And I couldn't take my eyes off George's wings. They lit up the whole room, like a snowbank at night.

The next morning I went back to see the minister again. "It all boils down to this," I said. "Why did God give George wings only to have them cut off?"

The minister told me that the ways of God were strange. "Why does He give man life," he said, "only to take it away again? Why did He create the sky and not allow the fish to see it?" He continued in this vein for several minutes, and then concluded: "You know in your heart that the doctor and I are right—the child's wings must be removed."

"Maybe he's right," I thought. "Maybe they're both right." I was dizzy from thinking. It was time to tell Katie; I left the minister and started for home, determined to go ahead, to do something. Katie and I would have to sit down and talk this thing out.

I tried to get my arguments straight. It was just a simple choice: was George to have a normal, happy life, or was he to be a strange, lonely boy with wings? I saw George as a real boy, with a crowd of others, playing; there he was with his wife and his own children; then a boy again running unencumbered across a short grass field. But there were two Georges: the other was thin, delicate, dark in color. His slight body was all but hidden by huge wings; his fingers were so thin that I could see the blood run through them. His great, dark eyes were marked with the light from his shining wings . . . Suddenly, I stopped and walked back to the doctor's office. This was no good; my thoughts were clouded with vision.

"Doctor," I said, "what will happen to the wings after they are removed? Will you take them off separately, or together? Will they stay bright and clean, or will they shrivel up and die?"

"Why," said the doctor, "we can do whatever you like with them. They will come off separately, and can easily be preserved. I had thought that you might want to give them to a museum or something. Or perhaps you might want to keep them; George could hang them on the wall of his room as a sort of trophy."

Well, I had beat around the bush too long. I went home. "Katie," I said, "the doctor says we should cut off George's wings—have them removed." She didn't say anything. "The minister says so, too, and so do I." I told her about how he would be an outcast, an emotional cripple. "He won't always be a baby," I said. "Look at the future."

She was holding him and watching me curiously as I spoke. I was watching him, older, still running in the field of short grass. But there was the other, the thin boy with dark eyes and great white wings. "Don't you see, Katie, he is alone!" It was hard for me to think; he was looking back at me, out of his dream. "He is a cripple. He can't run, can't dance, can't even sit down!" He was on a high hill, I could see that now, with the sea behind him. Katie looked toward the ocean, then back at me. As she began to speak, George began to turn into the wind, his wings trembling as he lifted them over his head . . .

"Oh no," said Katie. "He's not a cripple—he can fly!" We watched him fall forward and then up; as his feet lifted off the thick grass, his wings, held out, began to stir. Katie laughed: "Why should he want to ride a bus? Why should he walk when he can ride and float on the air?" Katie and I watched him all the way out of sight. Another watched him too: the boy running in the field suddenly stopped and looked up. The last light of the sun caught a flash of white, way up, and then the boy on the ground was lost in the great shadow of wings that covered half the hill.

The wind was suddenly quiet; the low sound of the water came in. Katie and I looked up as the gulls' wings stirred and they fell back toward the sea. Then it was dark; the wind came up again and George started to cry. Katie began to rock him and smiled at me across the room.

When spring came, we went back to the house on the hill. We stayed on through the next winter, and the next. George learned to walk before I tried to teach him to fly; then, during the third summer, I would take him out on the side of the hill and toss him into the air. At first he would fall with a wild flutter and thump, laughing. By the time cold weather came, he could rise off the ground by himself and stay up for a few seconds. By that time, he had a baby sister. Her wings were red, like fire.

⚜ NEXT ⚜

"NEXT!"

   "We want to get a marriage license, please."

   "Name?"

   "Johnson, Akisha."

   "Age?"

   "Eighteen."

   "Groom's name?"

   "Jones, Yusef."

   "Yusef? You with *him*? Honey, you kids are in the *wrong* line."

   "We are?"

   "Try that line over there, on the other side of the Pepsi machine. And good luck. You're gonna need it, child. Next!"

"Next!"

   "We want to apply for a marriage license."

   "For who, might I ask?"

   "For us. For me and him."

   "I beg your pardon?"

   "She told us to get in this line. I guess because—"

   "I can't give you a marriage license. He's black."

"I know, but I heard that if we get a special permit or something—"

"What you're talking about is a same-race certificate. But I can't give you one, and I wouldn't if I could. The very idea of blacks marrying *each other*, when—"

"So why'd she tell us to get in this line?"

"This line is for same-race certificate *applications.*"

"So what do we have to do to get one of those?"

"Under the law, just ask for it. Even though there's something disgusting about—"

"So look, lady, I'm asking."

"Here. Fill this out and return it to window A21."

"Does that mean we have to start in line all over again?"

"What do you think? Next!"

"Next!"

"Hello, I'm not even sure we're in the right line. We want to get one of those special certificates. To get married."

"A same-race certificate. You're in the right line. But under the Equal Access Provisions of the Melanin Conservation Act, we can't just hand those out. You have to have an Ozone Waiver to even apply for one."

"I already have the application filled out. See? That white girl over there told me about it."

"She told you wrong. What you filled out is the application for the *waiver*. But you can't get the waiver without twelve and a half minutes of counseling."

"Can't you just stamp it or whatever? We've already been standing in three lines for hours, and my feet are—"

"Excuse me? Maybe you know more about my job than I do?"

"No."

"Good. Then listen up. I'm trying to be helpful. What I'm going to give you is an appointment slip to see the marriage counselor. Take it to Building B and give it to the clerk at the first desk.''

"We have to go outside?"

"There's a covered walkway. But stay to the left, several panels are missing. Next!"

"Next!"

"We have an appointment slip."

"For what?"

"Counseling. To get a waiver, so we can apply for a certificate, or something. So we can get married."

"Sit down over there. The Sergeant Major will call you when he's ready."

"The Sergeant Major? We were supposed to see a marriage counselor."

"The Sergeant Major is the Marriage Counselor. Has been ever since the Declaration of Marital Law, under the Ozone Emergency Act. Where have you been?"

"We don't get married every day."

"Are you getting smart with me?"

"I guess not."

"I hope not. Take a seat, in those hard chairs, until I call you. Next!"

"Next! At ease. State your business."

"We need to get the counseling for—"

"I wasn't talking to you. I was talking to him."

"Me?"

"You're the man, aren't you?"

"Uh, yes, sir! We, uh, want to get married, sir!"

"Speak up. And don't call me sir. I'm not an officer. Call me Sergeant Major."

"Yes, sir; I mean, Sergeant."

"Sergeant Major."

"Sergeant Major!"

"Now tell me again what it is you want."

"This is ridiculous. Yusef already told you—"

"Did I ask you to speak, young lady? Maybe you think because I'm black I'll tolerate your insolence?"

"No. Sergeant. Major."

"Then shut up. Carry on, young man."

"We want to get married. Sergeant Major!"

"That's what I thought I heard you say. And I guess you want my approval as your marriage counselor? My blessing, so to speak?"

"Well, yes."

"Well, you can forget it! For Christ's sake, boy, show a little backbone. A little social responsibility. You kids are the kind who are giving our kind a bad name. You don't see white folks lining up trying to evade the law, do you?"

"They don't need to line up."

"Watch your mouth, young lady. And nobody told you to sit down. This is a military office."

"She's been standing for hours, Sarge. Major. My fiancée is, uh—"

"I'm pregnant."

"Will you quit butting in, young lady! Now, let me get this straight. Is she pregnant?"

"She is."

"Why didn't you say so in the first place?"

"That's why we want to get married. Sergeant Major."

"You're in the wrong office. I'll need to see a Melanin Heritage Impact Statement and a release from the Tactical Maternity Officer before I can even begin to counsel you. Take this slip to Office Twenty-three in Building C."

"Outside again?"

"Only for a few yards."

"But the sunscorch factor is eight point four!"

"Quit whining. Show a little pride. Imagine what it's like for white people. Next!"

* * *

"Next!"

"We were told to come here and see you because I'm—"

"I'm a woman too, I can tell. At ease. Sit down, you both look tired. Want a cigarette?"

"Isn't smoking bad for the baby?"

"Suit yourself. Now, how can I help you? Captain Kinder, here; Tactical Maternity."

"All we want is a certificate so we can get married."

"Negative, honey. No way. If you were both sterile, or overage, *maybe*. But nobody's going to give you kids a same-race if you are already PG. Not with active replicator AAs in such short supply. Who are all us white folks going to marry?"

"Each other?"

"Very funny. And watch our kids fry. But seriously, you don't have to get married to have a child. You can have all the AAs you want OW. What's the problem?"

"We want to keep it."

"Keep it? Negative. You know that under the Melanin Heritage Conservation Act, Out-of-Wedlock African American children must be raised in Protective Custody."

"You mean prison."

"Haven't you heard that old saying, 'stone walls do not a prison make'? And this is not like the bad old days; since the Ozone Emergency, AA children are a precious resource. You should be glad to see them in such good homes."

"But they *are* prisons. I've seen them."

"So what? Does an NB, that's newborn, know the diff? And it's for the child's own good as well as the good of the society. Do you realize the culture shock for African American youth when they find themselves in prison at age sixteen or so? If they are raised in prison from infancy, the TA or Transitional Adaptation goes much more smoothly. Besides, they get out as soon as they marry, anyway."

"What if we don't want our kid to go to prison at all?"

"Whoa, Akisha! Do you mind if I call you Akisha? Are we back in the Dark Ages here, where the parents decide the child's future even before it is born? This is a free country and kids as well as parents have rights. Sure you don't want a cigarette?"

"I'm sure."

"Suit yourself. Let's cut the BS. You're nice kids, but under the Melanin Distribution Provisions of the Ozone Emergency Act, the law is clear. If you want to raise your own children, you'll have to marry legally."

"Which means marry a white person."

"As a white person myself, I'll overlook your racist tone of voice, which I'm sure you didn't mean. Is there something so terrible about marrying a white person?"

"No. I don't guess so."

"Okay. Now why don't you get with the program. Don't you know some nice white boy to marry?"

"Then I can keep my baby?"

"Not this one, but the next one. This one's double M and belongs to Uncle Sam, or at least to the Natural Resources Administration of HEW and M."

"But what if I don't want to marry some damn white boy!"

"Jones, I was hoping we could handle this without emotional outbursts of naked bigotry. I see I was wrong. You are in danger of making me feel like an inadequate counselor with this racist attack on my professional self-image. Is it because I'm white?"

"It's because I want to marry Yusef."

"Who just *happens* to be black? Let's get real, girl. There's nothing subtle about you same-race couples. The way you strut around, as if daring the world to rain on your disgusting little intraracial parade."

"But—"

"Whoa! Before you go blaming all white people because of your personal problems, let me warn you that you are already in violation of several applicable federal Civil Rights statutes. I'm afraid you've taken this matter out of my hands. I have no choice but to send you up to see the Colonel."

"The Colonel?"

"The Civil Rights Prosecutor. In the big office on the top floor of the main building."

"What about me?"

"You can go with her if you want, Yusef. But if I were you—"

"You're not."

"—I'd find a nice white girl and get married. Fast. Before you both get in more trouble than you can handle. Dismissed. Next!"

"Next!"

"We're here to see the Colonel."

"I am the Colonel. I'm here to help you if I can. And let me begin by warning you that anything you say will be used against you."

"Will be?"

"Can be, will be, whatever. Young lady, are you splitting hairs with me?"

"No."

"Good. Now, I see you are under indictment for Discrimination and Conspiracy."

"Conspiracy? All we wanted to do was get married."

"Which is against the law. Surely you knew that or you wouldn't have gone to the Marital Law Administration in the first place."

"We were trying to get a special license."

"Precisely. And what is that if not trying to evade the Melanin Redistribution Act which prohibits black intramarriage? The mere presence of you two in line A21 is in itself evidence of a conspiracy to circumvent the provisions of the Melanin Hoarding Ban."

"But we were trying to *obey* the law!"

"That makes it even worse. The law is a just master, but it can be harsh with those who try to sabotage its spirit by hypocritically observing its letter. However, I'm going to delay sentencing on Conspiracy and Hoarding because we have an even more serious charge to deal with here."

"Sentencing? We haven't even been convicted yet."

"Young lady, are you splitting hairs with me?"

"No."

"Good. Now let's move on to the Discrimination charge. Deep issues are involved here. You two aren't old enough to remember the Jim Crow Days in the South, when blacks weren't permitted to swim in the public pools. But I remember. Do you know what Discrimination is?"

"I read about it in school."

"Well, then you know that it is wrong. And blacks who don't marry whites are denying them the right to swim in their gene pool. Discriminating against them."

"Nobody's denying anybody the right to do anything! I just want to marry Yusef."

"That's a conveniently simplistic way of looking at things, isn't it? But it won't wash in a court of law. You can't marry Yusef without refusing to marry Tom, Dick, or Harry. It's the same difference. If you marry a black person, you are denying a white person the *right* to marry you; and that's a violation of his rights under the Fourteenth Amendment. Do you recognize those two pictures on the wall?"

"Sure. Martin Luther King and John Kennedy."

"John *F.* Kennedy. Somehow your generation has lost sight of the ideals they died for. Let me pose a purely hypothetical question—would it be fair to have a society in which one racial grouping, such as yours, had special rights and privileges denied to the rest of us?"

"It never bothered anybody before."

"Are you getting smart?"

"No. But what about the Fourteenth Amendment? Doesn't it apply to me?"

"Certainly it does. To you as an individual, and to your young man as well. But as African Americans you are more than just individuals; you are also a precious natural treasure."

"Huh?"

"Under the Melanin Heritage Act, your genetic material is a national resource, which America is now claiming for all its people, not just for a privileged few. It is the same genetic material that was brought across the ocean (bought and paid for, I might add) in the eighteenth and nineteenth centuries."

"But the slaves were freed."

"And their descendants as well. But genetic material, being immortal, can be neither slave nor free. It is an irreplaceable natural resource, like the forests or the air we breathe. And whether you kids like it or not, the old days when our resources were squandered and hoarded by special interests are over. Your genetic heritage is a part of the priceless national endowment of every man, woman, and child in America, not just your private property to dispose of as you please. Am I making myself clear?"

"I guess."

"You guess! Would it be fair to have an African American child born double M; while a white child, denied his or her Melanin Birthright, was doomed to twice the chance of skin cancer and god-knows-what-else?"

"Nobody ever worried about white kids being born with twice everything before."

"Enough, young lady. I am sentencing you to nine months at Catskill Tolerance Development Camp, or until the baby is born, followed by nine years at Point Pleasant Repeat Pregnancy Farm. I sincerely hope you will use your time at Point Pleasant to think about how racist attitudes such as yours threaten the rainbow fabric of our multiethnic democracy.''

"What about me?''

"I'm putting you on probation, Yusef, and taking you home for dinner as soon as court is over. I want you to meet my daughter. Marshal, put the cuffs on this one and take her away. Pay no heed to her crocodile tears: they are masters of deceit.

"Next!''

✦ NECRONAUTS ✦

THE FIRST TIME I died was an eye-opener. Literally.

I got a call from a researcher at Duke. He said he had seen my paintings in the *National Geographic* and *Smithsonian* magazines and wanted to engage me as illustrator for an expedition he was planning.

I explained that I was blind and had been for eighteen months.

He said he knew; he said that was why they wanted me.

The next morning I was dropped in front of the university's Psy Studies Institute by my ex. You can tell a lot about a space by its echoes and the one I entered was drab and institutional, like a hospital waiting room.

Dr. Philip DeCandyle's hand was moist and cold, two qualities that don't always go together. I form a mental picture of those I am dealing with and I saw an overweight, soft man, almost six feet tall; later I was told I was not far off.

After introducing himself, DeCandyle introduced the woman standing beside him as Dr. Emma Sorel. She was only a little shorter, with a high-pitched voice and a cold, tentative touch that told me she was more skilled at withdrawing from the world than engaging it; a common quality in a scientist, but curious for an explorer. I wondered what sort of expedition these two could be planning.

"We're both very excited that you could come, Mr. Ray," said Dr. DeCandyle. "We saw the work you did for the undersea Mariana Trench expedition, and your paintings prove that there are some things that the camera just can't capture. It's not just a technical problem of lack of light. You were able to convey the grandeur of the ocean depths; its cold, awesome terror."

He did all the talking. It was my introduction to a manner of speech that struck me as exaggerated, almost comical— before I had experienced the horrors to which he held the key.

"Thank you," I said, nodding first to his position and then to hers, even though she had said nothing yet. "Then you both undoubtedly also know that I lost my eyesight on the expedition, as a result of a decompression incident."

"We do," said Dr. DeCandyle. "But we also read the feature in the *Sun;* and we know that you have continued to paint, even though blind. And to great acclaim."

This was true. After the accident, I learned that my hand hadn't lost the confidence that almost forty years of training and work had built. I didn't need to see to paint. The papers called it a psychic ability, but to me it was no more remarkable than the sketcher who watches his subject and not his pad. I had always been precise in how I lined up and laid on my colors; the fact I was still able to sense their shape and intensity on my canvas had more to do with moisture and smell, I suspected, than with ESP.

Whatever it was, the newspapers loved it. I had discussed it in several interviews over the past year; what I hadn't told anyone was how badly the work had been going lately. An artist is not just a creator of beauty but also its primary consumer, and I had lost heart. After almost two years of blindness, I had lost all interest in painting scenes from my past, no matter how remarkable they might appear to others. My art had become a trick. The darkness that had fallen over my world was becoming total.

"I still paint, it's true," was all I said.

"We are engaged in a unique experiment," said Dr. DeCandyle. "An expedition to a realm even more exotic and beautiful—and dangerous—than the ocean depths. Like the Mariana Trench, it is impossible to photograph and therefore has never been illustrated. That is why we want you to be a part of our team."

"But why me?" I said. "Why a blind artist?"

DeCandyle didn't answer. His voice took on a new authority. "Follow me and I'll show you."

Ignoring the awful irony of his words, and somewhat against my better judgment, I did.

Dr. Sorel fell in behind me; we passed through a door and entered a long corridor. Through another door, we entered a room larger and colder than the first. It sounded empty but wasn't; we walked to the center and stopped.

"Twenty years ago, before beginning my doctoral work," said DeCandyle, "I was part of a unique series of experiments being performed in Berkeley. I don't suppose you are familiar with the name of Dr. Edwin Noroguchi?"

I shook my head.

"Dr. Noroguchi was experimenting in techniques for reviving the dead. Oh, nothing as dramatic and sinister as Frankenstein. Noroguchi studied and adapted the recent successes in reviving people who had drowned or suffered heart attacks. Learning to *induce death* for as long as an hour, we—I say we, for I joined him and have since devoted my life to the work—began to explore and, you might say, map the areas of existence immediately following death. LAD or Life After Death experience."

My aunt Kate, who raised me after my parents were killed, always told me I was a little slow. It was only at this point that

I began to understand what DeCandyle was getting at. If I had been nearer the door, I would have walked out. As it was, in the middle of a room where I had no bearings, I began backing away.

"Using chemical and electrical techniques on volunteers, we were able to confirm the stories those who had been revived told about their spirits looking down on their own bodies; about floating toward a light; about an intense feeling of peace and well-being—all this was scientifically investigated and confirmed. Though not, of course, photographed or documented. There was no way to share what we discovered with the scientific world."

I had reached the wall; I started feeling along it for the door.

"Then legal and funding problems intervened, and our work was interrupted. Until recently. With the help of the university and interest from the *National Geographic,* Dr. Sorel and I have been able to continue the explorations that Dr. Noroguchi and I began. And your ability to paint will enable us to share with the world what we discover. The last unexplored frontier, the 'undiscovered country' of which Shakespeare wrote, is now within the reach of—"

"You're talking about killing yourselves," I interrupted. "You're talking about killing me."

"Only temporarily," said Dr. Sorel. It was the first thing she'd said; I felt her hand on my arm and I shuddered. "Dr. Sorel has been to LAD space many times," DeCandyle said, "and as you can see—forgive me; I mean tell—she has returned. Can it be called true death, if it is not final? And the compensations are—"

"Sorry," I interrupted again. Feeling behind me for the door, I was stalling for time. "What with insurance and royalties, I'm pretty well fixed."

"I am not speaking of money," Dr. DeCandyle said, "Although you will of course be paid. There is another and, perhaps for you, more important compensation than money.''

I found the door. I was just about to go through it when he said the only words that could have turned me around:

''In LAD space, you will once again be able to see.''

By two that afternoon I had completed my physical and was being strapped into what DeCandyle and Sorel called ''the car'' for my first mission into LAD space.

Of all the scenes of heaven and hell and the regions between which I was to witness, the one I most wish I was able to paint is that empty-sounding room and the car that was to carry me beyond this life. All I had was DeCandyle's description of the car. It was a black (appropriately) open fiberglass cockpit with two seats: I visualized it as a Corvette without the wheels.

Dr. Sorel strapped me in, while DeCandyle explained that the frame contained the electroshock revival mechanism and the monitoring systems. Around my left wrist, she fastened a Velcro gauntlet which contained the intradermal injector for the atropine chemical mix that would shut down my sympathetic nervous system.

In what I later realized was a shrewd psychological move, I was seated on the left: the first time I had been in a driver's seat since I had lost my sight.

''Give you a lift to the cemetery?'' I joked.

''You must take this first trip alone,'' Sorel said; I was to learn that she had no sense of humor whatsoever. This brief orientation trip (or ''LAD insertion''; DeCandyle was fond of NASA-type jargon) was supposed to be perfectly safe; it was to provide a chance for me to experience LAD space, and for them to evaluate my reaction, both physical and psychological, to induced death.

Sorel clipped the belt over my shoulder with her big, cold hands, and I heard her footsteps walking away. I had the image of her and DeCandyle hiding behind a lead curtain like X-ray technicians. The car's monitoring systems started up with a low hum.

"Ready?" DeCandyle called.

"Ready." But I had to say it twice before the word came out.

I felt a brief sting in my wrist. "Mr. Ray? Can you hear me now?" asked DeCandyle, who had somehow acquired a high, tinny edge to his voice, like Sorel's. I tried to answer but couldn't, wondering why, until I realized that the injection was working, that the trip was beginning.

That I was dying.

I felt an instant of panic and reached to pull off the wrist cuff, but my reflexes were slowing and by the time the impulse reached my left arm I was too weak to lift it. Dr. Sorel (or was it DeCandyle?) was saying something now, but the voice was receding from me. I tried again to lift my hand; I can't remember whether or not I succeeded. I felt a sudden strong sense of shame, as if I had been caught doing something terribly, irrevocably wrong; then the shame was gone. It had blown away. There seemed to be a wind blowing through the room as if a new door had opened. My skin grew cooler and seemed to be expanding; I felt like a balloon being inflated.

In those first moments, I didn't have the experience of which so many have spoken, of floating upward and looking down on their own bodies. Perhaps because of my blindness I had lost the impulse to "look" back. I was conscious only of floating upward, faster and faster, with no desires and nothing tying me to what was below: I felt myself dwindling, and there was a gladness in it, as if I were dwindling toward some tiny bright point which all of me had always yearned to be.

My naturalist's instincts, which I have carefully nurtured over the years as an essential balance to my artistic vision, were somehow missing in all this: I had no objectivity. I *was* what I was experiencing, which is just another way of saying there was no "me" to experience my experiencing it. Somehow this pleased me, like an accomplishment.

It was as I was becoming conscious of this pleasure that I saw the light, a lattice of light, toward which I was floating, as if it were the surface of a pond in which I had been submerged so long, and so deeply, as to forget that it had a surface at all.

I saw! I was seeing! It seemed perfectly natural, as if I had never stopped; and yet a great joy filled me.

I grew closer to the light and I seemed to slow; I felt myself spinning and "looked" back, or "down." For the first time, all in a rush, I remembered the car, my blindness, my life, the world. I saw specks floating like dust in shafts of light and wondered if that was all it had ever amounted to. Even as I puzzled over this I was turning back toward the lattice of light, which drew me toward it almost like a lover.

In their preliminary briefing, Sorel and DeCandyle had warned of the "chill" of LAD space; but I didn't feel it. I felt only awe and peacefulness, like the feeling one gets gazing down from a mountaintop onto a sea of clouds. Perhaps my experience was moderated by the wonderful new gift of vision; or perhaps somewhere in my bones I knew that this death was not final and that I would soon return to Earth.

I turned back toward the lattice of light (or was it turning toward me?) and saw that it was a display of light and light, no shade. I bathed in it, floating under it with a kind of bliss that I can compare only with that of orgasm, though it lasted for a long time, never peaking, never diminishing—a never-ending climax of quiet joy.

Was this, then, Heaven? Whether I asked that question then, or later, on reflection, I have no way of knowing; for memory and experience and anticipation were one to me then.

"After" (there is no sense of time in LAD space) I had

bathed in this glory for what seemed an eternity I felt myself drifting back, down, away from the light. The light was receding and the darkness below was growing closer. I could see both in front and behind as I "fell" and I was vaguely conscious (or did memory add this later?) of the darkness reaching up toward me, like welcoming arms.

And I was blind again. Blind! I pulled back, toward death—and the light—and suddenly felt a sharp shock, and the outrage that pain brings. Reeling, I felt another shock; both, I learned later, were from the electroshock system built into the car, bringing me back to life.

I was conscious of hands on my face. I tried to raise my own hands but they were tied. Then I realized they weren't tied, but dead.

Dead.

To describe what I felt as "fear" understates the wave of terror that filled me. Though something—my consciousness? my soul?—had been revived, my body was dead. I had no sensation and couldn't move. My mouth was open, but not by my own will, nor could I close it.

It was only when I tried to scream that I realized I wasn't breathing.

The third electroshock came as a friend: I welcomed its violence as it ripped through me. I *felt*, for the first time in my life (or was this my life?), my heart stir in my breast as it clutched itself inward, sucking for blood greedily, like a child sobbing; I heard it bubbling as it filled. Then the blood flooded into my brain, ice-cold, and I could hear screaming all around me.

It was my own scream, echoing.

I must have lost consciousness again, or perhaps there was an injection to smooth out the reentry process. When I awoke I was breathing smoothly, relaxed, lying on a two-person wheeled gurney. It was 4:03 P.M. according to my braille watch; only two hours since my trip had begun.

I heard voices and sat up; a paper cup of hot tea laced with bourbon was thrust into my hand. My lips were numb.

"That first retrocution can be rough," DeCandyle said.

"How do you feel?" Sorel asked, at the same time: "Are you with us?"

I hurt all over but I nodded.

Thus began my journey to the Other Side.

"There's something creepy about those two," my ex said when she picked me up at 5 P.M. as arranged.

"They're okay," I said.

"She has no chin but her nose makes up for it."

"They're researchers, not models," I said. "It's an experiment where I paint dream-induced images. Perfect job for a blind man." This was the agreed-on lie; there was no way I could tell the truth.

"But why a blind man?" she asked.

My ex is a cop. It is to her that I owe the independence I have enjoyed since the accident that blinded me. It was she who brought me home from the hospital and stayed with me, commuting daily from Durham where she works. It was she who managed the contractors and used the financial settlement from the Mariana Institute to rework my mountainside studio so that I was able to move (at first on ropes, like a puppet, and then independently) from bed to bath, from kitchen to studio, with as little hassle as possible.

Then it was she who went ahead with the divorce she had been planning even before the accident.

"Maybe they want somebody who can paint with his eyes closed," I said. "Maybe I'm the only fool who'll do it. Maybe they like my work; though I realize you would find that a little farfetched—"

"You should see her hair," she said. "It's white at the

roots." She turned off the highway up the short, steep driveway to my studio. The low-slung police cruiser scraped on the high spots. "This driveway needs fixing."

"First thing in the spring," I said.

I couldn't wait to get to work. That night, I began my first new painting in almost four months—the one that appeared on the cover of the "Undiscovered Country" issue of the *National Geographic* and now hangs in the Smithsonian as "The Lattice of Light."

One week later, at 10 A.M., as arranged, Dr. Sorel picked me up at my studio. I could tell by the door handles that she was driving a Honda Accord. Funny how the blind see cars.

"You're probably wondering what a blind man's doing with a shotgun," I said. I had been cleaning mine when she came. "I like the feel of it even though I don't shoot. It was a gift from the Outer Banks Wildlife Association. I did a series of paintings for them."

She said nothing. Which is different from not saying anything.

"Ducks and sand," I said. "Anyway, it's real silver. It's English; a Cleveland. Eighteen seventy-one."

She turned on the radio to let me know she didn't want to talk; the college FM station was playing Roenchler's "Funeral for Spring." She drove like a bat out of hell. The road from my studio to Durham is narrow and winding. For the first time since the incident, I was glad I couldn't see.

I decided I agreed with my ex; Sorel was creepy.

Dr. DeCandyle was waiting for us in the lobby, eager to get started, but first I had to stop by his office to "sign" the voiceprint contract; that is, affirm our agreement on tape. I was to join them on five "insertions into LAD space" one week apart. *National Geographic* (which already knew my work) was to get first reproduction rights to my paintings. I was to own the prints and the originals and get a first-use fee, plus a fairly handsome advance.

I signed, then said: "You never answered my question. Why a blind artist?"

"Call it intuition," DeCandyle said. "I saw the *Sun* article and said to Emma—that's Dr. Sorel—'Here's our man!' We need an artist who is not, shall we say, distracted by sight. Who can capture the intensity of the LAD experience without throwing in a lot of visual referents. Also, quite frankly, we need someone with a reputation; for the *Geographic*, you understand."

"Also you need somebody desperate enough do it."

His laugh was as dry as his palms were moist. "Let's just say 'adventurous.' "

Sorel joined us in the hall on the way to what DeCandyle called the "launch lab." I could tell by the rustling sound of her walk that she had changed clothes. I later learned that she wore a NASA-type nylon jumpsuit on our "LAD insertions."

I was pleased to find myself in the driver's seat again. Sorel strapped herself in beside me this time.

My left hand was free but my right hand was guided into an oversized stiff rubber mitten.

"The purpose of this glove, which we call the handbasket," DeCandyle said, "is to join our two LAD voyagers more closely together. We have learned that through constant physical contact, some perceptual contact is maintained in LAD space. The name is our little joke. To hell in a handbasket?"

"I get it," I said. Then I heard a *click* and realized he had not been talking to me but into a tape recorder. "How long will this trip last?" I asked.

"Insertion," DeCandyle corrected. "And we have found it's best not to discuss duration; that way we avoid clashes between objective and subjective time. As a matter of fact, we prefer that you not verbalize your experiences at all, but commit them strictly to canvas. You will be driven home immediately after retrocution, or reentry, and not expected to participate in any debriefings with Dr. Sorel and myself."

Click.

"Now, if you have no further questions—"

If I had any further questions, I couldn't think of them. How much can you want to know about getting yourself killed?

"Good," DeCandyle said. I heard his footsteps walking away, and then I heard the drawing of the curtain that meant the trip—insertion—was about to begin.

"Ready, Dr. Sorel?" The car's monitoring systems started up with a low hum, like an idling engine.

Sorel said, "Ready." Her hand joined mine in the glove. It felt awkward. Rather than hold hands, we turned them so that only the backs of our hands touched.

"Series forty-one, insertion one." *Click.*

Again I felt the tiny sting; the sudden sense of shame and then the wind from somewhere else; and I was floating once more upward toward the lattice of light. This time, alarmingly, I could "see" a dark shape below that could only be the car, with two bodies slumped forward hideously, one of them mine— But I was gone. Then far off I saw the Blue Ridge, and Mount Mitchell, which I had painted from every side in every season, even though I knew it was not visible from Durham. The mountains are lost forever to the blind and I felt a sharp sorrow; then my sorrow, with my mountain, was lost in the light. The light! A shadow, chasing from below, drew closer and flowed into me, and then out again as light. I felt it as an *other:* a presence not quite separate, womanly yet part of me, linked to me like two fingers on one hand as under the lattice of light we spun. Again I felt the sweet warmth like unending orgasm—only there was no "again": each moment was as the first. The lattice of light stayed always at the same distance, almost close enough to touch, and yet as distant as a galaxy. Space was as indistinct and undifferentiated as Time. The presence linked with me somehow doubled my own ecstasy; I felt, I was, twice everything.

Then something pulled me downward, and I was alone, unlinked (unwhole?) again, spinning away from the light, feeling the warmth fade behind. Life from here looked as dark and lonesome as the grave. As before, there was the shock, the insult of pain, the agony as the cooled blood with its cold understandings rushed in . . .

Bringing another darkness.

"Retrocution at five thirty-three P.M." *Click.*

I was on the gurney again. Sorel must have revived (or "retrocuted") first, for she was helping DeCandyle. I sat dazed, silent, numb, while they recorded my vital signs. Her fingers felt familiar and I wondered if we had held hands while we were dead.

"How long?" I asked, finally.

"I thought we weren't going to ask that question," DeCandyle said. "I'll drive him home," said Sorel. She drove even faster than before. For the twenty-minute ride we listened to the radio—Mahler—and didn't speak. I didn't invite her in; I didn't have to. We both knew exactly what was going to happen. I heard her steps behind me on the gravel, on the step, on the floor. While I knelt to light the space heater—for the studio was cold—I heard the long pull of the zipper on her jumpsuit. By the time I had turned around she was helping me with my clothes, silent, efficient, and fast, and her mouth was cold; her tongue and her nipples were cold; I was naked like her and falling with her into my own cold unmade studio bed, exploring that body that was so strange and yet so utterly familiar. When I entered her it was she who entered me: we came together in a way that I had forgotten was possible.

Forgotten? I had never known, never dreamed of passion like this.

Twenty minutes later, she was dressed and gone without a word.

My ex came by on Thursday with her boyfriend—excuse me, partner—to drop off some microwavables. She left him in the cruiser with the engine idling. "You're painting again?" she said. I could hear her shuffling through my canvases, even though she knows it annoys me. "That's good. They say abstract art's good therapy."

She was looking at "The Lattice of Light"; or perhaps "Spinners." My ex thinks all art is therapy.

"It's not therapy," I said. "Remember the experiment? The dreams? The professors at Duke." I felt a sudden foolish impulse to explain myself to her. "And it's not an abstract, either. In the dreams, I can see."

"That's nice," she said. "Only, I had those two checked out. I have a friend in the dean's office. They're not professors. At least, not at Duke."

"They're from Berkeley," I said.

"Berkeley? That explains everything."

On Monday at ten, Sorel picked me up in the Honda. I offered her my hand, and from the tentative, almost reluctant way she shook it, I could tell that our sexual encounter had taken place in another realm altogether. That was fine with me. I found the university's FM station on the van's radio and we listened to Shulgin all the way to Durham. "The Dance of the Dead." I was beginning to like the way she drove.

DeCandyle was waiting impatiently in the launch lab. "On this second insertion, we're going to try and penetrate a little deeper," he said. *Click.*

"Deeper?" I asked. How could you get deeper than dead?

He spoke to me and the tape at the same time. "So far on

this series we have seen only the outer regions of LAD space. Beyond the threshold of light, there lies yet another LAD realm. It, also, seems to have an objective reality. On this insertion we will observe without penetrating that realm." *Click.*

Sorel entered the room; I recognized the swishing of her nylon jumpsuit. I was strapped into the car and my hand was guided into the glove—and I recoiled in disgust. Something was in there. It was like putting my hand into a bucket of cold entrails.

"The handbasket now contains a circulating plasma solution," DeCandyle said. "Our hope is that it will keep a more positive contact between our two LAD voyagers." *Click.*

"You mean necronauts," I said.

He didn't laugh; I hadn't expected him to. I slid my hand into the handbasket. The stuff was slick and sticky at the same time. Sorel's hand joined mine. Our fingers met with no awkwardness; even with a kind of comfortable, lascivious hunger. DeCandyle asked: "Ready?"

Ready? For a week I had thought of nothing but the intensity, the excitement—the *light* of LAD space. The lab's machines started with their low harmony of hums. It seemed to be taking forever. The solution in the glove began to circulate while I waited for the injection that would free me from the prison of my blindness.

"Series forty-one, insertion two," DeCandyle said. *Click.*

Oh death, where is thy sting? My heart was pounding.

Then it stopped.

I could feel my blood pool, grow thick, grow cool. My body seemed to elongate—then suddenly I was gone; peeling away, up from the car, away from my body, into the light.

I was rising as if being pulled. There was no time to look back at my own body, or the mountains. Faster and faster, we were ascending into the realm of the dead: LAD space. I say *we*, for I was a shadow pursuing a shadow, yet together we were a circle of light, spinning in a dance harmonious. I ached for Sorel as a planet aches for its sun. The light loved us—and we spun basking in its sweet climactic endless glow, luxuriating in a nakedness so total that the body itself has been stripped off and set aside. I felt like the gods must feel, knowing that the world we lurch through in life is only their cast-off clothes. We rose into the lattice of light and it opened before us . . .

And I felt a sudden fear. It was slight, like the chill on the back of your neck when a door opens that shouldn't be opened. The light was darkening around me and the presence at the end of my fingertips was suddenly gone. I was alone. I thought (yes, dead, but I "thought"!) something had gone wrong in the lab.

All was still. I was in a new darkness. Only this was a darkness unlike the darkness of blindness: here somehow I could see. I was alone on a gray plain that stretched forever in every direction, but instead of space I felt claustrophobia, for every horizon was close enough to touch. The chill had become a deep, cruel, vicious, bone cold. I tried to move and the darkness itself moved with me . . .

"Retrocution at three oh seven," DeCandyle was saying; Sorel was slapping my cheeks. "We lost contact," I heard her say.

I wasn't in the car; I was lying down on the wheeled gurney. I was freezing. "Duration one hundred thirty-seven minutes," DeCandyle said. *Click.*

I sat up and held my face in my hands. Both cheeks were cold. Both hands were shaking.

"I'll drive him home," Sorel said.

"Where were we?" I asked, but she wouldn't answer me. Instead she drove faster and faster.

My studio was cold and I knelt to light the space heater. I fumbled with the damp matches, afraid she would leave, until I felt her hand on the back of my neck. She was undressed already, pulling me toward the bed, toward her plump, taut, cool breasts; her opening thighs. I forgot the chill I had felt in her womb, as cold and sweet as her mouth. How backward romance's metaphors are! For it is the flesh, scorned in song for so many centuries, that leads the spirit toward the light. Underneath our nakedness we discovered more nakedness still, entering and opening one another, until together we soared like creatures that cannot fly alone, but only joined; the naked flesh going where our naked spirits had been only hours before. What we made was more than love.

"Does he know?" I asked, afterward, when we were lying in the dark. I like the darkness; it equalizes things.

"Know? Who?"

"DeCandyle. Who do you think?"

"What I do is none of his business," she said. "And what he knows, is none of yours." It was the end of our first and longest conversation. I slept for six hours and when I woke up she was gone.

"Turns out I have a friend at Berkeley too," my ex said when she came by on Thursday to drop off some microwavables. Cops have friends everywhere; at least they think of them as friends.

"DeCandyle was in the medical school until he was kicked out for selling drugs. The other one was in comparative lit until she was kicked out in her junior year. All very hush-hush but it seems she was using drugs to recruit students for experiments. I think there was even a death involved. I have another friend who's checking the PD files."

"Dum de-dum dum," I said.

"I'm just giving you the facts, Ray. What you do with them, if anything, is up to you." She was shuffling through my stacked canvases again. "I'm glad to see you're doing mountains again. They were always your best sellers. And what have we here? Pornography?''

"Eye of the beholder," I said.

"Bullshit. Don't you think this is a little—gynecological—for *Natural Geographic?* I know they show tits and all, but—''

"It's *National,*" I said. "And do me a favor—'' I nodded toward her partner, who was standing just inside the door, foolishly thinking that if he stood perfectly still I wouldn't know he was there. "As long as you and your boyfriend are playing Sergeant Friday, check out one more name for me."

On Monday I was supposed to deliver the first batch of paintings in the series. DeCandyle sent a hired van to pick me up. I knew the driver. He was a local part-time preacher and abortion-clinic bomber. I was careful to keep the paintings covered as we loaded them in.

"I hear you're working with the Hell Docs," he said.

"I don't know what you're talking about; I'm just going in for a treatment," I lied. "I am blind, you know."

"Whatever you say," he said. "I hear they're sending a man and a woman to Hell. Sort of a new Adam and Eve."

He laughed. I didn't.

"Magnificent," said DeCandyle, when he unwrapped the paintings in his office. "How can you do it? I could understand touch, sculpture; but painting? Colors?"

"I know what it looks like while I'm working on it," I said. "After it's dry, no. If you need a theory, my theory is that colors have smells; smells that are pitched too high for most people. So I'm like a dog that can hear a high-pitched whistle. That's why I paint in oil and not acrylic."

"So you don't agree with the article in the *Sun* that it's a psychic ability?"

"As a scientist, surely you don't believe that crap."

"As a scientist," DeCandyle said, "I don't know what I believe anymore. But let's go to work."

There was something different about the echoes in the launch lab. I was led directly to the gurney, and helped onto it. "Where's the car?" I protested.

"We are dispensing with the car for the rest of this series," DeCandyle said. I knew he was only partly talking to me when I heard the *click* of his recorder. "With this insertion we will begin using the C-T or Cold Tissue chamber developed while I was in Europe. It will allow us to penetrate deeper into LAD space." *Click.*

"Deeper?" I was alarmed; I didn't like lying down. "By staying dead longer?"

"Not necessarily longer," DeCandyle said. "The C-T chamber will cool the home tissue more rapidly, allowing faster LAD penetration. We hope on this insertion to actually penetrate the threshold barrier." *Click.*

By home tissue he meant the corpse. "I don't like this," I said. I sat up on the gurney. "It's not in my contract."

"Your contract calls for five LAD insertions," DeCandyle said. "However, if you don't want to go—"

Just then Sorel came into the room in her jumpsuit. I could hear the swishing of the nylon between her legs.

"I didn't say I didn't want to go," I said. "I just want—" But I didn't know what I wanted. I lay back down and she lay down beside me. I heard the snap of tubes being attached; guided by hers, my hand slid into the smelly, cold mash of the glove. Our fingers met and entertwined. They were like teenagers, getting together in secret, each with its own little libido.

"Series forty-one, insertion three," DeCandyle said. *Click.*

The gurney was rolling and we were pushed into a small chamber. I felt rather than heard a door close just behind my head: a softer *click.* I panicked but Sorel clutched my hand and the smell of atropine and formaldehyde filled the air. I felt myself falling—no, rising, with Sorel, linked, hand in hand, toward the light. This time we went more slowly and I saw our bodies laid out, spinning, naked as the day we were born. We rose into the lattice of light and it parted around us like a song.

And it was gone.

All around was the gray darkness.

We were on the Other Side.

I felt nothing. It filled me. I was frozen.

Sorel's presence now had a form; she who had been all light was all flesh. I find it impossible to describe even though I was to paint it several times. She had legs but they were strangely segmented; breasts but not the breasts my lips and fingers knew; her hands were blunt, her face was blank and her hips and what I can only call her mind were bone-white. She moved away into the gray distance and I moved with her, still linked "hand" to "hand."

I felt—I *knew*—I had always been dreaming and only this was real. The space around me was a blank and endless gray. "Life" had been a dream; this was all there was.

I drifted. I seemed to have a body again, although it was not in my control. For hours, centuries, eternities we drifted through a world as small as a coffin, yet never reached an end. At the still center of it all was a circle of stones. I followed Sorel down toward them. Somebody—or something—was inside.

Waiting.

She passed through the stones toward the Other, pulling me with her. I pushed back; then pulled away, filled with terror. For I had touched stone. Nothing here was real and yet—I had touched stone. Suddenly I knew I was awake because everything was dark, only I could no longer see.

Beside me was her body; its dead hand clutching mine. I had never before awakened—retrocuted—before Sorel. I reached up with my left hand, fearfully, tentatively, until I felt the lid of my coffin just where I knew it would be. It was porcelain or steel, not stone. But cold as stone.

I tried to scream but there was no air. Before I could scream there was a shock, and I fell into another, a darker, darkness.

"What you felt was the roof of the C-T chamber," DeCandyle was saying. "It enables you to remain in LAD space longer without damage to the home tissue. And with ultrasonic blood cooling, to cross directly to the Other Side." It was the first time I had heard the term yet I knew immediately what he meant.

Someone was clutching my right hand; it was Sorel. She was still dead. I was lying on the gurney; it rocked on its wheels as I struggled to sit up.

I shuddered as I remembered. "Before I touched the lid, while I was still dead, I touched stone."

DeCandyle went on: "Apparently there are realms in LAD space whose accessibility depends on residual electrical fields in the home tissue." I waited for the click, which never came, and realized he was talking only to me. "There is a magnetic polarity in the body that endures for several days after death. We want to find out what happens as the electrical field decays. The C-T chamber allows us to explore this without waiting on the actual mortification of the flesh."

Mortification. "So there's dead and then there's deader."

"Something like that. Let me drive you home."

I was still holding Sorel's hand. I pried my fingers loose.

I couldn't sleep. The horror of the Gray Realm (as I was to call it in a painting) kept leaking back in. I felt like a man halfway up the Amazon, afraid to go on but afraid to turn back, because no matter what horrors lay ahead, he knows too well the horror that lies behind. The Devil's Island of blindness.

I ached for Sorel. We blind are said to be connoisseurs of masturbation, perhaps because our imaginations are so practiced at summoning up images. Afterward, I turned on the lights and tried to paint. I always work in the light. Painting is a collaboration between the artist and his materials. I know paint loves light; I figure canvas at least likes it.

But it was no good. I couldn't work. It wasn't till after dawn, amid the harsh din of the awakening birds, that I realized what was bothering me.

I was jealous.

My ex came by a day early (I thought) to drop off some microwavables. "Where have you been?" she asked. "I was trying to call you all day."

"I was at the university on Monday, as usual," I said.

"I'm talking about Tuesday."

"Yesterday?"

"Today is Thursday; you've lost a day. Anyway, we struck paydirt with your other name. Noroguchi was the real thing, a tenured professor at Berkeley, in the medical school, no less. That is, until he was murdered."

I could hear her flipping through my canvases, waiting for me to respond. I could imagine her half-smile.

"Don't you want to know who murdered him?"

"Let me guess," I said. "Philip DeCandyle."

"Ray, I always said you should have been a cop," she said. "You take the fun out of everything. Manslaughter. Plea-bargained down from Murder Two. Served six years at San Rafael. The creepy one was an accessory but she never went to jail."

"I thought you said they were both creepy."

"She's creepier. Did you know her tits are different sizes?

Don't answer that. Did you know you have a blank canvas here in the finished pile?"

"It belongs there," I said. "It's called 'The Other Side.' "

On Monday, it was DeCandyle who picked me up in the Honda. "Where's Sorel?" I asked. I had to know. Even if she was dead I wanted to be with her.

"She's okay. She's waiting for us at the lab."

"I'm dying to see her," I said. I didn't expect DeCandyle to laugh and he didn't.

He drove maddeningly slowly. I missed Sorel's breathtaking speed. I asked him to tell me about Noroguchi.

"Dr. Noroguchi died during an insertion; that is, failed to retrocute. I was blamed. But I get the distinct feeling you've heard the whole story."

"And he's still there."

"Where else?"

"But why him? Millions of people are dead but we don't see them."

"You've *seen* Edwin?" DeCandyle stopped and there was a scream of brakes as someone almost hit us from behind. He stepped on the gas. "We don't know why," he said. "Apparently the connection persists when it's strong enough. He and Emma were partners on many insertions. Too many. Emma's convinced that it's possible to penetrate deep enough to find him."

"To bring him back?"

"Of course not. He's dead. Edwin always insisted on going deeper and deeper even though we didn't have the C-T chamber then. It's Emma's obsession now. If anything, she's worse than him; than he was."

"Were they—"

"Were they lovers?" It wasn't what I was going to ask, but it was what I wanted to know.

"Toward the end, they were lovers," he said. He laughed; a bitter little laugh. "I don't think they knew I knew."

When we got to the institute I heard rhythmic shouts and the unfamiliar crunch of gravel.

"We'll have to enter through the back," DeCandyle said. "We have demonstrators out front. A local preacher has been telling the natives that we are trying to duplicate the Resurrection in the laboratory."

"They always get it backward," I said.

We entered through a side door, directly into the lab. I sat on the gurney waiting to hear the swish of Sorel's nylon jumpsuit between her legs. Instead I heard the *suss* of rubber tires and the faint ringing of spokes.

"You're in a wheelchair?"

"Temporarily," she said.

"Thrombophlebitis," said DeCandyle. "The blood clots when it pools in the veins for too long. But don't worry; the C-T chamber diffusion fluid now contains a blood thinner."

We lay down together, side by side. My hand found the glove, which was between us. Was the solution getting old? There was a funny smell. Sorel's hand found mine and our fingers met in their familiar lascivious fond embrace, except—

She was missing a finger. Two.

Stumps.

My hand froze, wanting to pull away; the handbasket started gurgling and we were rolled forward, then stopped.

"Ready?"

"Ready." A part of me was scared; another part of me was amazed at how impatient a third part of me was to die. We were rolled forward again, feet first, into the cold, slightly acrid air of the chamber. A door closed behind my head. Before I had time to panic, Sorel's fingers found mine and comforted them, opening them like petals, and there was the sting. My heart stopped, like a TV that has been turned off.

Or on. For there came a kaleidoscope of colors, through which I arose, faster and faster. There was no floating, no looking back, no basking in the lattice of light; for no sooner had I seen—no, glimpsed—the familiar splendors of LAD space than they were gone and we were in that other darkness.

The Other Side.

It stretched around us endless and yet enclosing. The "sky" was low like a coffin lid. Sorel and I moved stiffly, drifting, no longer spirit but all flesh. I was dead awake. I was conscious of her buttocks, the flesh on her arms which was fluted somehow like toadstool skin; the cold insect smell as we circled the stone pillars that pinned the low sky down.

We seemed to get no closer as we circled "The Pens" (as I was to call them in a painting): they spun slowly in the center of our immobility, like a system of stone stars. Again someone, some Other, waited inside. Under the lattice of light there was no sense of time's passage, perhaps because the spirit (unlike the body) moved at time's exact speed; but here, on the Other Side, time no longer buoyed us in its stream. There was no movement. Every forever was inside another forever, and the moments were no longer a stream but a pond: concentric circles that went nowhere.

There were other differences. In LAD space I had known, even dead, that I was alive. Here I knew that I was dead. That even alive, I was dead: that I had always been dead. That this was the reality into which all else flowed, from which nothing came. That this was the end of things.

My terror never diminished, nor did it grow: a still panic filled every cell of my body like uncirculating blood. Yet I was unmoved; I watched myself suffer as dispassionately as a boy watches a bug burn.

Sorel was dead-white. She was somehow closer to the pens

and when she reached out the stone was right there. She turned toward me and her face was blank, a gaze of bone. Mine back at her was the same; our nothingness was complete. We were at the standing stones and through them I could see a figure. He (it was a he) beckoned and Sorel passed through the stones, but I pulled back: then I, too, touched the stone (colder than cold) and I was with her again. We were inside the pens and now there were three of us, and it was as if there had always been. We were following Noroguchi (it was surely he) into a sort of dark water, which grew deeper. It was I who stopped; it took all my will. I turned away and this time Sorel, her face bone-blank, turned away with me.

I woke up in darkness, the blind darkness of the world.

I touched the lid of our coffin. It was porcelain, smooth and cold. I felt Sorel's hand locked in mine in the steel grip of the dead. I felt not panic but peace.

There was a shock, then another shock, and darkness came over the darkness, and all was still.

"We made contact," I heard Sorel's voice say. I was glad. Wasn't I?

I was on the gurney. I sat up. My hands were burning; my fingertips were on fire.

"The pain is just the blood coming back around," said DeCandyle. "You were inserted into LAD space for over four hours."

It was unusual for him to volunteer a duration. And there was no *click*. I knew he was lying.

"I'll take him home," Sorel said. Her voice sounded tinny and far away, as when we were dying. "I can still drive."

It was morning. Dawn may not "come up like thunder" as Kipling put it, but it does have a sound. I rolled down the Honda's window and bathed in the cold air, letting the new day cover over the night's horror like a fresh coat of paint.

But the horror kept bleeding back through.

"We were gone all night," I said.

Sorel laughed. "Try two nights," she said. It was the first time I had heard her laugh. She seemed happy.

She pulled up in my drive but left the engine running. I reached over and turned the key off. "I'll come in if you want me to," she said. "You'll have to help me in the door."

I did. She could hop on one leg okay. Under her nylon NASA-style jumpsuit I was surprised to find smooth silk underwear with lace through the crotch; I could tell by my fingertips that it was white. One leg was puffy like a sausage. Her skin was tight and cool.

"Sorel," I said. I couldn't call her Emma. "Are you trying to bring him back or go with him?"

"There's no coming back," she said. "No body to come back to." She pressed my hand to the stumps of her fingers, then to her cold lips, then between her cold thighs.

"Then stay here with me," I said.

We fumbled for each other, our lips and fingers numb. "Don't take my bra all the way off," she said. She pulled one cup down and her nipple was cold and sticky and sweet. Too sweet. "It's too late," she said.

"Then take me with you," I said.

That was the end of our last conversation.

"Sort of a Stonehenge," my ex said when she came by on Thursday with some microwavables. She was shuffling through my paintings again. "And what's this? My God, Ray. Porn is one thing; this is, this is—"

"I told you, they're images from dreams."

"That makes it even worse. I hope you're not going to show these to anybody. It's against the law. And what's that smell?"

"Smell?"

"Like something died. Maybe a raccoon or something. I'm going to send William over to check under the studio."

"Who's William?"

"You know perfectly well who William is," she said.

Saturday night I was awakened by a banging on the studio door.

"DeCandyle, it's two in the morning," I said. "I'm not supposed to see you till Monday anyway."

"I need you now," he said, "or there won't be a Monday." I got into the Honda with him; even when he was hurrying he drove too slowly. "I can't get Emma to retrocute. She's been in LAD space for over four days now. This is the longest she's ever gone. The home tissue is starting to deteriorate. Excessive signs of morbidity."

She's dead, I thought. This guy just can't say it.

"I let her go too often," he said. "I left her inserted too long. Too deep. But she insisted; she's been like a woman obsessed."

"Step on it or we'll get hit from behind," I said. I didn't want to hear any more. I turned up the radio and we listened to *Carmina Burana,* an opera about a bunch of monks singing their way to Hell.

It seemed appropriate.

DeCandyle helped me up onto the gurney and I felt the body beside me, swollen and stiff. I quickly got used to the smell. Tentatively, with a feeling of fear, I slipped my hand into the handbasket.

Her hand in the glove felt soft, like old cheese. Her fingers, for the first time, didn't seek mine but lay passive. But of course—she was dead.

I didn't want to go. Suddenly, desperately, I didn't want to go. "Wait," I said. But even as I said it, I knew I hadn't a chance. He was sending me after her. The gurney was already rolling and the small square door shut with a soft *click*.

I panicked; my lungs filled with the sour smell of atropine and formaldehyde. I felt my mind shrink and grow manageable. My fingers in the glove felt tiny, miserable, alone until they found hers. I expected more stumps but there were only the two. I made myself quiet and waited like a lover for the sting that would— Oh! I floated free at last, toward light, and saw the dark lab and the cars on the highway like fireflies and the mountains in the distance, and I realized with a start that I was totally conscious. Why wasn't I dead? The lattice of light parted around me like a cloud and suddenly I was standing on the Other Side, alone; no, she was beside me. She was with the Other. We drifted, the three of us, and time looped back on itself: we had always been here.

Why had I been afraid? This was so easy. We were inside the pens, which were a ring on the horizon in every direction, so many, so much stone; close enough to touch yet as far away as the stars I could barely remember . . . and at my feet, black still water.

Plenty of darkness but no stars on the Other Side.

I was moving. The water was still. I understood then (and I understand now) what physicists mean when they say that everything in the universe is in motion, wheeling around everything else, for I was in the black still water at the center of it all: the only thing that doesn't move. Was it a subjective or an objective reality? The question had no significance. This was more real than anything that had ever happened to me or ever would again.

There was certainly no joy. Yet no fear. We were filled with a cold nothingness; complete. I had always been here and will be here forever. Sorel is in front of me and in front of her—the Other—and we are moving again. Through the black water. Deeper and deeper. It is like watching myself go away and get smaller.

This is no dream. Noroguchi is going under. Sorel grows smaller, following him into the black water: and I know that there is another realm beyond this one, and other realms beyond that, and the knowing fills me with a despair as thick as fear.

And I am moving backward, alive with terror, ripping my hand from Sorel's even as she pulls me with her; then she too is gone under.

Gone.

I reach up with both hands and touch the lid of my coffin. My hand out of the glove drips cold plasma down on my face. I am screaming soundlessly without air.

Then a shock, and warm darkness. Retrocution. When I woke up I was colder than I'd ever been. DeCandyle helped me sit up.

"No good?" He was weeping; he knew it.

"No good," I said. My tongue was thick and tasted bad from the plasma. Sorel's hand was still in the handbasket, and when I reached in and and pulled it out her flesh peeled off like the skin of a rotten fruit, and stuck to my fingers. Outside, we could hear the protesters' chants. It was Sunday morning.

That was two and a half months ago.

DeCandyle and I waited until the demonstrators left for church, and then he drove me home. "I have killed them both," he said. Lamented. "First him and then her. With twenty years in between. Now there is no one left to forgive me."

"They wanted it. They used you," I said. Like they used me.

I made him let me off at the bottom of the drive. I was tired of him, sick of his self-pity, and I wanted to walk up to the studio alone. I couldn't paint. I couldn't sleep. I waited all day and all night, hoping irrationally to feel her cold touch on the back of my neck. Who says the dead can't walk? I paced the floor all night. I must have fallen asleep for I had a dream in which she came to me, naked and shining and swollen and all mine. I woke up and lay listening to the sounds coming through the half-open window over my bed. It's amazing how full of life the woods are, even in the winter. I hated it.

The next Wednesday I got a call from my ex. A woman's body had been found at the Psy Studies Institute, and there was a chance that I would be brought in to help identify it. Dr. DeCandyle had been arrested. I might be asked to testify against him, also.

As it turned out I was never questioned. The police aren't eager to press a blind man for an identification. "Especially when the university is trying to hush up the whole business," my ex said. "Especially when the body is as erratically decomposed as this one," said her boyfriend.

"What do you mean?"

"I have a friend in the coroner's office," he said. " 'Erratically' is the word he used. He said it was the most peculiar corpse he had ever seen. Some of the organs were badly decomposed and others almost fresh; it was as if the decedent had died in stages, over a period of several years."

Cops love words like "decedent" and "corpse." They, doctors, and lawyers are the only ones left that still speak Latin.

Sorel was buried on Friday. There was no funeral, just a brief graveside procedure so the proper papers could get signed. She was buried in the part of the cemetery set aside for amputated limbs and used medical school cadavers. It was odd mourning someone I had known better dead than alive. It felt more like a wedding; when I smelled the dirt and heard it hit the coffin lid I felt I was giving away the bride.

DeCandyle was there, handcuffed to my ex's boyfriend. They had let him come as the next of kin.

"How's that?" I asked.

"She was his wife," my ex said as she led me to her cruiser so she could drive me home. "Student marriage. Separated but never divorced. I think she ran off with the Jap. The one he killed first. See how it all fits together? That's the beauty of police work, Ray."

The rest of the story you already know, especially if you subscribe to the *National Geographic*. The story was a Ballantine Prize nominee: the first pictures ever from the other side, the far realm, or as Shakespeare put it best, the Undiscovered Country. DeCandyle even made it into *People* magazine:

> The Magellan of the Styx
> Speaks from his Prison Cell

and my gallery show in New York was a huge success. I was able to sell, for an astonishing price, a limited edition of prints, while donating (for a generous tax break) the paintings to the Smithsonian.

My ex and her boyfriend picked me up at the Raleigh-Durham airport when I flew back from New York. They were getting married. He had checked under the studio but found nothing. She was pregnant.

"What's this I hear about your fingers?" my ex asked when she called last Thursday. She no longer has time to stop by; a country woman cooks for me. I explained that I had lost the tips of two fingers to what my doctor claims is the only case of frostbite in North Carolina during the exceptionally mild winter of 199–. Somehow my touch for painting has gone with them, but no one needs to know that yet.

It's spring at last. The wet earth smells remind me of the

grave and awaken in me a hunger that painting can no longer fill, even if I had my fingers. I have painted my last. My ex—excuse me, the future Mrs. William Robertson Cherry—and her boyfriend—excuse me, fiancé—have assured me that they will send a driver to pick me up and bring me to the wedding next Sunday.

I may not make it, though. I have a silver shotgun behind the door that I can ride like a rocket anytime I want to.

And I hate weddings. And spring.

And envy the living.

And love the dead.

♦ Are There Any Questions? ♦

WELCOME.

I'm glad to see you all looking so alert, so eager, so prosperous this morning. I promise you that at the end of our little talk and tour, you'll be even more eager, and potentially more prosperous, because you didn't come here to be entertained. You came here to get in on the ground floor, and "ground" is a good word for it, of the most unique investment opportunity since the opening of the American West.

So let's get down to the nitty-gritty, as my grandad used to say. We're here to talk about something people don't usually like to talk about. Even though there's plenty of it around. Last year, in 1999, the average family in the New York metropolitan area produced 157.4 pounds of it in a week. This comes to 645,527 cubic yards of it a day, or—uncompacted—an Empire State Building every 16.4 days or a truckload every six and a half minutes.

What in the world is he talking about? Well, we all know, don't we? You there, madam, on the second row. I can see your lips forming the very word itself.

But you're wrong.

I'm not talking about garbage. Not anymore. I'm talking about real estate. I'm talking about land.

"Land," my granddad used to say, "is the only surefire investment there is, because God's not making any more of it."

He was right about it being a surefire investment. But he was wrong about why. Because even though God's not making any more of it, we at Eden-Prudential are. But I don't have to tell you folks that. That's why you're here.

I see some of you are getting your calculators out. Good. Let's look at those numbers again. 11,987,058 cubic meters of solid waste, and that's what we can collect, process, transport, and place in a month, can, in the right hands, translate to a quarter acre of beautiful mountain view property, or sixteen feet of ocean front. Notice I say "in the right hands." That's where Eden-Prudential comes in. Even as you and I speak, EP's trucks are running and EP's barges are under sail. We have four fleets of 138 trucks apiece—all independent contractors, by the way; real mom 'n' pop types—operating from our catchment and processing center on Staten Island. Every eighteen minutes sees five trucks dispatched, three to south Jersey, and two to Montauk; all working around the clock to make America not only more prosperous than ever, but a little bit bigger. And more valuable.

But enough poetry. Let's talk opportunity. What area produces the most solid waste in the world, per square mile of already existing land? The New York metropolitan area. And what area contains the world's most valuable real estate? Or to put it another way: is there any other place in the world where land is in such short supply and where people are so willing—not to mention able—to pay for it?

Again, you just can't beat the New York area.

A surplus of garbage. A shortage of land. Put those two facts together in the right equation, and you come up with what we at EP call IP, or Investment Potential. But it was only potential, and potential only, until the invention of the Eden Land Developer, the solid-waste transformer that turns ordinary garbage of any kind, shape, or origin, into quality, consistent, durable *real estate.*

If you will be kind enough to take one of the foil-wrapped souvenir samples Miss Crumb is passing around the room . . . Go ahead, open it. It's going to make you rich. Don't be afraid of getting your hands dirty because you won't. Does it look like dirt? Not with that attractive gold color, it doesn't. It's Eden Earth. Go ahead, sniff it. Taste it if you want to. My great-great-granddad was a farmer, God rest his soul, out in Iowa, I think it was, and he never judged a piece of land without putting a piece of it on his tongue.

No takers. Well, I understand.

You can take my word for it: what you hold in your hand is a piece of solid waste that has been not only recycled but reconstituted, not to mention eye- and odor-enhanced, to make an earth that is the equal to, and in many ways actually superior to, the earth that the Earth itself is made of.

Do I see eyebrows lifting?

Well, try to crumble it. This cookie doesn't crumble. Dunk it—it's water-resistant and therefore it doesn't turn into mud. You'll notice it doesn't soil your hands or stain your shirt. Its epoxy polymer additives mean that smells and stains are locked in, and that once we put it in place it stays there—it doesn't dry up and blow away like the Great Plains in the dust bowl, or wash away like the beaches of Long Island in a hurricane. Eden Earth is *real estate,* in the true, biblical meaning of the word, not ephemeral dirt and dust that is dependent on every caprice of Nature.

But people who know Real Estate—and I can see that you are all professionals in the field—know that the value of land depends on its location. We at Eden-Prudential not only collect and process Eden Earth by the tons every day; we truck and barge it to the areas where people want to be. The locations people are most hungry for and most willing to pay big money for. We're creating the kind of real estate that is in short supply and high demand.

A home in the mountains. A home by the sea.

Eden-Prudential is making America grow, with two areas currently under development. In the no-longer-barren Pine Barrens of south Jersey, our environmental designers are right now putting the finishing touches on an attractive range of small mountains called the Crestfills. Miss Crumb, could we have the first video please? The magnificent peak in the background is Eden Peak. It soars to an elevation of 2,670 feet, almost a thousand feet higher than any other mountain in New Jersey, and over half again the height of Fresh Kills Peak on Staten Island.

Eden Peak's lovely summit is a nature preserve. If you want to see the breathtaking view from the top, as we're seeing it here on video, you'll have to park your 4X4 and walk up one of our beautiful nature trails—the first trails I might add that were planned and built along *with* a mountain, not added as an afterthought.

Of more interest to yourselves, as brokers and developers, are the winding drives along the crest of Atlantic City Ridge, so named because it overlooks the lights of that great capital of chance only forty-five minutes away by car. The three planned neighborhoods here—Eaglefill Estates, Hawkfill Glade, and Baronfill Manor—will be open to the public in October, and sold through selected brokers only. Our hope is that you will be among them.

The foundation for another quality ridge is even now being laid to the west, nearer to Philadelphia.

There will be those who will want to live in the Crestfills year-round, but for most these will be vacation homes, hideaways for busy executives who want to lay aside the world's cares and communicate with nature. And here in the Crestfill Mountains, nature is at its best. Your clients will hear birds singing winter and summer. They are drawn to the Crestfills not only by the pleasant pine scent, renewed monthly, but by the fact that the mountainsides are warmed several degrees by the gentle internal action of Eden Earth as it ages, making the Crestfills a unique and precious winter wildlife sanctuary.

These pine-covered slopes, with their cunningly spaced "rocky" outcrops—there's one right now—were created by a team of environmental designers who spared no expense, even dropping fill from container-copters to create those hard-to-reach spots that give wilderness areas their special appeal. Free-range deer and even an occasional bear roam the rugged slopes. There's a deer now. Put it on "pause," Miss Crumb, and let's have another look. How many here are old enough to remember the original *Bambi?* How many took their children to see it?. Their grandchildren?

Me too.

But suppose your clients and prospective buyers dream of a home by the sea? What if Fire Island, Cape Cod, Nantucket are the kind of names that fire their souls and loosen their checkbooks?

How does Bayfill Island sound to you?

If we may, Miss Crumb, let's cut away to our second video, and another type of paradise—a rocky, fogbound New England-style island of the kind featured in so many romantic movies. How many of you have dreamed of the opportunity to buy and sell summer homes on one of these exclusive sites? Well, hang on—your dreams are about to come true.

Bayfill Island lies at the opening of Long Island Sound, between Montauk and one of the older glacial debris islands, Block Island. It is by comparing Bayfill with the rather run-down—geologically speaking—islands in the area, that we can best understand why we say Eden Earth puts standard earth to shame. Large areas of Nantucket Island are carved away by the ocean waves every winter—valuable real estate becoming silt and sand in the ocean deeps. Not so on Bayfill Island. Since Eden Earth is both salt- and water-resistant, it stands firm against the weather. Large areas of Martha's Vineyard are swamps and marshes, filled with vicious insects. In contrast, there are no wastelands on Bayfill Island, where all the land is dry land and rain runs off as clear and clean as when it fell. Large areas of Block Island are out of sight and sound of the ocean, drastically lowering property values. On ingeniously S-shaped Bayfill Island, every property is ocean-front property; there are no "cheap seats" in the house.

But enough poetry. It's time to go and see for ourselves. Miss Crumb has just signaled me that Eden-Prudential's chartered airbus has arrived to take us on our tour of the two sites. We only have to walk a block to board. As you leave the office here, we'll be crossing the East Thirty-fourth Street Extension. Watch your step; the ground is still a little springy.

Are there any questions?

↯ Two Guys from the Future ↯

"WE ARE TWO guys from the future."

"Yeah, right. Now get the hell out of here!"

"Don't shoot! Is that a gun?"

That gave me pause; it was a flashlight. There were two of them. They both wore shimmery suits. The short one was kind of cute. The tall one did all the talking.

"Lady, we are serious guys from the future," he said. "This is not a hard-on."

"You mean a put-on," I said. "Now kindly get the hell out of here."

"We are here on a missionary position to all mankind," he said. "No shit is fixing to hang loose any someday now."

"Break loose," I said. "Hey, are you guys talking about nuclear war?"

"We are not allowed to say," the cute one said.

"The bottom line is, we have come to salvage the artworks of your posteriors," the tall one said.

"Save the art and let the world go. Not a bad idea," I said. "But, *mira*, it's midnight and the gallery's closed. Come back *en la mañana*."

"*Que bueno! No hay mas necesididad que hablar en inglés,*" the tall one said. "Nothing worse than trying to communicate in a dead language," he went on in Spanish. "But how did you know?"

"Just a guess," I said, also in Spanish; and we spoke in the mother tongue from then on. "If you really are two guys from the future, you can come back in the future, like tomorrow after we open, right?"

"Too much danger of Timeslip," he said. "We have to come and go between midnight and four A.M., when we won't interfere with your world. Plus we're from far in the future, not just tomorrow. We are here to save artworks that will otherwise be lost in the coming holocaust by sending them through a Chronoslot to our century in what is, to you, the distant future."

"I got that picture," I said. "But you're talking to the wrong girl. I don't own this art gallery. I'm just an artist."

"Artists wear uniforms in your century?"

"Okay, so I'm moonlighting as a security guard."

"Then it's your boss we need to talk to. Get him here tomorrow at midnight, okay?"

"He's a her," I said. "Besides, *mira*, how do I know you really are, on the level, two guys from the future?"

"You saw us suddenly materialize in the middle of the room, didn't you?"

"Okay, so I may have been dozing. You try working two jobs."

"But you noticed how bad our *inglés* was. And how about these outfits?"

"A lot of people in New York speak worse *inglés* than you," I said. "And here on the Lower East Side, funny suits don't prove anything." Then I remembered a science fiction story I had once heard about. (I never actually *read* science fiction.)

"You did *what*?" said Borogove, the gallery owner, the next morning when I told her about the two guys from the future.

"I lit a match and held it to his sleeve."

"Girl, you're lucky he didn't shoot you."

"He wasn't carrying a gun. I could tell. Those shimmery suits are pretty tight. Anyway, when I saw that the cloth didn't burn, I decided I believed their story."

"There's all sorts of material that doesn't burn," Borogove said. "And if they're really two guys from the future who have come back to save the great art of our century, how come they didn't take anything?" She looked around the gallery, which was filled with giant plastic breasts and buttocks, the work of her dead ex-husband, "Bucky" Borogove. She seemed disappointed that all of them were still hanging.

"Beats me," I said. "They insist on talking to the gallery owner. Maybe you have to sign for it or something."

"Hmmm. There have been several mysterious disappearances of great art lately. That's why I hired you; it was one of the conditions of Bucky's will. In fact, I'm still not sure this isn't one of his posthumous publicity stunts. What time are these guys from the future supposed to show up?"

"Midnight."

"Hmmm. Well, don't tell anyone about this. I'll join you at midnight, like Macbeth on the tower."

"Hamlet," I said. "And tomorrow's my night off. My boyfriend is taking me to the cockfights."

"I'll pay you time and a half," she said. "I may need you there to translate. My *español* is a little rusty."

Girls don't go to cockfights and I don't have a boyfriend. How could I? There aren't any single men in New York. I just didn't want Borogove to think I was easy.

But in fact, I wouldn't have missed it for the world.

I was standing beside her in the gallery at midnight when a column of air in the center of the room began to shimmer and glow and . . . But you've seen *Star Trek*. There they were. I decided to call the tall one Stretch and the cute one Shorty.

"*Bienvenidos* to our century," said Borogove, in Spanish, "and to the Borogove Gallery." Her Spanish was more than a little rusty; turned out she had done a month in Cuernavaca in 1964. "We are described in *Art Talk* magazine as 'the traffic control center of the Downtown Art Renaissance.' "

"We are two guys from the future," Stretch said, in Spanish this time. He held out his arm.

"You don't have to prove anything," said Borogove. "I can tell by the way you arrived here that you're not from our world. But if you like, you could show me some future money."

"We're not allowed to carry cash," said Shorty.

"Too much danger of Timeslip," explained Stretch. "In fact, the only reason we're here at all is because of a special exemption in the Chronolaws, allowing us to save great artworks that otherwise would be destroyed in the coming holocaust."

"Oh dear. What coming holocaust?"

"We're not allowed to say," said Shorty. It seemed to be the only thing he was allowed to say. But I liked the way that no matter who he was talking to, he kept stealing looks at me.

"Don't worry about it," said Stretch, looking at his watch. "It doesn't happen for quite a while. We're buying the art early to keep the prices down. Next month our time (last year, yours) we bought two Harings and a Ledesma right around the corner."

"Bought?" said Borogove. "Those paintings were reported stolen."

Stretch shrugged. "That's between the gallery owners and their insurance companies. But we are not thieves. In fact—"

"What about the people?" I asked.

"You stay out of this," Borogove whispered, in *inglés*. "You're just here to translate."

I ignored her. "You know, in this coming holocaust thing. What happens to the people?"

"We're not allowed to save people," said Shorty.

"No big deal," said Stretch. "People all die anyway. Only great art is forever. Well, almost forever."

"And Bucky made the short list!" said Borogove. "That son of a bitch. But I'm not surprised. If self-promotion can—"

"Bucky?" Stretch looked confused.

"Bucky Borogove. My late ex-husband. The artist whose work is hanging all around us here. The art you came to save for future generations."

"Oh no," said Stretch. He looked around at the giant tits and asses hanging on the walls. "We can't take this stuff. It would never fit through the Chronoslot anyway. We came to give you time to get rid of it. We're here for the early works of Teresa Algarín Rosado, the Puerto Rican neoretromaximinimalist. You will hang her show next week, and we'll come back and pick up the paintings we want."

"I beg your pardon!" said Borogove. "Nobody tells me who will or will not hang in this gallery. Not even guys from the future. Besides, who's ever heard of this Rosado?"

"I didn't mean to be rude," said Stretch. "It's just that we already know what will happen. Besides, we've already deposited three hundred thousand dollars in your account first thing tomorrow."

"Well, in that case . . ." Borogove seemed mollified. "But who is she? Do you have her phone number? Does she even have a phone? A lot of artists—"

"How many paintings are you going to buy?" I asked.

"You stay out of this!" she whispered in *inglés*.

"But I am Teresa Algarín Rosado," I said.

I quit my job as a security guard. A few nights later I was in my apartment when I noticed a shimmering by the sink. The air began to glow and . . . but you've seen *Star Trek.* I barely had time to pull on my jeans. I was painting and I usually work in a T-shirt and underpants.

"Remember me, one of the two guys from the future?" Shorty said, in Spanish, as soon as he had fully appeared.

"So you can talk," I said, in Spanish also. "Where's your *compañero?*"

"It's his night off. He's got a date."

"And you're working?"

"It's my night off too. I just—uh—uh . . ." He blushed.

"Couldn't get a date," I said. "It's all right. I'm about ready to knock off anyway. There's a Bud in the refrigerator. Get me one too."

"You always work at midnight? Can I call you Teresa?"

"Please do. Just finishing a couple of canvases. This is my big chance. My own show. I want everything to be just right. What are you looking for?"

"A bud?"

"A Bud is a *cerveza,*" I said. "The top twists off. To the left. Are you sure you guys are from the future and not the past?" (Or just the country, I thought to myself.)

"We travel to many different time zones," he said.

"Must be exciting. Do you get to watch them throw the Christians to the lions?"

"We don't go there, it's all statues," he said. "Statues won't fit through the Chronoslot. You might have noticed, Stretch and I broke quite a few before we quit trying."

"Stretch?"

"My partner. Oh, and call me Shorty."

It was my first positive illustration of the power of the past over the future.

"So what kind of art do you like?" I asked while we got comfortable on the couch.

"I don't like any of it, but I guess paintings are best; you can turn them flat. Say, this is pretty good *cerveza*. Do you have any roll and rock?''

I thought he meant the beer but he meant the music. I also had a joint, left over from a more interesting decade.

"Your century is my favorite," Shorty said. Soon he said he was ready for another petal.

"Bud," I said. "In the fridge."

"The *cerveza* in your century is very good," he called out from the kitchen.

"Let me ask you two questions," I said from the couch.

"Sure."

"Do you have a wife or a girlfriend back there, or up there, in the future?"

"Are you kidding?" he said. "There are no single girls in the future. What's your second question?"

"Do you look as cute out of that shimmery suit as you do in it?"

"There's one missing," said Borogove, checking off her list as the workmen unloaded the last of my paintings from the rented panel truck and carried them in the front door of the gallery. Other workmen were taking Bucky's giant tits and asses out the back door.

"This is all of it," I said. "Everything I've ever painted. I even borrowed back two paintings that I had traded for rent."

Borogove consulted her list. "According to the two guys from the future, three of your early paintings are in the Museo de Arte Inmortal del Mundo in 2255: 'Tres Dolores,' 'De Mon Mouse,' and 'La Rosa del Futuro.' Those are the three they want."

"Let me see that list," I said.

"It's just the titles. They have a catalogue with pictures of what they want, but they wouldn't show it to me. Too much danger of Timesplits."

"Slips," I said. We looked through the stacked canvases again. I am partial to portraits. "De Mon Mouse" was an oil painting of the super in my building, a rasta who always wore Mickey Mouse T-shirts. He had a collection of two. "Tres Dolores" was a mother, daughter, and grandmother I had known on Avenue B; it was a pose faked up from photographs—a sort of tampering with time in itself, now that I thought of it.

But "La Rosa del Futuro"? "Never heard of it," I said.

Borogove waved the list. "It's on here. Which means it's in their catalogue."

"Which means it survives the holocaust," I said.

"Which means they pick it up at midnight, after the opening Wednesday night," she said.

"Which means I must paint it between now and then."

"Which means you've got four days."

"This is crazy, Borogove."

"Call me Mimsy," she said. "And don't worry about it. Just get to work."

"There's pickled herring in the *nevera*," I said, in Spanish.

"I thought you were Puerto Rican," said Shorty.

"I am, but my ex-boyfriend was Jewish, and that stuff keeps forever."

"I thought there were no single men in New York."

"Exactly the problem," I said. "His wife was Jewish too."

"You're sure I'm not keeping you from your work?" said Shorty.

"What work?" I said forlornly. I had been staring at a blank canvas since ten P.M. "I still have one painting to finish for the show, and I haven't even started it."

"Which one?"

"La Rosa del Futuro," I said. I had the title pinned to the top corner of the frame. Maybe that was what was blocking me. I wadded it up and threw it at the wall. It only went half-way across the room.

"I think that's the most famous one," he said. "So you know it gets done. Is there a blossom—"

"A Bud," I said. "In the door of the fridge."

"Maybe what you need," he said, with that shy, sly futuristic smile I was growing to like, "is a little rest."

After our little rest, which wasn't so little, and wasn't exactly a rest, I asked him, "Do you do this often?"

"This?"

"Go to bed with girls from the past. What if I'm your great-great-grandmother or something?"

"I had it checked out," he said. "She's living in the Bronx."

"So you do! You bastard! You do this all the time."

"Teresa! *Mi corazón!* Never before. It's strictly not allowed. I could lose my job! It's just that when I saw those little . . ."

"Those little what?"

He blushed. "Those little hands and feet. I fell in love."

It was my turn to blush. He had won my heart, a guy from the future, forever.

"So if you love me so much, why don't you take me back to the future with you?" I asked, after another little rest.

"Then who would paint all the paintings you are supposed to paint over the next thirty years? Teresa, you don't understand how famous you are going to be. Even I have heard of Picasso, Michelangelo, and the great Algarín—and art is not my thing. If something happened to you, the Timeslip would throw off the whole history of art."

"Oh. How about that." I couldn't seem to stop smiling. "So why don't you stay here with me."

"I've thought about it," he said. "But if I stayed here, I wouldn't be around to come back here and meet you in the first place. And if I had stayed here, we would know about it anyway, since there would be some evidence of it. See how complicated Time is? I'm just a delivery guy and it gives me a headache. I need another leaf."

"Bud," I said. "You know where they are."

He went into the kitchen for a *cerveza* and I called out after him: "So you're going to go back to the future and let me die in the coming holocaust?"

"Die? Holocaust?"

"The one you're not allowed to tell me about. The nuclear war."

"Oh, that. Stretch is just trying to alarm you. It's not a war. It's a warehouse fire."

"All this *mischigosch* for a warehouse fire?"

"It's cheaper to go back and get the stuff than to avoid the fire," he said. "It all has to do with Timeslip insurance or something."

The phone rang. "How's it going?"

"It's two in the morning, Borogove!" I said, in *inglés*.

"Please, Teresa, call me Mimsy. Is it finished?"

"I'm working on it," I lied. "Go to sleep."

"Who was that?" Shorty asked, in Spanish. *"La Gordita?"*

"Don't be cruel," I said, pulling on my T-shirt and underpants. "You go to sleep, too. I have to get back to work."

"Okay, but wake me up by four. If I oversleep and get stuck here—"

"If you had overslept we would already know about it, wouldn't we?" I said, sarcastically. But he was already snoring.

"I can't put it off for a week!" said Borogove the next day at the gallery. "Everybody who's anybody in the downtown art scene is going to be here tomorrow night."

"But—"

"Teresa, I've already ordered the wine."

"But—"

"Teresa, I've already ordered the cheese. Plus, remember, whatever we sell beyond the three paintings they're coming for is gravy. *Comprende?*"

"*En inglés,* Borogove," I said. "But what if I don't finish this painting in time?"

"Teresa, I insist, you must call me Mimsy. If you weren't going to finish it, they would have arranged a later pickup date, since they already know what will happen. For God's sake, girl, quit worrying. Go home and get to work! You have until tomorrow night."

"But I don't even know where to start!"

"Don't you artists have any imagination? Make something up!"

I had never been blocked before. It's not like constipation; when you're constipated you can work sitting down.

I padded and paced like a caged lion, staring at my blank canvas as if I were trying to get up the appetite to eat it. By eleven-thirty I had started it and painted it out six times. It just didn't feel right.

Just as the clock was striking midnight, a column of air near the sink began to shimmer and . . . but you've seen *Star Trek.* Shorty appeared by the sink, one hand behind his back.

"Am I glad to see you!" I said. "I need a clue."

"A clue?"

"This painting. 'La Rosa del Futuro.' Your catalogue from the future has a picture of it. Let me see it."

"Copy your own painting?" Shorty said. "That would cause a Timeslip for sure."

"I won't copy it!" I said. "I just need a clue. I'll just glance at it."

"Same thing. Besides, Stretch carries the catalogue. I'm just his helper."

"Okay, then just *tell* me what's it a picture of."

"I don't know, Teresa . . ."

"How can you say you love me if you won't even break the rules to help me?"

"No, I mean I *really* don't know. Like I said, art is not my thing. I'm just a delivery guy. Besides—" He blushed. "You know what my thing is."

"Well, my thing *is* art," I said. "And I'm going to lose the chance of a lifetime—hell, of more than that, of artistic *inmortalidad*—if I don't come up with something pretty soon."

"Teresa, quit worrying," he said. "The painting's so famous even I've heard of it. There's no way it can *not* happen. Meanwhile, let's don't spend our last—"

"Our what? Our last what? Why are you standing there with your hands behind your back?"

He pulled out a rose. "Don't you understand? This Chronolink closes forever after the pickup tonight. I don't know where my next job will take me, but it won't be here."

"So what's the rose for?"

"To remember our . . . our . . ." He burst into tears.

Girls cry hard and fast and it's over. Guys from the future are more sentimental, and Shorty cried himself to sleep. After comforting him as best I could, I pulled on my T-shirt and underpants and found a clean brush and started pacing again. I left him snoring on the bed, a short brown Adonis without even a fig leaf.

"Wake me up at four," he mumbled, then went back to sleep.

I looked at the *rosa* he had brought. The roses of the future had soft thorns; that was encouraging. I laid it on the pillow next to his cheek and that was when it came to me, in the form of a whole picture, which is how it always comes to me when it finally does. (And it always does.)

When I'm painting and it's going well, I forget everything. It seemed like only minutes before the phone rang.

"Well? How's it going?"

"Borogove, it's almost four in the morning."

"No, it's not, it's four in the afternoon. You've been working all night and all day, Teresa, I can tell. But you really have to call me Mimsy."

"I can't talk now," I said. "I have a live model. Sort of."

"I thought you didn't work from live models."

"This time I am."

"Whatever. Don't let me bother you while you're working; I can tell you're getting somewhere. The opening is at seven. I'm sending a van for you at six."

"Make it a limo, Mimsy," I said. "We're making art history."

"It's beautiful," Borogove said, as I unveiled "La Rosa del Futuro" for her. "But who's the model? He looks vaguely familiar."

"He's been around the art world for years and years," I said.

The gallery was packed. The show was a huge success. "La Rosa," "De Mon Mouse," and "Los Tres" were already marked SOLD, and SOLD stickers went up on my other paintings at the rate of one every twenty minutes. Everybody wanted to meet me. I had left Shorty directions and cab fare by the bed, and at eleven-thirty he showed up wearing only my old boyfriend's trenchcoat, saying that his shimmery suit had disappeared into thin air while he was pulling it on.

I wasn't surprised. We were in the middle of a Timeslip, after all.

"Who's the barefoot guy in the fabulous Burberry?" Borogove asked. "He looks vaguely familiar."

"He's been around the art world forever and ever," I said.

Shorty was looking jet-lagged. He was staring dazedly at the wine and cheese and I signaled to one of the caterers to show him where the beer was kept, in the backroom.

At eleven fifty-five, Borogove threw everybody else out and turned down the lights. At midnight, right on time, a glowing column of air appeared in the center of the room, then gradually took on the shape of . . . But you've seen *Star Trek*. It was Stretch, and he was alone.

"We are—uh—a guy from the future," Stretch said, starting in English and finishing *en español*. He was wobbling a little.

"I could have sworn there were two of you guys," said Borogove. "Or did I make that up?" she whispered to me, in *inglés*.

"Could be a Timeslip," said Stretch. He looked confused himself, then brightened. "No problem, though! Happens all the time. This is a light pickup. Only three paintings!"

"We have all three right here," said Borogove. "Teresa, why don't you do the honors. I'll check them off as you hand them to this guy from the future."

I handed him "De Mon Mouse." Then "Los Tres Dolores." He slipped them both through a dark slot that appeared in the air.

"Whoops," Stretch said, his knees wobbling. "Feel that? Slight aftershock."

Shorty had wandered in from the back room with a Bud in his hand. In nothing but a raincoat, he looked very disoriented.

"This is my boyfriend, Shorty," I said. He and Stretch stared at each other blankly and I felt the fabric of space/time tremble just for a moment. Then it was over.

"Of course!" said Stretch. "Of course, I'd recognize you anywhere."

"Huh? Oh." Shorty looked at the painting I was holding, the last of the three. "La Rosa del Futuro." It was a full-length nude of a short brown Adonis, asleep on his back without even a fig leaf, a rose placed tenderly on the pillow by his cheek. The paint was still tacky but I suspected that by the time it arrived in the future it would be dry.

"Reminds me of the day I met Mona Lisa," said Stretch. "How many times have I seen this painting, and now I meet the guy! Must feel weird to have the world's most famous, you know . . ." He winked toward Shorty's crotch.

"I don't know about weird," said Shorty. "Something definitely feels funny."

"Let's get on with this," I said. I handed Stretch the painting and he pushed it through the slot, and Shorty and I lived happily ever after. For a while. More or less . . .

But you've seen *I Love Lucy*.

✧ THE TOXIC DONUT ✧

HI, I'M RON, the Host's Chief Administrative Assistant, but you can just call me Ron. Let me begin, at the risk of seeming weird, by saying congratulations.

Of course I know. I've been doing this show every year for six years; how could I not know? But look at it this way, Kim—do you mind if I call you Kim? You have been chosen to represent all humanity for one evening. All the birds and beasts too. The worms and the butterflies. The fishes of the sea. The lilies of the field. You are, for one half hour tonight, the representative of all life on the planet. Hell, all life in the Universe, as far as we know. That calls for congratulations, doesn't it? You have a right to be proud. And your family, too.

Did you, I mean do you have a family? How nice. Well, we all know what they'll be watching tonight, don't we? Of course, I know, everybody watches it anyway. More than watch the Academy Awards. Eight to ten points more. A point is about thirteen million people these days, did you know that?

Okay. Anyway. Have you ever been on TV before? "Long shot at a ball game"—that's good. I loved Bill Murray too. God rest his soul. Anyway. Okay. TV is ninety-nine percent preparation, especially live TV. So if you'll walk over here with me, let's take this opportunity to run through the steps for our lighting people, as well as yourself; so you will be able to concentrate on the Event itself.

After all, it's your night.

Watch your step. Lots of wires.

Okay. We call this Stage Left. At 8:59, one minute to Airtime, one of the Girls will bring you out. Over there, in the little green outfits. What? Since you're a woman it should be guys in bikinis? I get it, a joke. You have quite a sense of humor, Kim. Do you mind if I call you Kim?

Right, we did.

Anyway. Okay. You'll stand here. Toes on that mark. Don't worry, the cameras won't linger on you, not yet. You'll just be part of the scene at the beginning. There will be one song from the International Children's Rainbow Chorus. "Here Comes the Sun," I think. All you have to do is stand here and look pretty. Dignified, then. Whatever. You're the first woman in two years, by the way; the last two Consumers were men.

I don't know why, Consumers is just what we call them; I mean, call you. What would you want us to call you?

That's another joke, right? Whatever.

Okay. Anyway. Song ends, it's 9:07. Some business with the lights and the Host comes on. I don't need to tell you there'll be applause. He walks straight up to you, and—kiss or handshake? Suit yourself. After the handshake, a little small talk. Where you're from, job, etc. Where are you from, by the way?

How nice. I didn't know they spoke English, but then it was British for years, wasn't it?

Anyway. Okay. Don't worry about what to say; the Host has been briefed on your background, and he'll ask a question or two. Short and sweet, sort of like *Jeopardy*.

To meet him? Well—of course—maybe—tonight right before the show, if time allows. But you have to understand,

Mr. Crystal's a very busy man, Kim. Do you mind if I call you Kim?

Right, we did. I remember. Sorry.

Okay. Anyway. A little ad-lib and it's 9:10. I have it all here on my clipboard, see? To the minute. At 9:10 there's some business with the lights, then the Girls bring out the Presidents of the Common Market, the African Federation, the Americas, Pacific Rim, etc. Five gentlemen, one of them a lady this year, I believe. There's a brief statement; nothing elaborate. "Your great courage, protecting our way of life" sort of thing. A few words on how the Lottery works, since this was the first year people were allowed to buy tickets for others.

I'm sorry you feel that way. I'm sure voluntary would be better. But somebody must have bought you a ticket; that's the way it works.

Anyway. Okay. Where were we? 9:13, the Presidents. They have a plaque that goes to your family after. Don't take it; it's just to look at. Then a kiss; right, handshake. Sorry. I'll make a note of it. Then they're out of here, Stage Right. Don't worry, the Girls manage all the traffic.

Okay. 9:14, lights down, then up on the Native People's presentation. You're still standing here, Stage Left, watching them, of course. You might even like it. Three women and three men, clickers and drums and stuff. While the women dance, the men chant. "Science, once our enemy, now our brother" sort of thing. You'll feel something on the back of your neck; that's the wind machine. They finish at 9:17, cross to here, give you a kind of bark scroll. Take it but don't try to unroll it. It's 9:18 and they're out of here, Stage Left. That's the end of the—

What? No, the corporations themselves don't make a presentation. They want to keep a very low profile.

Anyway. Okay. It's 9:19 and that's the end of the warm-up, as we call it. The Host comes back out, and you walk with him—here, let's try it—across to Center Stage. He'll help you stay in the spotlight. He admires the scroll, makes a joke, ad-lib stuff; don't worry about it. He's done it every year now for six years and never flubbed yet.

There won't be so many wires underfoot tonight.

Okay. It's 9:20. You're at Center Stage, toes here. That's it, right on the mark. There's more business with the lights, and the Host introduces the President of the International Institute of Environmental Sciences, who comes out from Stage Left. With the Donut. We don't see it, of course. It's in a white paper sack. He sets it here, on the podium in front of you.

He stands out there, those green marks are his—we call him the Green Meany—and gives his Evils of Science rap, starting at 9:22. "For centuries, poisoned the Earth, fouled the air, polluted the waters, etc., etc." It's the same rap as last year but different, if you know what I mean. A video goes with it; what we call the sad video. You don't have to watch if you don't want to, just look concerned, alarmed, whatever. I mean it all really happened! Dead rivers, dead birds, dioxins. Two minutes' worth.

Okay. Anyway. It's 9:24, and he starts what we call the glad video. Blue sky, birds, bears, etc. Gives the Wonders of Science rap where he explains how they have managed to collect and contain all the year's toxic wastes, pollutants, etc., and keep them out of the environment—

How? I don't know exactly. I never listen to the technical part. Some kind of submolecular-nano-mini-mumbo-jumbo. But he explains it all, I'm pretty sure. I think there's even a diagram. Anyway, he explains how all the toxic wastes for the year have been collected and concentrated into a single Donut. The fiscal year, by the way. That's why the Ceremony is tonight and not New Year's Eve.

Okay. Anyway. Hands you the bag.

Exits Stage Right, 9:27. Now it's just you and the Host, and of course, the Donut, still in the bag.

It might be a little greasy. You can hold it at the top if you want to. Whatever.

Anyway. Okay. It's 9:28. You'll hear a drumroll. It might sound corny now but it won't sound corny then. I know because I've been here every year for six years, standing right over there in the wings, and I get a tear in my eye every time. Every damn time. The camera pulls in close. This is your moment. You reach in the bag and—

Huh? It looks like any other donut. I'm sure it'll be glazed, if that's what you requested.

Okay. Anyway. 9:29, but don't worry about the time. This is your moment. Our moment, really, everybody in the world who cares about the environment, and these days that includes everybody. You reach in the bag, you pull out the Donut—

What happens next? I get it, still joking. I admire somebody with your sense of humor. Kim.

Anyway. Okay. We all know what happens next.

You eat it.

↓ CANCIÓN AUTÉNTICA DE ↓ OLD EARTH

"QUIETLY," OUR GUIDE said.

Quietly it was.

We glided over ancient asphalt, past ghost-gray buildings that glowed in the old, cold light of a ruined Moon that seemed (even though we have all seen it in pictures a thousand times) too bright, too close, too dead.

Our way was lighted by our photon shadow guide, enclosing us and the street around us in an egg of softer, newer light.

At the end of a narrow lane, four streets came together in a small plaza. At one end was a stone church; at the other a glass-and-brick department store façade; both dating (my studies coming through at last) from the High European.

"There's no one here," one of us said.

"Listen . . ." said our guide.

There came a rumbling. A synthesizer on a rubber-tired wood-and-wire cart rolled into the plaza out of an alley beyond the department store. It was pulled by an old man in black sweaters, layered against the planet's chill, and a boy in a leather jacket. An old woman, also all in black, and a smiling man who looked to be about forty walked behind. His smile was the smile of the blind.

"They still live here?" someone asked.

"Where else could they live?"

They stopped and a small yellow dog jumped down from the cart. The old man opened the synthesizer's panels and connected its cables to a moldering fuel cell. Sparks flew. The boy took a dirty bundle from the cart and unwrapped a strat and a tambourine. He handed the tambourine to the blind man.

The old lady carried a black vinyl purse. She watched not them, but us; and I had the "feeling" she was trying to remember who we were.

The blind man was smiling past us, over us, as if at a larger crowd that had come into the plaza behind us. He was so convincing that I even "turned" to look. But of course, the plaza was empty. The city was empty except for us and them; the planet was empty. It had been empty for a thousand years, empty while the seas fell and rose then fell again; empty since the twist.

The old lady watched while our guide flowed out and narrowed into a crescent, arranging us in a half circle around the musicians. Her face was as rough as the stones of the front of the church; her façade as fallen in.

Except for the boy's leather jacket, which was too shiny, everything they wore was old. Everything was cheap. Everything was black or gray.

The old man switched on the synthesizer and started to play chords in blocks of three. An electronic drumbeat kept time, a slow waltz. After a few bars the boy came in on the strat, high wailing tremolos.

"What about the singing?" someone complained in a whisper. "We came all the way across the Universe"—a slight exaggeration!—"for the singing."

"They used to sing for the tourists," our guide said. "Now there's only the occasional special group such as ours."

The blind man began to dance. With the dog at his feet, he waltzed around our little half circle and then back, beating the tambourine first against the heel of one hand and then against his hip. Where his feet brushed our photon shadow guide, his shoes sparkled and looked almost new.

As suddenly as he had started, he stopped, and the old man spoke in a shout:

"Hidalgos y damas estimadas—"

It was a variant of Latin which I could almost follow, Catalan or Spanish or Romany perhaps. Looking over us (just as the blind man had) the old man welcomed us back to our ancient, our ancestral home, where we would always be welcome, no matter how far we strayed, no matter how many centuries we stayed away, no matter what form it pleased us to take, etc.

"Y ahora, una canción autentica de old Earth . . ."He gave a nod to the boy, who played a blues figure high in the cutaway—

The blind man looked up to where a moon, *the* Moon, half filled the sky; then rose toward it on his tiptoes, and opened his mouth revealing blackened shards of teeth; and there was the singing we had come halfway across the Universe to hear.

The little dog following him, he walked as he sang—up, then down our half circle. It was quite beautiful. It sounded just as we had always imagined it might. His eyes were closed (now that he was singing) but the dog looked directly at us, one by one, from our "feet" upward, as if searching for something or someone. I could only partly follow the words, but as the song rose and fell I knew he sang of the seas and of the cities, and of the centuries before the twist, when genetics locked our parents to a single planet and a single form. His song soared to a wail as he sang of the centuries after, and of the Universe that was ours at last. Listening, we huddled together inside our photon shadow guide; everything outside it, under that ruined Moon, even the little yellow dog, looked abandoned and lost.

"They are the last?" one of us whispered.

"According to them," our guide said, in its low tone, "there will be no more."

The song was over. The singer bowed until the echo had died away. When he straightened and opened his eyes, they were filled like little seas.

"The *canción autentica* is said to be a very sad song," said our guide.

The old lady stepped forward at last. She opened the purse and someone produced a coin: the two met with a *clink* as if a long chain had just been closed. The dog followed in her footsteps as she walked around our half circle, holding out the purse, and each of us put in the coin we had brought. I wished I had brought two. Though where would I have found another? God knows what she did with them anyway. There was no trade, no commerce, nothing left to buy.

"The *canción autentica* seemed very sad to me," someone said. I "nodded" in agreement. Certainly we can no longer sing, and it is said that since the twist we no longer feel sadness, but what is hearing a thing if not feeling it? What is the difference? How else account for the desolate colors where our faces might once have been?

Closing the purse, the old woman returned to stand beside the cart. The blind man seemed ready to sing again, but the old man began closing the synthesizer, folding its panels in on themselves. The boy wrapped the strat, and then the tambourine, in the blanket. The photon shadow guide pulled in, gathering us into its egg of light, while the dog watched.

It was time to go.

When the others began moving, I hesitated at the edge of the department store's shadow, just out of the Moon's light. The singer stood watching us leave with his shining eyes, dead as moons. It struck me that he hadn't come for the coins, but for something else; someone to sing for. Perhaps he wanted us to applaud, but of course that was impossible; perhaps he was still hoping we would all come home some-day.

The old man and the boy began pulling the cart away. The old woman called to the blind man and he turned and followed; the rumbling of the cart was all the guide he needed. The yellow dog stopped at the edge of the shadow, and turned, and looked back at me, as if he . . . as if I . . . But the blind man whistled, and the dog too was gone, following the cart; and without further ado I caught up with the others, and we left for our flyer, our starship, and our faraway home.

⍆ Partial People ⍆

QUESTIONS ARE BEING raised about people only incompletely seen, or found in boxes, perhaps under benches. Lips and eyes stuck under theatre seats like gum. Feet *in shoes* in rude doorways.

Whatever mystery may have surrounded them can be cleared up at once. These are partial people.

Partial people are not entire in themselves. They do not merit your consideration though they may vie for it.

Partial people may seem to need medical attention, because of lacking a leg, a side, an essential attribute, etc. Their partial quality [sic] is not however indication of a genuine medical condition. They do not need medical treatment, and if so, only a little.

They may (they will!) claim to be dying, but how can that be? As a wise man once said, how can they truly die, who have only partially lived.

Read my lips: these are partial people.

* * *

There has been speculation that they are from another or a parallel Universe. Science, however, has confirmed that this is not so; or that if they are from another Universe, it is not an important one.

The question of food is bound to come up. In general, it is best to pretend that partial people have already eaten.

Appearance is an issue. The grotesque and often unpresentable appearance of partial people may provoke discussion. Particularly among those looking for something ugly to talk about. Such discussion should be kept to a minimum.

Traffic. It is rarely that they undertake to drive. Automotive controls, even with automatic transmission (most cars these days!), may prove daunting. Not to mention rentals.

Partial people can cause traffic delays, however: as Leslie R—— drove toward a box in his/her lane on G—— Ave in M——, he/she was surprised to find an arm sticking out of it. He/she was able to judge from *the size* of the rest of the box, however, that it was not large enough to contain an entire person, and therefore was able to maintain speed and direction, thus avoiding lane changing with its potential for accidents.

To make a long story short, Leslie was not distracted by frantic hand waving. Crushing the box.

Partial people may try to pass themselves off as entire people. Sometimes all, or almost all, the customary visual aspects may be present. It may be an internal organ or aspect that is missing, not apparent to the eye (or *eyes,* among the entire). For this reason, it is best to assume that importunate strangers are partial people.

* * *

Travel. Partial people must pay full fare but may not go the whole way. This limits their travel.

Police experience with partial people is inconclusive. They are sometimes worth a beating, but rarely an Arrest.

Money. Partial people usually have a little but are certain to ask for more. On the subway do not take their cards.

In crowds, they stand cunningly so that three or four together may look like an entire person, or even two embracing. This marks the limit of their ability to cooperate.

Neither *p* is capitalized in "partial people."

When they insist on having children, their children are also partial people (partial children). They hardly play.

They may claim to be veterans, especially those which are dis- or un-figured.

They may have trouble counting (being less than one to begin with). Their ideas may appear in contradiction to the ones you hold. Their speech is riddled with sentence fragments and futile attempts at dogma. Even a hello can lead to a loud harangue.

Frantic hand waving is not a friendly greeting with partial people. It is a blatant attempt to gain attention.

Do yourself and society a favor. Don't be taken in. Just say no to partial people.

Thank you.

✦ CARL'S LAWN & GARDEN ✦

LET'S STOP MOURNING FOR THE GOOD OLD DAYS.
WE ARE LARGELY LIVING IN THEM STILL.
—EUELL GIBBONS

MY LAST WEEK on the job started (as usual) with a crisis. "Code Four, Gail," Carl said, throwing me my cap. He never could pronounce my name. "It's the Barbers, out in Whispering Woods subdivision, south of New Brunswick, just off Route One." He backed the pickup to the shed end of the greenhouse and quizzed me while I threw equipment into the back. "Got the drip nozzles? Got the 4 plus 6? Got the Sylovan, the Di50Si? The lawn injectors? The Thumper, just in case? Oh, and a Dutch Elm chip for the mall. We might make it by there today."

It was a bright, mournful June day. The traffic was colorful and hard. The roadsides were brilliant green; newly painted for spring.

"Here we are, Gail. Whispering Woods." We pulled past the wrought-iron gates between the two big laser maples with Dolby rustling leaves, and around the curved drive lined with big houses set on wide pseudolawns. It was all "nerf and turf" (that's what Carl calls verdachip and astrolawn) until the Barbers' house, at the turnaround.

Their lawn was not green but yellow-green. It was the only organic lawn in the sub. We put it in for them four years ago, and for two years it almost made it; then last summer we had to put it on twenty-four-hour IV, and now this looked like the end of the line.

Mrs. Barber was standing at the door looking worried. Her husband pulled in the drive just as we did. She must have called us both at the same time.

"Jesus," Mr. Barber said as he got out of his Chrysler Iacocca and looked at his yellowing hundred thousand dollars ($104,066.29 to be precise; I sometimes watched Carl do the books). "It's not too late, is it, Carl?"

"It's never too late, Mr. Barber," Carl said. The greenest part of the lawn made a crisscross pattern like an X ray showing the underground grid where the drip saturators were buried; the rest of the grass was jaundiced-yellow. A darker brown edge ran all around the yard, like paper just before it bursts into flame.

"Code Six, Gail," Carl said, revising his original assessment. "Give me 4.5 liters of straight Biuloformicaine on a speed inject. And be quick about it. I'll load up the ambulofogger."

The nutritank was built onto the side of the ranch-style home, disguised as a shed. I spilled in a four-can of Bi, added some Phishphlakes for good measure, and set the underpumps whining on super. Out front, Carl trotted up and down the lawn with a Diprothemytaline sprayer, while the Barbers looked on, worried, from the doorway. A few neighbors had gathered at the curb, a mixture of concern and poorly disguised pleasure on their faces. I could tell that the Barbers and their organic lawn were not popular.

The quick Dipro fix gives a green flush to the skinny little leaves of the grass. I could hear them sigh with relief through the soles of my feet. But unless the saturasolution coming up from the IV grid found living roots, the whole thing would be a waste.

Carl looked grave as he put the sprayer back into the truck. "If it's not looking better by Wednesday, call me," he said to the Barbers. "You have my home phone number. We'll stop by on Friday to adjust the IV solution, and I'll check it then."

"How much is this—going to cost?" Mr. Barber whispered, so his wife and the neighbors couldn't hear. Carl gave him a mournful, disapproving look, and Mr. Barber turned away, ashamed.

"Hell, I understand where he's coming from, though," Carl told me when we were back on the road. "It used to be that when you bought a lawn you could get insurance, especially with a new house, but these days nobody is insured. You can insure a tree, a potted one, anyway, or a cybershrub, and of course any kind of holo. But a living lawn? Jesus, Gail, no wonder the guy's worried."

Carl's empathy is his best quality.

We stopped for lunch at Lord Byron's on the Princeton bypass; it's the only place that'll allow a girl with no shoes. Lord Byron was a cook at a veterans' hospital for twenty years before he saved enough to start his own place. Because of this medical background, he thinks he's a doctor.

"The usual," said Carl. Two beers and a sloppy joe on a hard roll.

Lord Byron lifted my cap and his huge warm black hand covered the top of my head. "Just as I thought," he said. "Cold as ice. Sure you can't find something on the menu you can eat, Gay?"

He never could say my name right either.

After lunch we changed the motherboard on a flower bed at a funeral home on Route 303. The display was one of those cheap, sixteen-bit jobs that you can't walk through, that only looks right from a hundred yards or so. Carl had sold it to them last fall. It was supposedly upgradable, but in fact the company that made it had gone out of business over the winter, and now the chip was an orphan; you couldn't change the variety or even the colors of the flowers without a whole new unit.

Carl explained this hesitantly, expecting an argument, but the funeral home manager signed for the new chip, a Hallmark clone, in a minute. "It's one of these franchise operations, Gail," Carl said on the way back to the shop. "They don't care what they spend. Hell, why should they? It's all tax deductible under the Environmental Upgrade Act. I never liked flowers much anyway. Even organic ones."

Tuesday was a better day because we got to dig. We put in ten meters of Patagonian Civet Hedge at Johnson, Johnson, & Johnson. Pat is not really Patagonian; the name is supposed to suggest some kind of hardy stock. It's actually cyberhedge, a fert-saturated plastate lattice with dri-gro bud lodgements at 20 mm intervals on a 3-D grid. But the tiny leaves that grow out of it are as real as I am. They bask in the sun and wave in the wind. The bugs, if there were any, would be fooled.

Carl was in a good mood. Ten meters of pat at $325 a meter is a nice piece of change. And since the roots themselves are not alive, you can put them directly into untreated ground. There's something about the sliding of a shovel into the dirt that stirs the blood of a nurseryman.

"This is the life, right, Gail?" Carl said.

I nodded and grinned back at him. Even though something about the dirt didn't smell right. It didn't smell wrong. It just didn't smell at all.

After lunch at Lord Byron's, Carl sold two electric trees at the Garden State Mall. The manager wanted the trees for a display at the main entrance, and Carl had to talk him out of organics. Carl doesn't like the electrics any better than I do, but sometimes they are the only alternative.

"I sort of wanted real trees," the manager said.

"Not outdoors you don't," Carl said. "Look, organic trees are too frail. Even if you could afford them—and you can't—they get weird diseases, they fall over. You've got to feed them day and night. Let me show you these new Dutch Elms from Microsoft." He threw the switch on the holoprojector while I started piecing together the sensofence. "See how great they look?" Carl said. "Go ahead, walk all the way around them. We call them the Immortals. Bugs don't eat on them, they never get sick, and all you have to feed them is 110. We can set this projector up on the roof, so you don't have to worry about cars running over it."

"I sort of wanted something that cast a shadow," the manager said.

"You don't want shadows here at the mall anyway," said Carl, who had an answer for everything when he was selling. "And you won't have to worry about shoppers walking through the trees"—he passed his hand through the trunk—"and spoiling the image, either. That's what this fence is for, which my lovely assistant is setting up. Ready, Gail?"

I set two sections of white picket fence next to the tree and snapped them together.

"That's not a holo," said the manager.

"No sir. Solid plastic," Carl said. "And it does a lot more than just keep people from walking or driving though the trees. The pickets themselves are sophisticated envirosensors. Made in Singapore. Watch."

I turned on the fence, and since there was no wind, Carl blew on a picket. The leaves on the trees waved and wiggled. He covered a picket with his hand and a shadow fell over the treetops. "They respond to actual wind and sun conditions, for the utmost in total realism. Now let's suppose it looks like rain . . ."

That was my cue. I handed Carl a paper cup and he sprinkled water on the pickets with his fingertips, like a priest giving a blessing. The leaves of the trees shimmered and looked wet. "We call them the Immortals," Carl said again, proudly.

"What about birds?"

"Birds?"

"I read somewhere that birds get confused and try to land in the branches or something," the manager said. "I forget exactly."

Carl's laugh was suddenly sad. "How long since you've seen a bird?"

Wednesday was the day we had set aside to service Carl's masterpiece, the Oak Grove at Princeton University. These were not ailanth-oaks or composite red "woods"; these were full-sized white oaks of solid wood that grew not out of pots but straight out of the "ground"—a .09-acre ecotrap colloid reservoir saturated with a high electrolyte forced-drip solution of Arborpryzinamine Plus, the most effective (and expensive) IV arbo-stabilizer ever developed. The ground colloid was so firm that the trees stood without cables, fully forty-four feet tall. They were grand. The Grove was seven oaks in all, only two less than the state forest in Windham. Princeton was the only private institution in New Jersey that could afford so many organic trees.

But something was wrong. There wasn't a leaf on any of them.

"Code Seven, Gail," said Carl with an undertone of panic in his voice. I limped up the hill as fast as I could and checked the vats under the Humanities Building, but they were almost full and the solution was correct, so I left them. Trees aren't like grass; there was no point in cranking up the IV pump pressure.

Carl was honking the horn, so I got back in the truck and we left to look for the Dean of Grounds. He wasn't in his office. We found him at Knowledge Hall, watching an outfit from Bucks County do a scan-in on the north wall ivy. The ivy wasn't quite dead yet; I could hear its faint brown moaning as the software scanned and replicated each dying tendril, replacing it with a vivid green image. Then the old stuff was pulled down with a long wall rake and bagged. I was getting a headache.

"I just came from the Grove," Carl demanded. "How long have the oaks been bare like that? Why didn't you call me?"

"I figured they were automatic," said the Grounds Dean. "Besides, nobody's blaming you."

The image-ivy came complete with butterflies, hovering tirelessly.

"It's not a question of blame," said Carl. Exasperated with the Grounds Dean, he put the pickup into gear. "Jump in, Gail," he said. "Let's head back to the Grove. I think we've got a Code Seven here. It's time for the Thumper."

The Thumper is a gasoline-powered induction coil the size of the "salamander" we used to warm the greenhouse back when the winters were cold. While Carl cranked it up, I pulled the two cables attached to it out of the truck bed and started dragging them toward the trees; they grew heavier as they grew longer.

"We haven't got all day!" Carl yelled. I clipped the red cable to a low branch on the farthest tree, and clipped the black one to a steel rod driven into the ground-colloid. Then I got back in the truck.

The Grounds Dean pulled up on his three-wheeler just as Carl hit the switch. A few students hurrying to class stopped and looked around, bewildered, as the current ripped through the pavement under them. Carl hit it twice more. I could see the topmost twigs of the trees flutter, but there was no feeling there, and hardly any far below where the taproots were curled in on themselves in dark and silent misery.

"That oughta wake 'em up!" the Grounds Dean called out cheerily.

Carl ignored him. He was in the Grove, kneeling at the

base of one of the oaks, and he motioned for me to come over. "Volunteer," he whispered, brushing four tiny blades of fescue with his fingertips. "I haven't seen volunteer in years." I felt it with my fingertips, an incredibly delicate green filigree, eagerly and shamelessly alive. It was feeding on the nutrients that should have gone to the tree roots, which had somehow lost their will to live.

"I'm sorry I yelled at you, Gail," Carl said, brushing his knees off as we stood up; awkwardly, he leaned over and brushed mine off too. "I don't know what's getting into me." And it was true: it was the first time he had yelled at me since I had sought refuge in his nursery six springs before.

Carl told the Grounds Dean that we would check on the Oak Grove tomorrow, and we left. But we both knew the electroshock was too little, too late. On the way back to the nursery, Carl didn't talk about his beloved oaks at all. Instead, he talked about the volunteer. "Remember when grass just grew, Gail?" he said. "It was everywhere. You didn't have to feed it, or force it, or plant it, or anything. Kids made money cutting it. Hell, you couldn't stop it! It grew on the roadsides, grew in the medians, grew up through the cracks in the sidewalk. Trees, too. Trees grew wild. Leave a field alone and it turned into a forest in a few years. Life was in the air, like wild yeast; the whole damn world was like sourdough bread. Remember, Gail? Those were the good old days."

I nodded and looked away, but not before tears of self-pity sprang unbidden to my eyes. How could I forget the good old days?

By noon on Wednesday the Barbers hadn't called, so we swung by their place on the way to lunch. The ominous brown edge was still there, but the grass toward the center of the lawn was a brighter green, almost feverish-looking in spots. "At least it's still alive," Carl said, but a little uncertainly. I shrugged. I didn't feel good.

"That girl doesn't look right to me," said Lord Byron at lunch. I had to find a chair because I couldn't balance on a counter stool. "She'll be all right," said Carl. Next to empathy, optimism is his best quality. "And I'll have the usual."

Carl spent the afternoon doing the books while I dozed on a cot at the office end of the greenhouse. "What I lose in plants I make up in cybers," he said. "I'm the only nurseryman in the state who still services organics—but you know that. Funny how it all balances out, Gail. First I make money poisoning or cutting the grass; then I make more trying to keep it alive. When that goes, there's a fortune in greenlawn. Paint it every spring. Same with trees. First it was sales. Then it was maintenance, life supports. Now it's electrics. Hell, I don't know what I'm complaining about, Gail. I'm making more money than ever, yet somehow I can't help feeling like I'm going out of business . . ."

He talked on and on all afternoon, while I tossed and turned, trying to sleep.

Thursday morning we approached the university with a mounting sense of dread. I had known it all along; Carl knew it as soon as he pulled up beside the trees and shut off the engine. I didn't even have to get out of the truck to feel the silence through the soles of my feet. There was no life in the Oak Grove. Carl's pride and joy was dead forever.

The volunteer fescue was gone, too. We got out to look, but it had dried up overnight and only brown blades were left, withering in the network shadows of the bare branches. Maybe the Thumper had killed it; or maybe it had just run out of life, like everything else seemed to be doing these days.

"Nobody's blaming you," said the Grounds Dean. He had come up behind us unnoticed and put his hand on Carl's shoulder. "To tell the truth, Carl, we've been having funding problems. I'm not sure how long we could have afforded to keep the ground feed going anyway. What would you think of going to videoleaf? Or we could even try silicyberbud branch implants, at least for a season or two. But don't worry, we're not going to take out these stately oaks until we absolutely have to. They're like old friends to the students, Carl. Do you know what they call the Grove?" The Dean looked at me and winked; I guess because he thought I was young. "The students call it the Kissing Grove!"

"It's not a question of blame," Carl said. I'd never seen him so depressed. I wasn't feeling so hot myself.

"You should send this girl home, Carl," Lord Byron said when we stopped for lunch. "How long has she worked for you? Gay, honey, have you ever taken a sick day?"

"She lives in the greenhouse," Carl said. "She doesn't exactly work for me. And leave her cap alone; nobody wants to look at a bald head."

We spent the afternoon pulling IV fittings. The Delaware Valley Golf Club is one of the fanciest clubs in the Garden State, and the fairways as well as the greens had been organic not so many years ago. This year we had finally lost the battle on the greens. Thursday was the deadline for us to get our hardware out so they could lay the permaturf.

Carl drove the pickup straight up the fairways, ignoring the angry shouts and curses of the golfers. The greens looked like the moon. Carl angrily unscrewed the nozzles and the fittings and threw them into the back of the pickup, but left the pipes under the ground; they weren't worth the trouble it would take to get them out, at least for one person working alone. I was too dizzy to do much more than watch.

"Every spring it gets worse," Carl muttered as he bounced across the last fairway, through the ditch, and onto the county road. "Are you okay? Do you want me to pull over?"

I tried to throw up but nothing would come.

* * *

Friday I could barely get up. My once dark skin looked pale reflected in the windows of the greenhouse. Carl was tapping on the glass with the truck key. It was already ten o'clock.

"Code Eight, Gail!" he said. "I'm getting the truck."

It was the Barbers. "I couldn't understand what she was saying," Carl said as he pulled out into traffic. He gave me the emergency flasher to plug in and set up on the dash. "But it must be bad. Hell, she was screaming."

It was a bright, hard spring day; the sky was cruel blue. Route One was jammed and Carl turned on the siren as well as the light. He drove on the shoulder, with one wheel on the asphalt and the other on the green-painted rocks.

By the time we got to Whispering Woods I could see it was already too late.

The neighbors were standing around the edges of the Barbers' front yard, watching the grass turn yellow, then yellow-green, then yellow again, flickering like an alcohol fire in sickening waves. There was a faint crackling noise and a thin dying smell.

"Sounds like cereal when you pour the milk on!" said one of the kids.

Carl knelt down and pulled up a clump of grass and smelled the roots; then he sniffed the air and looked over at me as if for the first time. "Code Ten," he said in a curiously flat voice. Hadn't we both known this day had to come?

"Look out!" one of the neighbors shouted. "Get back!"

The brown at the edges of the yard was starting to darken and spread inward. The crackling grew louder as it closed on the still-green center; it pulled back once, then again, each wave leaving the yellow-green grass a little paler. Then the grass all darkened at once like an eye closing, and there was silence. I felt my knees give out, so I leaned back against the truck.

"It's not too late, is it, Carl?" asked Mr. Barber, coming to the end of the walk. His wife followed him, sniffling with fear, keeping her feet on the center of the walk, away from the dead ground. The thin dying smell had given way to a foul, wet, loathsome ugly stench as if some great grave had yawned open.

"What's that smell?" a neighbor asked.

"Hey, mister, your boy is falling over," said one of the kids, tugging at Carl's sleeve. "His hat came off."

"She's not a boy," said Carl. "And her name is Gaea." I'd never heard him get it right before.

"What's that smell?" asked another neighbor. She was sniffing not the lawn but the wind, the long one, the one that blows all the way around the world.

"Excuse me," Carl said to the Barbers. He ran over and tried to pick me up, but I was too far gone.

"It *is* too late, isn't it, Carl?" said Mr. Barber, and Carl, nodding, began to cry, and so would I if I could have anymore.

✴ THE MESSAGE ✴

THE VOICE ON the phone was distinct if faint: "Our call came through."

"I'll be right there."

Although I had wanted this for years, had anticipated it, had worked for it and dreamed of it even when working for other things, it was still hard to believe. And harder still to explain to Janet.

"That was Beth on the phone," I said.

"And you're leaving." It was a statement, not a question.

"We both knew this might happen."

"Don't bother coming back."

"Janet . . ."

But she had already rolled over and was pretending to be asleep. I could almost hear the fabric ripping: the seam of an eight-year marriage that had held us together from small colleges in the Midwest to oceanic exploration centers, to the long winters at Woods Hole.

Once it started to tear, it tore straight and true. I took a cab to the airport.

The flight to San Diego was interminable. As soon as I got off the plane I called Doug at Flying Fish.

"Remember when you said you would drop everything to

take me to the island if what we were trying to do came through?''

"I'll meet you at the hangar," he said.

Doug's ancient Cessna was already warming up when I got there. I carried two coffees, the black one for him. We were in the air and heading west over Point Loma before we spoke.

"So the fish finally got through," he said.

"Dolphins aren't fish and you know it," I said.

"I wasn't talking about them; I was talking about Leonard. He spends so much time underwater he ought to grow gills."

Doug flew out to the island twice a month to deliver supplies to my partners. As the mainland diminished to a smudge behind us, I thought of the years of research that had brought us to this remote Pacific outpost.

Our funding had been cut off by the Navy when we had refused to allow them to use our data for weapons research. It had been cut off by Stanford when we had refused to publish our preliminary results. Grant after grant had fallen away like leaves; like my marriage, which I now could see was only another leaf hitting the ground. Janet and I had been going in different directions for several years, ever since I had turned down tenure in order to continue my life's work.

The Project.

"There it is, Doc."

The island had been loaned to us by Alejandro Martinez, the nitrate millionaire who was even now on his deathbed in Mexico City. It was a mile-long teardrop of rock, inhabited at one end by seals and at the other by the gray (dolphin-colored, I realized for the first time) fiberglass modulars of the Project.

Doug brought the little 172 straight in to the short strip bulldozed out of the side of a hill. I wondered how he managed in a fog or a wind. There were only about ten feet left at the end, when he snubbed the brakes hard to keep the prop out of the rocks.

Beth was waiting in the jeep with the engine running. Seeing the radiant smile on her broad, plain face, I wondered what my life would have been like if I had married not for beauty but for harmony. She and Leonard were partners before anything else.

"Welcome!" she shouted over the wind and crashing surf. "Want to join us, Doug? This is our big day!"

"Wouldn't miss it for the world," he said, shutting down the engine. "Where's the fish?"

"Down in the pool, I imagine," Beth said. "Comes and goes. What kind of intelligent creature would communicate with us if we kept it confined?"

"He's pulling your leg," I told her. "He's talking about Leonard."

"So am I," she laughed.

Expertly, terrifyingly ("This *is* Mexico, after all!"), Beth raced down the island's only half mile of road to the lab, which was built out over the rocks. It looked like a gray and pink coral shelf left behind by the tide. The pool it enclosed was open on three sides to the sea.

Leonard was on the sheltered upper deck, dripping in the wet suit he always wore, munching a seaweed sandwich and staring at a computer screen.

"It came?" I asked.

"The message. It came," he said, looking up at me, his face shining with either sea water or tears.

We embraced, and Beth joined us both. It was a shared triumph. Leonard and I had started the Project twelve years before. He had done the undersea field work, she had designed and built the voice synthesizer, and I had written the program.

While I got into my wet suit, Beth explained to a puzzled Doug what we had done. It had all been top secret until now.

"The previous attempts to communicate with dolphins always failed because of the time factor," she said. "It was Doc who figured out that they think not as individuals but collectively. The first problem was to convince them that we, a race that lives and dies as individuals, is even capable of thought, much less communication. Their feeling was, I think, that all our activity was reactive behavior."

"What about cities? Ships?" said Doug. "We've been active on the sea for centuries."

"Oh, they know that. But they have seen coral reefs and seashells, all built objects. The Australian Barrier Reef, for example, is a made object, and it's vaster than all our cities put together. They don't make things. They don't put value in things."

"The work of their civilization is thought," put in Leonard. "They are building a thought, a concept that they have been working out over the millennia. It's a grand project beyond anything we could imagine."

"So they think they're too good to talk to us," said Doug.

"Don't get your fur up," said Beth, laughing. "They don't think in words, like we do. Words are an extension of the hand—a grasping mechanism, and they don't grasp and manipulate ideas in the way we do. So what we've been working to do over the years is to try and break their concepts down into words."

I was almost ready. I had another gulp of coffee. My hand was shaking.

"The main problem was the time frame," Leonard said. "We talk in bites. Their conversations run in long, centuries-old strings. They are not interested in communicating individual to individual. They communicate with their own developing selves and their descendants. Ready?"

This last was to me. I nodded.

Leonard led me down the stairs to the pool level. Beth

and Doug followed. The surf outside was booming like a great heart.

"It still sounds like what you're saying is that they don't want to talk to us," Doug protested.

"Oh, they do, as it turns out," Leonard said. "They were very glad to hear from us. You see, they know who we are."

"They remember," said Beth.

"They have a message for us," said Leonard.

"It took thirty-one months for them to say it," said Beth. "It was the work of thousands of individuals."

"So let's have it!" said Doug. We all laughed at his impatience, so typically human.

"Doc first," said Leonard. "The synthesizer only works under the water." He led me to the end of the pool, where several dolphins, dignified and pearl-gray, waited like envoys in the reception room of an embassy.

I slipped into the water. It was cold but it felt good. The dolphins nuzzled at me, then dove. I felt like diving with them, but I had only my wet suit and no breathing gear.

"Ready?" Leonard asked.

I nodded.

"Put your head under, and listen."

I floated. A deep, slow voice echoed through my bones, like the voice I remembered from a long-ago dream:

"Come home. All is forgiven."

⚹ England Underway ⚹

MR. FOX WAS, he realized afterward, with a shudder of sudden recognition like that of the man who gives a cup of water to a stranger and finds out hours, or even years later, that it was Napoleon, perhaps the first to notice. Perhaps. At least no one else in Brighton seemed to be looking at the sea that day. He was taking his constitutional on the Boardwalk, thinking of Lizzie Eustace and her diamonds, the people in novels becoming increasingly more real to him as the people in the everyday (or "real") world grew more remote, when he noticed that the waves seemed funny.

"Look," he said to Anthony, who accompanied him everywhere, which was not far, his customary world being circumscribed by the Boardwalk to the south, Mrs. Oldenshield's to the east, the cricket grounds to the north, and the Pig & Thistle, where he kept a room—or more precisely, a room kept him, and had since 1956—to the west.

"Woof?" said Anthony, in what might have been a quizzical tone.

"The waves," said Mr. Fox. "They seem—well, odd, don't they? Closer together?"

"Woof."

"Well, perhaps not. Could be just my imagination."

Fact is, waves had always looked odd to Mr. Fox. Odd and tiresome and sinister. He enjoyed the Boardwalk but he never walked on the beach proper, not only because he disliked the shifty quality of the sand but because of the waves with their ceaseless back-and-forth. He didn't understand why the sea had to toss about so. Rivers didn't make all that fuss, and they were actually going somewhere. The movement of the waves seemed to suggest that something was stirring things up, just beyond the horizon. Which was what Mr. Fox had always suspected in his heart; which was why he had never visited his sister in America.

"Perhaps the waves have always looked funny and I have just never noticed," said Mr. Fox. If indeed "funny" was the word for something so odd.

At any rate, it was almost half past four. Mr. Fox went to Mrs. Oldenshield's, and with a pot of tea and a plate of shortbread biscuits placed in front of him, read his daily Trollope—he had long ago decided to read all forty-seven novels in exactly the order, and at about the rate, in which they had been written—then fell asleep for twenty minutes. When he awoke (and no one but he knew he was sleeping) and closed the book, Mrs. Oldenshield put it away for him, on the high shelf where the complete set, bound in morocco, resided in state. Then Mr. Fox walked to the cricket ground, so that Anthony might run with the boys and their kites until dinner was served at the Pig & Thistle. A whisky at nine with Harrison ended what seemed at the time to be an ordinary day.

The next day it all began in earnest.

Mr. Fox awoke to a hubbub of traffic, footsteps, and unintelligible shouts. There was, as usual, no one but himself and Anthony (and of course, the Finn, who cooked) at breakfast; but outside, he found the streets remarkably lively for the time of year. He saw more and more people as he headed downtown, until he was immersed in a virtual sea of humanity. People of all sorts, even Pakistanis and foreigners, not ordinarily much in evidence in Brighton off season.

"What in the world can it be?" Mr. Fox wondered aloud. "I simply can't imagine."

"Woof," said Anthony, who couldn't imagine either, but who was never called upon to do so.

With Anthony in his arms, Mr. Fox picked his way through the crowd along the King's Esplanade until he came to the entrance to the Boardwalk. He mounted the twelve steps briskly. It was irritating to have one's customary way blocked by strangers. The Boardwalk was half filled with strollers who, instead of strolling, were holding on to the rail and looking out to sea. It was mysterious; but then the habits of everyday people had always been mysterious to Mr. Fox; they were so much less likely to stay in character than the people in novels.

The waves were even closer together than they had been the day before; they were piling up as if pulled toward the shore by a magnet. The surf where it broke had the odd character of being a single continuous wave about one and a half feet high. Though it no longer seemed to be rising, the water had risen during the night: it covered half the beach, coming almost up to the seawall just below the Boardwalk.

The wind was quite stout for the season. Off to the left (the east) a dark line was seen on the horizon. It might have been clouds but it looked more solid, like land. Mr. Fox could not remember ever having seen it before, even though he had walked here daily for the past forty-two years.

"Dog?"

Mr. Fox looked to his left. Standing beside him at the rail of the Boardwalk was a large, one might even say portly, African man with an alarming hairdo. He was wearing a tweed coat. An English girl clinging to his arm had asked the question. She was pale with dark, stringy hair, and she wore an oilskin cape that looked wet even though it wasn't raining.

"Beg your pardon?" said Mr. Fox.

"That's a dog?" The girl was pointing toward Anthony.

"Woof."

"Well, of course it's a dog."

"Can't he walk?"

"Of course he can walk. He just doesn't always choose to."

"You bloody wish," said the girl, snorting unattractively and looking away. She wasn't exactly a girl. She could have been twenty.

"Don't mind her," said the African. "Look at that chop, would you."

"Indeed," Mr. Fox said. He didn't know what to make of the girl but he was grateful to the African for starting a conversation. It was often difficult these days; it had become increasingly difficult over the years. "A storm offshore, perhaps?" he ventured.

"A storm?" the African said. "I guess you haven't heard. It was on the telly hours ago. We're making close to two knots now, south and east. Heading around Ireland and out to sea."

"Out to sea?" Mr. Fox looked over his shoulder at the King's Esplanade and the buildings beyond, which seemed as stationary as ever. "Brighton is heading out to sea?"

"You bloody wish," the girl said.

"Not just Brighton, man," the African said. For the first time, Mr. Fox could hear a faint Caribbean lilt in his voice. "England herself is underway."

England underway? How extraordinary. Mr. Fox could see what he supposed was excitement in the faces of the other strollers on the Boardwalk all that day. The wind smelled somehow saltier as he went to take his tea. He almost told Mrs. Oldenshield the news when she brought him his pot and platter; but the affairs of the day, which had never intruded far into her tearoom, receded entirely when he took down his book and began to read. This was (as it turned out) the very day that Lizzie finally read the letter from Mr. Camperdown, the Eustace family lawyer, which she had carried unopened for three days. As Mr. Fox had expected, it demanded that the diamonds be returned to her late husband's family. In response, Lizzie bought a strongbox. That evening, England's peregrinations were all the news on the BBC. The kingdom was heading south into the Atlantic at 1.8 knots, according to the newsmen on the telly over the bar at the Pig & Thistle, where Mr. Fox was accustomed to taking a glass of whisky with Harrison, the barkeep, before retiring. In the sixteen hours hours since the phenomenon had first been detected, England had gone some thirty-five miles, beginning a long turn around Ireland which would carry it into the open sea.

"Ireland is not going?" asked Mr. Fox.

"Ireland has been independent since 19 and 21," said Harrison, who often hinted darkly at having relatives with the IRA. "Ireland is hardly about to be chasing England around the seven seas."

"Well, what about, you know . . . ?"

"The Six Counties? The Six Counties have always been a part of Ireland and always will be," said Harrison. Mr. Fox nodded politely and finished his whisky. It was not his custom to argue politics, particularly not with barkeeps, and certainly not with the Irish.

"So I suppose you'll be going home?"

"And lose me job?"

For the next several days, the wave got no higher but it seemed steadier. It was not a chop but a continual smooth wake, streaming across the shore to the east as England began its turn to the west. The cricket ground grew deserted as the boys laid aside their kites and joined the rest of the town at the shore, watching the waves. There was such a crowd on the Boardwalk that several of the shops, which had closed for the season, reopened. Mrs. Oldenshield's was no busier than usual, however, and Mr. Fox was able to forge ahead as steadily in his reading as Mr. Trollope had in his writing. It was not long before Lord Fawn, with something almost of dignity in his gesture and demeanor, declared himself to the young widow Eustace and asked for her hand. Mr. Fox knew Lizzie's diamonds would be trouble, though. He knew something of heirlooms himself. His tiny attic room in the Pig & Thistle had been left to him *in perpetuity* by the innkeeper, whose life had been saved by Mr. Fox's father during an air raid. A life saved (said the innkeeper, an East Indian, but a Christian, not a Hindu) was a debt never fully paid. Mr. Fox had often wondered where he would have lived if he'd been forced to go out and find a place, like so many in novels did. Indeed, in real life as well. That evening on the telly there was panic in Belfast as the headlands of Scotland slid by, south. Were the Loyalists to be left behind? Everyone was waiting to hear from the King, who was closeted with his advisors.

The next morning, there was a letter on the little table in the downstairs hallway at the Pig & Thistle. Mr. Fox knew as soon as he saw the letter that it was the fifth of the month. His niece, Emily, always mailed her letters from America on the first, and they always arrived on the morning of the fifth.

Mr. Fox opened it, as always, just after tea at Mrs. Oldenshield's. He read the ending first, as always, to make sure there were no surprises. "Wish you could see your great-niece before she's grown," Emily wrote; she wrote the same thing every month. When her mother, Mr. Fox's sister, Clare, had visited after moving to America, it had been his niece she had wanted him to meet. Emily had taken up the same refrain since her mother's death. "Your great-niece will be a young lady soon," she wrote, as if this were somehow Mr. Fox's doing. His only regret was that Emily, in asking him to come to America when her mother died, had asked him to do the one thing he couldn't even contemplate; and so he had been unable to grant her even the courtesy of a refusal. He read all the way back to the opening ("Dear Uncle Anthony") then folded the letter very small; and put it into the box with the others when he got back to his room that evening.

The bar seemed crowded when he came downstairs at nine. The King, in a brown suit with a green and gold tie, was on the telly, sitting in front of a clock in a BBC studio. Even Harrison, never one for royalty, set aside the glasses he was polishing and listened while Charles confirmed that England was, indeed, underway. His words made it official, and there was a polite "hip, hip, hooray" from the three men (two of them strangers) at the end of the bar. The King and his advisors weren't exactly sure when England would arrive, nor, for that matter, where it was going. Scotland and Wales were, of course, coming right along. Parliament would announce time-zone adjustments as necessary. While His Majesty was aware that there was cause for *concern* about Northern Ireland and the Isle of Man, there was as yet no cause for *alarm*.

His Majesty, King Charles, spoke for almost half an hour, but Mr. Fox missed much of what he said. His eye had been caught by the date under the clock on the wall behind the King's head. It was the fourth of the month, not the fifth; his niece's letter had arrived a day early! This, even more than the funny waves or the King's speech, seemed to announce that the world was changing. Mr. Fox had a sudden, but not unpleasant, feeling almost of dizziness. After it had passed, and the bar had cleared out, he suggested to Harrison, as he always did at closing time: "Perhaps you'll join me in a whisky"; and as always, Harrison replied, "Don't mind if I do."

He poured two Bells'. Mr. Fox had noticed that when

other patrons "bought" Harrison a drink, and the barkeep passed his hand across the bottle and pocketed the tab, the whisky was Bushmills. It was only with Mr. Fox, at closing, that he actually took a drink, and then it was always scotch.

"To your King," said Harrison. "And to plate tectonics."

"Beg your pardon?"

"Plate tectonics, Fox. Weren't you listening when your precious Charles explained why all this was happening? All having to do with movement of the Earth's crust, and such."

"To plate tectonics," said Mr. Fox. He raised his glass to hide his embarrassment. He had in fact heard the words, but had assumed they had to do with plans to protect the household treasures at Buckingham Palace.

Mr. Fox never bought the papers, but the next morning he slowed down to read the headlines as he passed the news stalls. King Charles's picture was on all the front pages, looking confidently into the future.

ENGLAND UNDERWAY AT 2.9 KNOTS; SCOTLAND, WALES
COMING ALONG PEACEFULLY;
CHARLES FIRM AT 'HELM' OF UNITED KINGDOM

read the *Daily Alarm*. *The Economist* took a less sanguine view:

CHUNNEL COMPLETION DELAYED;
EEC CALLS EMERGENCY MEETING

Although Northern Ireland was legally and without question part of the United Kingdom, the BBC explained that night, it was for some inexplicable reason apparently remaining with Ireland. The King urged his subjects in Belfast and Londonderry not to panic; arrangements were being made for the evacuation of all who wished it.

The King's address seemed to have a calming effect over

the next few days. The streets of Brighton grew quiet once again. The Esplanade and the Boardwalk still saw a few video crews which kept the fish and chips stalls busy; but they bought no souvenirs, and the gift shops all closed again one by one.

"Woof," said Anthony, delighted to find the boys back on the cricket ground with their kites. "Things are getting back to normal," said Mr. Fox. But were they really? The smudge on the eastern horizon was Brittany, according to the newsmen on the telly; next would be the open sea. One shuddered to think of it. Fortunately, there was familiarity and warmth at Mrs. Oldenshield's, where Lizzie was avoiding the Eustace family lawyer, Mr. Camperdown, by retreating to her castle in Ayr. Lord Fawn (urged on by his family) was insisting he couldn't marry her unless she gave up the diamonds. Lizzie's answer was to carry the diamonds with her to Scotland in a strongbox. Later that week, Mr. Fox saw the African again. There was a crowd on the old West Pier, and even though it was beginning to rain, Mr. Fox walked out to the end, where a boat was unloading. It was a sleek hydrofoil, with the Royal Family's crest upon its bow. Two video crews were filming, as sailors in slickers passed an old lady in a wheelchair from the boat to the pier. She was handed an umbrella and a tiny white dog. The handsome young captain of the hydrofoil waved his braided hat as he gunned the motors and pulled away from the pier; the crowd cried "hurrah" as the boat rose on its spidery legs and blasted off into the rain.

"Woof," said Anthony. No one else paid any attention to the old lady, sitting in the wheelchair with a wet, shivering dog on her lap. She had fallen asleep (or perhaps even died!) and dropped her umbrella. Fortunately it wasn't raining. "That would be the young Prince of Wales," said a familiar voice to Mr. Fox's left. It was the African. According to him (and he seemed to know such things), the Channel Islands

and most of the islanders, had been left behind. The hydrofoil had been sent to Guernsey at the Royal Family's private expense to rescue the old lady, who'd had a last-minute
change of heart; perhaps she'd wanted to die in England.
"He'll be in Portsmouth by five," said the African, pointing
to an already far-off plume of spray.

"Is it past four already?" Mr. Fox asked. He realized he
had lost track of the time.

"Don't have a watch?" asked the girl, sticking her head
around the African's bulk.

Mr. Fox hadn't seen her lurking there. "Haven't really
needed one," he said.

"You bloody wish," she said.

"Twenty past, precisely," said the African. "Don't mind
her, mate." Mr. Fox had never been called "mate" before.
He was pleased that even with all the excitement he hadn't
missed his tea. He hurried to Mrs. Oldenshield's, where he
found a fox hunt just getting underway at Portray, Lizzie's
castle in Scotland. He settled down eagerly to read about it. A
fox hunt! Mr. Fox was a believer in the power of names.

The weather began to change; to get, at the same time,
warmer and rougher. In the satellite pictures on the telly
over the bar at the Pig & Thistle, England was a cloud-
dimmed outline that could just as easily have been a drawing
as a photo. After squeezing between Ireland and Brittany,
like a restless child slipping from the arms of its ancient
Celtic parents, it was headed south and west, into the open
Atlantic. The waves came no longer at a slant but straight in
at the seawall. Somewhat to his surprise, Mr. Fox enjoyed his
constitutional more than ever, knowing that he was looking
at a different stretch of sea every day, even though it always
looked the same. The wind was strong and steady in his face,
and the Boardwalk was empty. Even the newsmen were
gone—to Scotland, where it had only just been noticed that

the Hebrides were being left behind with the Orkneys and the Shetlands. "Arctic islands with their own traditions, languages, and monuments, all mysteriously made of stone," explained the reporter, live from Uig, by remote. The video showed a postman shouting incomprehensibly into the wind and rain.

"What's he saying?" Mr. Fox asked. "Would that be Gaelic?"

"How would I be expected to know?" said Harrison.

A few evenings later, a BBC crew in the Highlands provided the last view of the continent: the receding headlands of Brittany seen from the 3,504-foot summit of Ben Hope, on a bright, clear day. "It's a good thing," Mr. Fox joked to Anthony the next day, "that Mrs. Oldenshield has laid in plenty of Hyson." This was the green tea Mr. Fox preferred. She had laid in dog biscuits for Anthony as well. Lizzie herself was leaving Scotland, following the last of her guests back to London, when her hotel room was robbed and her strongbox was stolen, just as Mr. Fox had always feared it would be. For a week it rained. Great swells pounded at the seawall. Brighton was almost deserted. The faint-hearted had left for Portsmouth, where they were protected by the Isle of Wight from the winds and waves that struck what might now be properly called the *bow* of Britain.

On the Boardwalk, Mr. Fox strolled as deliberate and proud as a captain on his bridge. The wind was almost a gale, but a steady gale, and he soon grew used to it; it simply meant walking and standing at a tilt. The rail seemed to thrum with energy under his hand. Even though he knew that they were hundreds of miles at sea, Mr. Fox felt secure with all of England at his back. He began to almost enjoy the fulminations of the water as it threw itself against the Brighton seawall.

Which plowed on west, into the Atlantic.

* * *

With the south coast from Penzance to Dover in the lead (or perhaps it should be said, the bow) and the Highlands of Scotland at the stern, the United Kingdom was making almost four knots. Or 3.8 to be precise.

"A modest and appropriate speed," the King told his subjects, speaking from his chambers in Buckingham Palace, which had been decked out with nautical maps and charts, a lighted globe, and a silver sextant. "Approximately equal to that of the great ships-of-the-line of Nelson's day."

In actual fact, the BBC commentator corrected (for they will correct even a king), 3.8 knots was considerably slower than an eighteenth-century warship. But it was good that this was so, Britain being, at best, blunt; indeed, it was estimated that with even a half knot more speed, the seas piling up the Plymouth and Exeter channels would have devastated the docks. Oddly enough, it was London, far from the headwinds and bow wave, that was hardest hit. The wake past Margate, along what used to be the English Channel, had sucked the Thames down almost two feet, leaving broad mud flats along the Victoria Embankment and under the Waterloo Bridge. The news showed treasure seekers with gum boots tracking mud all over the city, "a mud as foul-smelling as the ancient crimes they unearth daily," said BBC. Not a very patriotic report, thought Mr. Fox, who turned from the telly to Harrison to remark, "I believe you have family there."

"In London? Not hardly," said Harrison. "They've all gone to America."

By the time the Scottish mountaintops should have been enduring (or perhaps "enjoying" is the word, being mountains, and Scottish at that) the first snow flurries of the winter, they were enjoying (or perhaps "enduring") subtropical rains as the United Kingdom passed just to the north of the Azores. The weather in the south (now west) of England was springlike and fine. The boys at the cricket ground, who had usually put away their kites by this time of year, were out every day, affording endless delight to Anthony, who accepted with the simple, unquestioning joy of a dog, the fact of a world well supplied with running boys. *Our Day's Log,* the popular new BBC evening show, which began and ended with shots of the bow wave breaking on the rocks of Cornwall, showed hobbyists with telescopes and camcorders on the cliffs at Dover, cheering "Land Ho!" on sighting the distant peaks of the Azores. Things were getting back to normal. The public (according to the news) was finding that even the mid-Atlantic held no terrors. The wave of urban seasickness that had been predicted never materialized. At a steady 3.8 knots, Great Britain was unaffected by the motion of the waves, even during the fiercest storms: it was almost as if she had been designed for travel, and built for comfort, not for speed. A few of the smaller Scottish islands had been stripped away and had, alarmingly, sunk; but the only real damage was on the east (now south) coast, where the slipstream was washing away house-sized chunks of the soft Norfolk banks. The King was seen on the news, in muddy hip boots, helping to dike the fens against the wake. Taking a break from digging, he reassured his subjects that the United Kingdom, wherever it might be headed, would remain sovereign. When a reporter, with shocking impertinence, asked if that meant that he *didn't know* where his kingdom was headed, King Charles answered coolly that he hoped his subjects were satisfied with his performance in a role that was, after all, designed to content them with *what was,* rather than to shape or even predict *what might be.* Then, without excusing himself, he picked up his silver shovel with the Royal Crest, and began to dig again.

Meanwhile, at Mrs. Oldenshield's, all of London was abuzz with Lizzie's loss. Or supposed loss. Only Lizzie (and Messrs. Fox and Trollope) knew that the diamonds had been not in her strongbox but under her pillow. Mr. Fox's letter from his niece arrived a day earlier still, on the *third* of the month, underscoring in its own quiet manner that England was indeed underway. The letter, which Mr. Fox read in reverse, as usual, ended alarmingly with the words "looking forward to seeing you." Forward? He read on backward and found "underway toward America." America? It had never occurred to Mr. Fox. He looked at the return address on the envelope. It was from a town called, rather ominously, Babylon.

Lizzie was one for holding on. Even though the police (and half of London society) suspected that she had engineered the theft of the diamonds in order to avoid returning them to the Eustace family, she wasn't about to admit that they had never been stolen at all. Indeed, why should she? As the book was placed back up on the shelf day after day, Mr. Fox marveled at the strength of character of one so able to convince herself that what was in her interest, was in the right. The next morning there was a small crowd on the West Pier, waving Union Jacks and pointing toward a smudge on the horizon. Mr. Fox was not surprised to see a familiar face (and hairdo) among them.

"Bermuda," said the African. Mr. Fox only nodded, not wanting to provoke the girl, whom he suspected was waiting on the other side of the African, waiting to strike. Was it only his imagination, that the smudge on the horizon was pink? That night and the two nights following, he watched the highlights of the Bermuda Passage on the telly over the bar. The island, which had barely been visible from Brighton, passed within a mile of Dover, and thousands turned out to see the colonial policemen in their red coats lined up atop the coral cliffs, saluting the Mother Country as she passed. Even where no crowds turned out, the low broads of Norfolk, the shaley cliffs of Yorkshire, the rocky headlands of Scotland's (former) North Sea coast, all received the same salute. The passage took nearly a week, and Mr. Fox thought it was quite a tribute to the Bermudans' stamina, as well as their patriotism.

Over the next few days, the wind shifted and began to drop. Anthony was pleased, noticing only that the boys had to run harder to lift their kites, and seemed to need a dog yipping along beside them more than ever. But Mr. Fox knew that if the wind dropped much further, they would lose interest altogether. The Bermudans were satisfied with their glimpse of the Mother Country, according to BBC; but the rest of the Commonwealth members were outraged as the United Kingdom turned sharply north after the Bermuda Passage, and headed north on a course that appeared to be carrying it toward the USA. Mr. Fox, meanwhile, was embroiled in a hardly unexpected but no less devastating crisis of a more domestic nature: for Lizzie had had her diamonds stolen—for real this time! She had been keeping them in a locked drawer in her room at the loathsome Mrs. Carbuncle's. If she reported the theft, she would be admitting that they hadn't been in the strongbox stolen in Scotland. Her only hope was that they, and the thieves, were never found.

COMMONWEALTH IN UPROAR

CARIBBEAN MEMBERS REGISTER SHARP PROTEST

BRITS TO BASH BIG APPLE?

The British and American papers were held up side by side on BBC. Navigation experts were produced, with pointers and maps, who estimated that on its current course, the south (now north) of England would nose into the crook of New York harbor, where Long Island meets New Jersey; so that Dover would be in sight of the New York City skyline. Plymouth was expected to end up off Montauk, and Brighton somewhere in the middle, where there were no place names on the satellite pictures. Harrison kept a map under the bar for settling bets, and when he pulled it out after *Our Daily*

Log, Mr. Fox was alarmed (but not surprised) to see that the area where Brighton was headed was dominated by a city whose name evoked images too lurid to visualize:

Babylon.

On the day that Lizzie got her first visit from Scotland Yard, Mr. Fox saw a charter fishing boat holding steady off the shore, making about three knots. It was the *Judy J* out of Islip, and the rails were packed with people waving. Mr. Fox waved back, and waved Anthony's paw for him. An airplane flew low over the beach towing a sign. On the telly that night, Mr. Fox could see on the satellite picture that Brighton was already in the lee of Long Island; that was why the wind was dropping. The BBC showed clips from *King Kong.* "New York City is preparing to evacuate," said the announcer, "fearing that the shock of collision with ancient England will cause the fabled skyscrapers of Manhattan to tumble." He seemed pleased by the prospect, as did the Canadian earthquake expert he interviewed; as, indeed, did Harrison. New York City officials were gloomier; they feared the panic more than the actual collision. The next morning there were two boats off the shore, and in the afternoon, five. The waves, coming in at an angle, looked tentative after the bold swells of the mid-Atlantic. At tea, Lizzie was visited for the second time by Scotland Yard. Something seemed to have gone out of her, some of her fight, her spunk. Something in the air outside the tea-room was different too, but it wasn't until he and Anthony approached the cricket ground that Mr. Fox realized what it was. It was the wind. It was gone altogether. The boys were struggling to raise the same kites that had flown so eagerly only a few days before. As soon as they stopped running the kites came down. Anthony ran and barked wildly, as if calling on Heaven for assistance, but the boys went home before dark, disgusted.

That night, Mr. Fox stepped outside the Pig & Thistle for a moment after supper. The street was as still as he had always imagined a graveyard might be. Had everyone left Brighton, or were they just staying indoors? According to *Our Daily Log*, the feared panic in New York City had failed to materialize. Video clips showed horrendous traffic jams, but they were apparently normal. The King was . . . but just as the BBC was about to cut to Buckingham Palace, the picture began to flicker and an American game show came on. "Who were the Beatles," said a young woman standing in a sort of bright pulpit. It was a statement and not a question.

"The telly has arrived before us," said Harrison, turning off the sound but leaving the picture. "Shall we celebrate with a whisky? My treat tonight."

Mr. Fox's room, left to him by Mr. Singh, the original owner of the Pig & Thistle, was on the top floor under a gable. It was small; he and Anthony shared a bed. That night they were awakened by a mysterious, musical scraping sound. "Woof," said Anthony, in his sleep. Mr. Fox listened with trepidation; he thought at first that someone, a thief certainly, was moving the piano out of the public room downstairs. Then he remembered that the piano had been sold twenty years before. There came a deeper rumble from far away—and then silence. A bell rang across town. A horn honked; a door slammed. Mr. Fox looked at the time on the branch bank across the street (he had positioned his bed to save the cost of a clock): it was 4:36 A.M., Eastern Standard time. There were no more unusual sounds, and the bell stopped ringing. Anthony had already drifted back to sleep, but Mr. Fox lay awake, with his eyes open. The anxiety he had felt for the past several days (indeed, years) was mysteriously gone, and he was enjoying a pleasant feeling of anticipation that was entirely new to him.

"Hold still," Mr. Fox told Anthony as he brushed him and snapped on his little tweed suit. The weather was getting colder. Was it his imagination, or was the light through the window over the breakfast table different as the Finn served him his boiled egg and toast and marmalade and tea with milk? There was a fog, the first in weeks. The street outside the inn was deserted, and as he crossed the King's Esplanade and climbed the twelve steps, Mr. Fox saw that the Boardwalk was almost empty too. There were only two or three small groups, standing at the railing, staring at the fog as if at a blank screen.

There were no waves, no wake; the water lapped at the sand with nervous, pointless motions like an old lady's fingers on a shawl. Mr. Fox took a place at the rail. Soon the fog began to lift; and emerging in the near distance, across a gray expanse of water, like the image on the telly when it has first been turned on, Mr. Fox saw a wide, flat beach. Near the center was a cement bathhouse. Knots of people stood on the sand, some of them by parked cars. One of them shot a gun into the air; another waved a striped flag. Mr. Fox waved Anthony's paw for him.

America (and this could only be America) didn't seem very developed. Mr. Fox had expected, if not skyscrapers, at least more buildings. A white lorry pulled up beside the bathhouse. A man in uniform got out, lit a cigarette, looked through binoculars. The lorry said GOYA on the side.

"Welcome to Long Island," said a familiar voice. It was the African. Mr. Fox nodded but didn't say anything. He could see the girl on the African's other side, looking through binoculars. He wondered if she and the GOYA man were watching each other. "If you expected skyscrapers, they're fifty miles west of here, in Dover," said the African.

"West?"

"Dover's west now, since England's upside down. That's why the sun rises over Upper Beeding."

Mr. Fox nodded. Of course. He had never seen the sun rising, though he felt no need to say so.

"Everyone's gone to Dover. You can see Manhattan, the Statue of Liberty, the Empire State Building, all from Dover."

Mr. Fox nodded. Reassured by the girl's silence so far, he asked in a whisper, "So what place is this; where are we now?"

"Jones Beach."

"Not Babylon?"

"You bloody wish," said the girl.

Mr. Fox was exhausted. Lizzie was being harried like the fox she herself had hunted with such bloodthirsty glee in Scotland. As Major Mackintosh closed in, she seemed to take a perverse pleasure in the hopelessness of her situation: as if it bestowed on her a vulnerability she had never before possessed, a treasure more precious to her than the Eustace family diamonds. "Mr. Fox?" asked Mrs. Oldenshield.

"Mr. Fox?" She was shaking his shoulder. "Oh, I'm quite all right," he said. The book had fallen off his lap and she had caught him sleeping. Mrs. Oldenshield had a letter for him. (A letter for him!) It was from his niece, even though it was only the tenth of the month. There was nothing to do but open it. Mr. Fox began, as usual, at the ending, to make sure there were no surprises: but this time there were. "Until then," he read. As he scanned back through, he saw mention of "two ferries a day," and he couldn't read on. How had she gotten Mrs. Oldenshield's address? Did she expect him to come to America? He folded the letter and put it into his pocket. He couldn't read on.

That evening BBC was back on the air. The lights of Manhattan could be seen on live video from atop the cliffs of Dover, shimmering in the distance through the rain (for England had brought rain). One-day passes were being issued by both governments, and queues were already six blocks long. The East (now West) Kent Ferry from Folkestone to Coney Island was booked solid for the next three weeks.

There was talk of service to Eastbourne and Brighton as well. The next morning after breakfast, Mr. Fox lingered over his tea, examining a photograph of his niece which he had discovered in his letter box while putting her most recent (and most alarming) letter away. She was a serious-looking nine-year-old with a yellow ribbon in her light brown hair. Her mother, Mr. Fox's sister, Clare, held an open raincoat around them both. All this was thirty years ago but already her hair was streaked with gray. The Finn cleared the plates, which was the signal for Mr. Fox and Anthony to leave. There was quite a crowd on the Boardwalk, near the West Pier, watching the first ferry from America steaming across the narrow sound. Or was "steaming" the word? It was probably powered by some new type of engine. Immigration officers stood idly by, with their clipboards closed against the remnants of the fog (for England had brought fog). Mr. Fox was surprised to see Harrison at the end of the pier, wearing a windbreaker and carrying a paper bag that was greasy, as if it contained food. Mr. Fox had never seen Harrison in the day, or outside, before; in fact, he had never seen his legs. Harrison was wearing striped pants, and before Mr. Fox could speak to him, he sidled away like a crab into the crowd. There was a jolt as the ferry struck the pier. Mr. Fox stepped back just as Americans started up the ramp like an invading army. In the front were teenagers, talking among themselves as if no one else could hear; older people, almost as loud, followed behind them. They seemed no worse than the Americans who came to Brighton every summer, only not as well dressed.

"Woof, woof!"

Anthony was yipping over his shoulder, and Mr. Fox turned and saw a little girl with light brown hair and a familiar yellow ribbon. "Emily?" he said, recognizing his niece from the picture. Or so he thought. "Uncle Anthony?" The voice came from behind him again. He turned and saw a lady in a faded Burberry. The fog was blowing away and behind her he could see, for the first time that day, the drab American shore.

"You haven't changed a bit," the woman said. At first Mr. Fox thought she was his sister, Clare, just as she had been thirty years before, when she had brought her daughter to Brighton to meet him. But of course Clare had been dead for twenty years; and the woman was Emily, who had then been almost ten, and was now almost forty; and the girl was her own child (the niece who had been growing up inexorably) who was almost ten. Children, it seemed, were almost always almost something.

"Uncle Anthony?" The child was holding out her arms. Mr. Fox was startled, thinking she was about to hug him; then he saw what she wanted and handed her the dog. "You can pet him," he said. "His name is Anthony too."

"Really?"

"Since no one ever calls us both at the same time, it creates no confusion," said Mr. Fox.

"Can he walk?"

"Certainly he can walk. He just doesn't often choose to."

A whistle blew and the ferry left with its load of Britons for America. Mr. Fox saw Harrison at the bow, holding his greasy bag with one hand and the rail with the other, looking a little sick, or perhaps apprehensive. Then he took his niece and great-niece for a stroll along the Boardwalk. The girl, Clare—she was named after her grandmother—walked ahead with Anthony, while Mr. Fox and his niece, Emily, followed behind. The other Americans had all drifted into the city looking for restaurants, except for the male teenagers, who were crowding into the amusement parlors along the Esplanade, which had opened for the day.

"If the mountain won't come to Mahomet, and so forth," said Emily, mysteriously, when Mr. Fox asked if she'd had a nice crossing. Her brown hair was streaked with gray. He recognized the coat now; it had been her mother's, his sister's, Clare's. He was trying to think of where to take them for lunch. The Finn at the Pig & Thistle served a pretty fair shepherd's pie, but he didn't want them to see where he lived. They were content, however, with fish and chips on the Boardwalk; certainly Anthony seemed pleased to have chips fed to him, one by one, by the little girl named for the sister Mr. Fox had met only twice: once when she had been a student at Cambridge (or was it Oxford? he got them confused) about to marry an American; and once when she had returned with her daughter for a visit.

"Her father, your grandfather, was an Air Raid Warden," Mr. Fox told Emily. "He was killed in action, as it were, when a house collapsed during a rescue; and when his wife (well, she wasn't exactly his wife) died giving birth to twins a week later, they were each taken in by one of those whose life he had saved. It was a boarding house, all single people, so there was no way to keep the two together, you see; the children, I mean. Oh dear, I'm afraid I'm talking all in a heap."

"That's okay," said Emily.

"At any rate, when Mr. Singh died and his Inn was sold, my room was reserved for me, in accordance with his will, *in perpetuity,* which means as long as I remain in it. But if I were to move, you see, I would lose my patrimony entire."

"I see," said Emily. "And where is this place you go for tea?"

And so they spent the afternoon, and a rainy and an English afternoon it was, in the cozy tearoom with the faded purple drapes at the west (formerly east) end of Moncton Street where Mrs. Oldenshield kept Mr. Fox's complete set of Trollope on a high shelf, so he wouldn't have to carry them back and forth in all kinds of weather. While Clare shared her cake with Anthony, and then let him doze on her lap, Mr. Fox took down the handsome leather-bound volumes, one by one, and showed them to his niece and great-niece.

"They are, I believe, the first complete edition," he said. "Chapman and Hall."

"And were they your father's?" asked Emily. "My grandfather's?"

"Oh no!" said Mr. Fox. "They belonged to Mr. Singh. His grandmother was English and her own great-uncle had been, I believe, in the postal service in Ireland with the author, for whom I was, if I am not mistaken, named." He showed Emily the place in *The Eustace Diamonds* where he would have been reading that very afternoon, "were it not," he said, "for this rather surprisingly delightful family occasion." "Mother, is he blushing," said Clare. It was a statement and not a question.

It was almost six when Emily looked at her watch—a man's watch, Mr. Fox noted—and said, "We had better get back to the pier, or we'll miss the ferry." The rain had diminished to a misty drizzle as they hurried along the Boardwalk. "I must apologize for our English weather," said Mr. Fox, but his niece stopped him with a hand on his sleeve. "Don't brag," she said, smiling. She saw Mr. Fox looking at her big steel watch and explained that it had been found among her mother's things; she had always assumed it had been her grandfather's. Indeed, it had several dials, and across the face it said: "Civil Defense, Brighton." Across the bay, through the drizzle as through a lace curtain, they could see the sun shining on the sand and parked cars..

"Do you still live in, you know . . ." Mr. Fox hardly knew how to say the name of the place without sounding vulgar, but his niece came to his rescue. "Babylon? Only for another month. We're moving to Deer Park as soon as my divorce is final."

"I'm so glad," said Mr. Fox. "Deer Park sounds much nicer for the child."

"Can I buy Anthony a good-bye present?" Clare asked. Mr. Fox gave her some English money (even though the shops were all taking American) and she bought a paper of chips and fed them to the dog one by one. Mr. Fox knew Anthony would be flatulent for days, but it seemed hardly the sort of thing one mentioned. The ferry had pulled in and the tourists who had visited America for the day were streaming off, loaded with cheap gifts. Mr. Fox looked for Harrison, but if he was among them, he missed him. The whistle blew two warning toots. "It was kind of you to come," he said.

Emily smiled. "No big deal," she said. "It was mostly your doing anyway. I could never have made it all the way to England if England hadn't come here first. I don't fly."

"Nor do I." Mr. Fox held out his hand but Emily gave him a hug, and then a kiss, and insisted that Clare give him both as well. When that was over, she pulled off the watch (it was fitted with an expandable band) and slipped it over his thin, sticklike wrist. "It has a compass built in," she said. "I'm sure it was your father's. And Mother always . . ."

The final boarding whistle swallowed her last words. "You can be certain I'll take good care of it," Mr. Fox called out. He couldn't think of anything else to say. "Mother, is he crying," said Clare. It was a statement and not a question. "Let's you and me watch our steps," said Emily.

"Woof," said Anthony, and mother and daughter ran down (for the pier was high, and the boat was low) the gangplank. Mr. Fox waved until the ferry had backed out and turned, and everyone on board had gone inside, out of the rain, for it had started to rain in earnest. That night after dinner he was disappointed to find the bar unattended. "Anyone seen Harrison?" he asked. He had been looking forward to showing him the watch.

"I can get you a drink as well as him," said the Finn. She carried her broom with her and leaned it against the bar. She poured a whisky and said, "Just indicate if you need another.'' She thought indicate meant ask. The King was on the telly, getting into a long car with the President. Armed men stood all around them. Mr. Fox went to bed.

The next morning, Mr. Fox got up before Anthony. The family visit had been pleasant; indeed, wonderful; but he felt a need to get back to normal. While taking his constitutional, he watched the first ferry come in, hoping (somewhat to his surprise) that he might see Harrison in it; but no such luck. There were no English, and few Americans. The fog rolled in and out, like the same page on a book being turned over and over. At tea, Mr. Fox found Lizzie confessing (just as he had known she someday must) that the jewels had been in her possession all along. Now that they were truly gone, everyone seemed relieved, even the Eustace family lawyer. It seemed a better world without the diamonds.

"Did you hear that?"

"Beg your pardon?" Mr. Fox looked up from his book.

Mrs. Oldenshield pointed at his teacup, which was rattling in its saucer. Outside, in the distance, a bell was ringing. Mr. Fox wiped off the book himself and put it on the high shelf, then pulled on his coat, picked up his dog, and ducked through the low door into the street. Somewhere across town, a horn was honking. "Woof," said Anthony. There was a breeze for the first time in days. Knowing, or at least suspecting what he would find, Mr. Fox hurried to the Boardwalk. The waves on the beach were flattened, as if the water were being sucked away from the shore. The ferry was just pulling out with the last of the Americans who had come to spend the day. They looked irritated. On the way back to the Pig & Thistle Mr. Fox stopped by the cricket ground, but the boys were nowhere to be seen, the breeze being still too light for kiting, he supposed. "Perhaps tomorrow," he said to Anthony. The dog was silent, lacking the capacity for looking ahead.

That evening, Mr. Fox had his whisky alone again. He had hoped that Harrison might have shown up, but there was no one behind the bar but the Finn and her broom. King Charles came on the telly, breathless, having just landed in a helicopter direct from the Autumn White House. He promised to send for anyone who had been left behind, then commanded (or rather, urged) his subjects to secure the kingdom for the Atlantic. England was underway again. The next morning the breeze was brisk. When Mr. Fox and Anthony arrived at the Boardwalk, he checked the compass on his watch and saw that England had turned during the night, and Brighton had assumed its proper position, at the bow. A stout headwind was blowing and the seawall was washed by a steady two-foot curl. Long Island was a low, dark blur to the north, far off the port (or left).

"Nice chop."

"Beg pardon?" Mr. Fox turned and was glad to see a big man in a tweed coat, standing at the rail. He realized he had feared the African might have jumped ship like Harrison.

"Looks like we're making our four knots and more, this time."

Mr. Fox nodded. He didn't want to seem rude, but he knew if he said anything the girl would chime in. It was a dilemma.

"Trade winds," said the African. His collar was turned up, and his dreadlocks spilled over and around it like vines. "We'll make better time going back. If indeed we're going back. I say, is that a new watch?"

"Civil Defense chronometer," Mr. Fox said. "Has a compass built in. My father left it to me when he died."

"You bloody wish," said the girl.

"Should prove useful," said the African.

"I should think so," said Mr. Fox, smiling into the fresh

salt wind; then, saluting the African (and the girl), he tucked
Anthony under his arm and left the Boardwalk in their command. England was steady, heading south by southeast, and
it was twenty past four, almost time for tea.

↯ By Permit Only ↯

"WHAT ABOUT THE environmental costs?" my boss asked. My boss, Mr. Manning, always thinks about the environment. He's Personal Paints' Environmental Control Officer. Every company has one these days.

"That's the beauty of it, Manning," the salesman told him. (At least, I thought he was a salesman.) "Our system accommodates the scientific straight-through smokestack style that is the latest in environmental off-load technology. The fumes go directly into the atmosphere—"

"What? You want me to release the poisonous by-products of Personal Paints directly into the atmosphere, and you say there are no environmental costs?"

"I didn't say 'no,' I said 'low,' " the salesman said (at least, he talked like a salesman). "As you know, pollution is legal these days as long as it is properly licensed and paid for. And the new administration has lowered the toxic-particulate fee to twenty-five cents a ton. If you factor in your capital-improvements credit, and the discount you get if you buy the new smokestack from a U.S. company, you will save 39.8 percent the first year over your current smoke-scrubber system. Which doesn't do all that damn much good anyway, judging from what I see out the window."

"Hmmm! Well, you've got a point there. Are you getting all this down, Miss, Miss—"

" 'Mrs.,' and it's Robinson," I said, trying to ignore Mr. Manning's hand on my thigh. His sexual harassment permit (on file at the main office) didn't cover actual genital contact, so I didn't have to worry about him going much higher, thank God. "I'm writing it right here on my steno pad." (Recycled paper; I do my part.)

"It's all covered in the literature I gave you, anyway," the salesman went on (I was still thinking he was a salesman). "Unrestricted atmospheric off-load is only one element of a total waste-management system that also includes unlimited solid debris dispersal and full-flow aquatic effluent elimination, all for one low EPA fee."

(EPA! So he was a government man.)

"Well, now, you talk a good game!" Mr. Manning said. "But can you help with our solid-waste disposal crisis? We're talking heaps of stuff here."

"With our new accounting system, you no longer spend precious resources trucking trash all over creation looking for legal landfills," the Environmental Protection Agency representative (for that was what he was) said. "You pay a one-time pollution penalty fee and pile the shit in a big fucking heap on the poor side of town."

"I like that," said Mr. Manning. "But what about the sticky, stinky stuff? We have oodles of ordure that emit radioactive steam and drool dioxins directly into the groundwater. You're going to let us dump this anywhere we want?"

"No, we have a responsibility to protect the public," said the EPA rep. "The real stinky stuff, you dump it in the woods."

"I like that too," said Mr. Manning. "But what about the endangered species? You wouldn't believe the grief we get from the environmental do-gooders lately."

"Forget them," said the EPA rep. "If we listened to them, we'd be up to our assholes in owls."

"I thought it was eyebrows," I said.

"Don't worry your pretty little head about it," said Mr. Manning, his prowling paw pausing at the hem of my panties, where his permit ran out. "Just be sure you're getting all this down."

"It's all covered in the literature I gave you, anyway," said the EPA agent. "Since there are no endangered species left, the ES fees have been waived. That makes our direct environmental penalty payment plan even more attractive. According to the most conservative figures—"

While he droned on, I looked out the window. Mr. Manning's twenty-third-floor office commanded a beautiful view of the river, looking with its gleaming oil slicks like Joseph's coat of many colors. (I read the Bible every day. Do you?)

The EPA rep was showing Mr. Manning a four-color picture of a thirty-six-inch pipe. "The beauty of a scientific straight-through system is that it never clogs and rarely backs up," he said. "The effluents are taxed once only and dumped directly into the river, which runs conveniently into the sea. It's like a pay toilet."

"This guy's a poet," mused Mr. Manning, running his hand along the crack that separated my buttocks. I tried to ignore him (jobs are scarce these days) and kept looking out the window. It was a gorgeous day. You could almost see the sky. The radioactive dump across town glowed warmly, reminding me of home. Since the dump was in my neighborhood, the high-geiger penalty pennies (we called it clickety-clink, or mutation money) had provided bonus burial benefits for five of my six children.

"Plus, it's all plenty patriotic, since one hundred percent of the environmental penalty money goes directly into the U.S. treasury, and not to some high-tech Jap clean-up scam," the EPA rep said, winding up his spiel.

"I like that," said Mr. Manning.

I sneaked a glance at my watch. My chronically underemployed husband, Big Bill, would be waiting impatiently for me to get home to cook supper for himself and our last remaining child, the hideously deformed, demented little cripple, Tiny Tim.

It was 4:59. Mr. Manning and the EPA rep were still working out the details of the quarterly pollution payment plan, which meant I would have to work late, whether I wanted to or not.

Of course, I would get paid overtime.

Finally, at 5:59, the papers were signed and I headed home. The stairs were crowded but the elevator was almost empty. Lots of people are afraid to take the elevator, after the terrifying incidents of the past few weeks, but just knowing the inspection certificate is on file in the building superintendent's office (even if we're not allowed to see it) is enough for me.

The expressway was bumper-to-bumper with the big-finned fifties replicas that are popular now that leaded gasoline is available again. It warmed my heart to think of all the ethyl-penalty bucks going into the HEW budget. I knew it was helping to pay for the remedial education of my deranged, learning-dislocated, double-dyslexic little boy, Tiny Tim.

I drove only half listening to the ads and to Howard Stern, who was back on the air (his station had apparently purchased another obscenity authorization). I was tired and didn't really feel like listening, so I turned it down as low as it would go, longing for the day Big Bill and I could afford a car without a radio.

But it's better to light a candle than curse the darkness, so I concentrated on the beauty of the many-colored cars crawling through the magenta-tinted air. The carbon penalty fees

have certainly eased the tax burden on working wives like
me.

Traffic was slowed almost to a crawl near the airport. At
first I feared it was another crash (which can tie up the turn-
pike for hours) but it was only a set of landing gear that had
worked loose and fallen onto the highway. This was happening more and more lately since the Federal Aeronautics
Board had started selling maintenance waivers to the airlines
to augment the FAB retirement fund.

I was glad to see the lights of our peaceful suburb, Middle
Elm. My pleasure was spoiled a little (but only a little) by the
cross burning in the park. It looked like the KKK had purchased another bias license—not as expensive as actual violence permits. The lynching last week must have cost them a
pretty penny (if you can use the word "pretty" for such a
grim event).

It was almost nine when I pulled into the drive. I knew I
would be in trouble, so I hesitated at the door as long as I
could—until I started to gag on the stench from our next-
door neighbor's pigpen. It's a terrible odor, but what could
we do? Mrs. Greene had paid her feces fees, and the money
went to lower our property taxes, after all. Plus, her animals
were not eaten but tortured to death for science, and I knew
that these animal experiments were helping improve the
quality of life of my terminally-twisted, pus-encrusted, semi-
psychotic son, Tiny Tim.

Barbara (I will not call her Babs!) was in her doorway,
waving a rubber glove, but I didn't wave back. Not to be
snotty, but I hate it when ordinary people take on the airs of
giant corporations.

"Where the hell you been, bitch!" Big Bill muttered. He
took another swig of gin (ignoring the label, which said,
WARNING, DRINKING MAKES SOME PEOPLE ACT UGLY). He grabbed
my ass, and when I pulled away he made a fist like Ralph

Cramden (don't you love that old show?) and pointed not toward the Moon but toward his framed wife-beating authorization certificate hanging on the wall over the dinette table, next to our marriage license.

Ignoring his antics, I put the chicken in the oven, slamming the door quickly against the smell. I wondered how old it was but there was no way to tell. The expiration date was covered by an official USDA late-penalty override sticker, and it's against the law to pull them off, like mattress tags.

Where was Tiny Tim? Just then I heard automatic-weapons fire (everybody has a permit these days) and he burst in the door; or rather, rolled in, his face all bloody and his wheelchair bent out of shape.

"Where have you been?" I asked. (As if I didn't know! He's had to travel through a bad neighborhood lately, ever since the town floated a bond issue to buy a permit allowing them to bypass the handicapped-access laws.)

"Got mugged," he said, spitting broken teeth into one clawlike, grasping little hand.

"Who did it?" said his dad. "I'll kill them!"

"They had their papers, Pop!" whined our bruised, battered, blubbering baby boy. "They whipped it out and waved it in my face, and then it was whack whack whack!"

"Poor kid," I said, trying not to look at him. Never a pretty child, he looked even worse than usual. Instead, I looked out the window at the sunset. They say sunsets are better now than ever, now that pollution is controlled. Certainly they are colorful as all Hell (if you'll pardon my French)!

"God damn them every one," Tiny Tim said, wrinkling what was left of his little button nose. "What's for supper, chicken again?"

And that's the end of my story. If you don't like it, fuck

you. Please direct any complaints to the New York office of the National Writer's Union, Plot Department, where my Climax Bypass Permit Number 5944 is on file.

Fee paid.

✧ THE SHADOW KNOWS ✧

IF A LION COULD TALK, WE COULDN'T UNDERSTAND IT.
—WITTGENSTEIN

I

WHEN IT COMES to property, even old folks move fast. Edwards hadn't been abandoned for more than a year before the snowbirds began moving in. We turned the pride of the U.S. space program into a trailer park in six months, with Airstreams and Winneys parked on the slabs that had once held hangars and barracks.

I was considered sort of the unofficial mayor, since I had served in and out (or up and down, as earthsiders put it) of Edwards for some twenty years before being forced into retirement exactly six days short of ten years before the base itself was budget-cut out of existence by a bankrupt government. I knew where the septic tanks and waterlines had been; I knew where the electrical lines and roads were buried under the blowing sand. And since I had been in maintenance, I knew how to splice up the phone lines and even pirate a little electric from the LA-to-Vegas trunk. Though I didn't know everybody in Slab City, just about everybody knew me.

So when a bald-headed dude in a two-piece suit started going door to door asking for Captain Bewley, folks knew who he was looking for. "You must mean the Colonel," they would say. (I had never been very precise about rank.) Everybody knew I had been what the old-timers called an "astronaut," but nobody knew I had been a lunie, except for a couple of old girlfriends to whom I had shown the kind of tricks you learn in three years at .16g, but that's another and more, well, intimate story altogether.

This story, which also has its intimate aspects, starts with a knock at the door of my ancient but not exactly venerable 2009 Road Lord.

"Captain Bewley, probably you don't remember me, but I was junior day officer when you were number two on maintenance operations at Houbolt—"

"On the far side of the Moon. Flight Lieutenant J. B. 'Here's Johnny' Carson. How could I forget one of the most"—I searched for a word: what's a polite synonym for "forgettable"?—"agreeable young lunies in the Service. No longer quite so young. And now a civilian, I see."

"Not exactly, sir," he said.

"Not 'sir' anymore," I said. "You would probably outrank me by now, and I'm retired anyway. Just call me Colonel Mayor."

He didn't get the joke—Here's Johnny never got the joke, unless he was the one making it; he just stood there looking uncomfortable. Then I realized he was anxious to get in out of the UV, and that I was being a poor host.

"And come on in," I said. I put aside the radio-controlled model I was building; or rather, fixing, for one of my unofficial grandsons who couldn't seem to get the hang of landing. I don't have any grandkids, or kids, of my own. A career in space, or "in the out" as we used to say, has its down side.

"I see you've maintained an interest in flight," Here's Johnny said. "That makes my job easier."

That was clearly my cue, and since we lunies never saw much use in beating around the bush (there being no bushes on the Moon) I decided to let Here's Johnny off the hook. Or is that mixing metaphors? There are no metaphors on the Moon, either. Everything there is what it is.

Anyway, accommodatingly, I said, "Your job, which is—"

"I'm now working for the UN, Captain Bewley," he said. "They took over the Service, you know. Even though I'm out of uniform, I'm here on official business. Incognito. To offer you an assignment."

"An assignment? At my age? The Service threw me out ten years ago because I was too old!"

"It's a temporary assignment," he said. "A month, two months at most. But it means accepting a new commission, so they can give you clearance, since the whole project is Top Secret."

I could hear the caps on the *T* and the *S*. I suppose I was supposed to be impressed. I suppose I might have been, fifty years before.

"They're talking about a promotion to major, with increased retirement and medical benefits," said Here's Johnny.

"That would be a de facto demotion, since everybody here calls me Colonel already," I said. "Nothing personal, Here's Johnny, but you wasted a trip. I already have enough medical and retirment for my old bones. What's a little extra brass to a seventy-six-year-old with no dependents and few vices?"

"What about space pay?"

"Space pay?"

Here's Johnny smiled, and I realized he had been beating around the bush the whole time, and enjoying it. "They want to send you back to the Moon, Captain Bewley."

In the thrillers of the last century, when you are recruited for a top secret international operation (and this one turned out to be not just international but interplanetary; even interstellar; hell, intergalactic), they send a LearJet with no running lights to pick you up at an unmarked airport and whisk you to an unnamed Caribbean island, where you meet with the well-dressed and ruthless dudes who run the world from behind the scenes.

In real life, in the 2030s at least, you fly coach to Newark.

I knew that Here's Johnny couldn't tell me what was going on, at least until I had been sworn in, so on the way back East we just shot the bull and caught up on old times. We hadn't been friends in the Service—there was age and rank and temperament between us—but time has a way of smoothing out those wrinkles. Most of my old friends were dead; most of his were in civilian life, working for one of the French and Indian firms that serviced the network of communications and weather satellites that were the legacy of the last century's space program. The Service Here's Johnny and I knew had been cut down to a Coast Guard-type outfit running an orbital rescue shuttle and maintaining the lunar asteroid-watch base I had helped build, Houbolt.

"I was lucky enough to draw Houbolt," Here's Johnny said, "or I would probably have retired myself three years ago, at fifty."

I winced. Even the kids were getting old.

We took a cab straight through the Lincoln/Midtown Tunnel to the UN building in Queens, where I was recommissioned as a major in the Space Service by a bored lady in a magenta uniform. My new papers specified that when I retired again in sixty days I would draw a major's pension plus augmented medical with a full dental plan.

This was handsome treatment indeed, since I still had several teeth left. I was impressed; and also puzzled. "Okay, Here's Johnny," I said as we walked out into the perfect October sunlight (at my age you notice fall more than spring): "Let's have it. What's the deal? What's going on?"

He handed me a room chit for a midtown hotel (the Service had never been able to afford Queens) and a ticket on the first flight out for Reykjavik the next morning; but he held on to a brown envelope with my name scrawled on it.

"I have your orders in this envelope," he said. "They explain everything. The problem is, well—once I give them to you I'm supposed to stay by your side until I put you on the plane tomorrow morning."

"And you have a girlfriend."

"I figured you might."

So I did. An old girlfriend. At my age, all your girlfriends are old.

New York is supposed to be one of the dirtiest cities in the world; it is certainly the noisiest. Luckily I like noise and, like most old people, need little sleep. Here's Johnny must have needed more; he was late. He met me at the Icelandic gate at Reagan International only minutes before my flight's last boarding call and handed me the brown envelope with my name on it.

"You're not supposed to open it until you're on the plane, Captain," he said. "I mean, Major."

"Not so fast," I said, grabbing his wrist. "You got me into this. You must know something about it."

Here's Johnny lowered his voice and looked from side to side; like most lunies he loved secrets. "You know Zippe-Buisson, the French firm that cleans up orbital trash?" he said. "A few months ago they noticed a new blip in medium high earth. There weren't any lost sats on the db; it was too big to be a dropped wrench and too small to be a shuttle tank."

Ding, went the door. I backed into the gate and held it open with one foot. "Go on," I said.

"Remember *Voyager,* the interstellar probe sent out in the 1970s? It carried a disk with digital maps of Earth and pic-

tures of humans, even music. Mozart and what's-his-
name—"

Ding ding, went the door. "I remember the joke. 'Send
more Chuck Berry,' " I said. "But you're changing the subject."

No, he wasn't. Just as the door started to close and I had
to jump through, Here's Johnny called out: *"Voyager* is back.
With a passenger."

The sealed orders, which I opened on the plane, didn't add
much to what Here's Johnny had told me. I was officially as-
signed to the UN's SETI (Search for Extra-Terrestrial Intelligence) Commission, E Team, temporarily stationed at
Houbolt, Luna. That was interesting, since Houbolt had
been cut back to robot operation before my retirement, and
hadn't housed anybody (that I knew of) for almost fifteen
years.

I was to proceed to Reykjavik for my meds; I was to communicate with no one about my destination or my assignment. Period. There was no indication what the E Team was
(although I had of course been given a clue), or what my role
in it was to be. Or why I had been chosen.

Reykjavik is supposed to be one of the cleanest cities in
the world. It is certainly one of the quietest. I spent the afternoon and most of the evening getting medical tests in a spar-
kling new hospital wing, where it seemed I was the only
patient. The doctors seemed less worried about my physical
condition than my brain, blood, and bone status. I'm no
medical expert, but I can recognize a cancer scan when I am
subjected to one.

In between tests I met my new boss, the head of SETI's
E Team, by videophone from Luna. She was a heavyset fifty-
ish woman with perfect teeth (now that I had my dental
plan, I was noticing teeth again), short blond hair, piercing
blue eyes, and a barely perceptible Scandinavian accent.

She introduced herself as Dr. Sunda Hvarlgen and said: "Welcome to Reykjavik, Major. I understand you are part of Houbolt's history. I hope they are treating you well in my hometown."

"The films in the waiting room aren't bad," I said. "I watched *E.T.* twice."

"I promise an official briefing when you get to Houbolt. I just wanted to welcome you to the E team."

"Does this mean I passed my medicals?"

She rang off impatiently and it struck me as I hung up that the whole purpose of the call had been to get a look at me.

They finished with me at nine P.M. The next morning at seven, I was loaded into a fat-tired van and taken twelve miles north on a paved highway, then east on a track across a lava field. I was the only passenger. The driver was a descendant (or so he said) of Huggard the Grasping, one of the original lost settlers of Newfoundland. After an hour we passed through the gates of an abandoned air base. Huggard pointed to a small lava ridge with sharp peaks like teeth; behind it I noticed a single silver tooth, even sharper than the rest. It was the nose cone of an Ariane-Daewoo IV.

The Commission had given up the advantages of an equatorial launch in order to preserve the secrecy of the project; this meant that the burn was almost twenty-eight minutes long. I didn't mind. I hadn't been off planet in eleven years, and the press of six gravities was like an old lover holding me in her arms again. And the curve of the planet below—well, if I had been a sentimental man, I would have cried. But sentiment is for middle age, just as romance is for youth. Old age, like war, has colder feelings; it is, after all, a struggle to the death.

High Orbital was lighted and looked bustling from approach, which surprised me; the station had been shut down years ago except for fueling and docking use. We didn't go inside; just used the universal airlock for transfer to the lunar shuttle, the dirty but reliable old *Diana* in which I had made so many trips. She was officially Here's Johnny's command, but he was on rotation: presumably his reward for bringing me in alive.

When we old folks forget how decrepit and uninteresting we are, we can count on the young to remind us by ignoring us. The three-person crew of the *Diana* kept to themselves and spoke only Russo-Japanese. It made for a lonely day and a half, but I didn't mind. The trip to the Moon is one of the loveliest there is. You're leaving one ball of water and heading for another of rock, and there's always a view.

Since the crew didn't know I speak (or at least understand) a little R-J, I got my first clue as to what my assignment might be. I overheard two of them speculating about "ET" (a name that is the same in every language) and one said: "Who would have thought the thing would only relate to old folks?"

That night I slept like a baby. I woke up only once, when we crossed over what we lunies used to call Wolf Creek Pass— the top of the Earth's (relatively) long, steep gravitational well, and the beginning of the short, shallow slope to the Moon. In zero g there's no way this transition can be felt: yet I awoke, knowing exactly (even after eleven years) where I was.

I was on my way back to the Moon.

Situated on the farside of the Moon, facing always away from the Earth, Houbolt lies open to the Universe. In a more imaginative, more intelligent, more spirited age it would be a deep-space optical observatory; or at least a monastery. In our petty, penny-pinching, paranoid century it is used only as a semiautomated Near-Earth-Object or asteroid early-warning station. It wouldn't have been kept open at all if it were not for the near-miss of NEO 2201 Oljato back in '14, which had pried loose UN funds as only stark terror will.

Houbolt lies near the center of the farside's great Korolev crater, on a gray regolith plain ringed by jagged mountains unsmoothed by water, wind, or ice; as sheer as the lava sills of Iceland but miles instead of meters high; fantastic enough to remind you over and over, with every glance, that they are made of Moon, not Earth; and that you are in their realm; and that it is not a realm of living things.

I loved it. I had helped build and then maintain the base for four years, so I knew it well. In fact, on seeing that barren landscape again, in which life is neither a promise nor a memory, not even a rumor, I realized why I had stayed in the desert after retirement and not gone back to Tennessee, even though I still had people there. Tennessee is too damn green.

Houbolt is laid out like a starfish, with five small peripheral domes (named for the four winds, plus Other) all connected by forty-meter tubes to the larger central dome known as Grand Central. Hvarlgen met me at the airlock in South, which was still the shop and maintenance dome. I felt at home right away.

I was a little surprised to see that she was in a wheelchair; other than that, she looked the same as on the screen. The blue eyes were even bluer here on the blueless Moon.

"Welcome to Houbolt," she said as we shook hands. "Or back, maybe I should say. Didn't South here used to be your office?" The Moon with its .16g has always drawn more than its share of 'capped, and I could tell by the way she spun the chair around and ran it tilted back on two wheels, that it was just right for her. I followed her down the tube toward Grand Central.

I had been afraid Houbolt might have fallen into ruin, like High Orbital, but it was newly painted and the air smelled fresh. Grand Central was bright and cheerful. Hvarlgen's team of lunies had put in a few spots of color, but they hadn't overdone it. All of them were young, in bright yellow tunics. When Hvarlgen introduced me as one of the pioneers of Houbolt, none of them blinked at my name, even though it was one of twenty-two on a plaque just inside the main airlock. I wasn't surprised. The Service is like a mold, an organism with immortality but no memory.

A young lunie showed me to my windowless pie-shaped "wedgie" in North. A loose orange tunic with a SETI patch lay folded on the hammock. But I wasn't about to put on Hvarlgen's uniform until I learned what she was doing.

I found her back in Grand Central waiting by the coffee machine, a giant Russian apparatus that reflected our faces like a funhouse mirror. I was surprised to see myself. When you get to a certain age you stop looking in mirrors.

A hand-drawn poster over the machine read D=118.

"Hours until the *Diana* returns," Hvarlgen said. "The lunies see this as a hardship assignment, surprisingly enough. They're only used to being here a day or two at a time."

"You promised a briefing," I said.

"I did." She drew me a coffee and pointed out a seat. "I assume, since gossip is still the fuel of the Service, that in spite of our best efforts you have managed to learn something about our project here." She scowled. "If you haven't, you'd be too dumb to work with."

"There was a rumor," I said. "About an ET."

"An AO," she corrected. "At this point it's classified only as an Anomolous Object. Even though it's not in fact an object. More like an idea for an object. If my work—our work—is successful and we make contact, it will be upgraded to an ET. It was found in Earth orbit some sixteen days ago."

I was impressed. Here's Johnny hadn't told me how quickly all this had been pulled together. "You all move fast," I said.

She nodded. "What else did you hear?"

"Voyager," I said. " 'Send more Chuck Berry.' "

"Voyager II, actually. Circa 1977. Which left the heliosphere in 1991, becoming the first human-made object to enter interstellar space. Last month, more than fifty years after its launch, it was found in high Earth orbit with its batteries discharged, its nuclears dead, seemingly derelict. Space junk. How long it had been there, who or what returned it, and why—we still don't know. As it was brought into lock aboard the recovery vessel, the *Jean Genet,* what had appeared to be a shadow attached itself to one of the crew, one Hector Mersault, apparently while they were unsuiting. They didn't notice at first, until they found Mersault sitting in the airlock, half undressed and dazed, as if he had just come out from under anesthesia. He was holding his helmet and the shadow was pooled in it; apparently our AO likes small spaces, like a cat."

"Likes?"

"We allow ourselves certain anthropomorphisms, Major. We will correct for them later. If necessary. More coffee?"

While she poured us both another cup, I looked around the room; but with lunies it's hard to tell European from Asian, male from female.

"So where's this Mersault?" I asked. "Is he here?"

"Not exactly," Hvarlgen said. "He walked out of an airlock the next morning. But our friend the AO is still with us. Come. I'll show you."

We drained our coffee and I followed Hvarlgen down the tube toward the periphery dome known as Other. She ran with her chair tilted back, so that her front wheels were almost a foot off the floor; I was to learn that this angle of elevation reflected her mood. Other was divided into two semi-hemi-spherical rooms used to grow the environmental that we'd called "weed & bean." There was a small storage shed between the two rooms. We headed straight for the shed. A lunie with a ceremonial (I hoped) wiregun unlocked the door and let us into a gray closed wedgie, small as a prison cell. The door closed behind us. The room was empty except for a plastic chair facing a waist-high shelf, on which sat a clear glass bowl, like a fishbowl, in which was—

Well, a shadow.

It was about the size of a keyboard or a cantaloupe. It was hard to look at; it was sort of there and sort of not there. When I looked to one side, the bowl looked empty; whatever was (or wasn't) in it, didn't register on my peripheral vision.

"Our bio teams have been over it," Hvarlgen said. "It does not register on any instruments. It can't be touched, weighed, or measured in any way, not even an electrical charge. It's not even *not* there. As far as I can guess, it's some kind of antiparticle soup. Don't ask me how our eyes can see it. I think they just see the *isn't* of it, if you know what I mean."

I nodded even though I didn't.

"It doesn't show up on video; but I am hoping it will register on analog."

"Analog?"

"Chemical. We're filming it." Hvarlgen pointed to a gun-like object jerry-rigged to one wall, which whirred and followed her hand, then aimed back at the bowl. "I had this antique shipped up especially for the job. Everything our AO does is captured on film, twenty-four hours a day."

"Film!" I said. I was impressed again. "So what exactly does it do?"

"Sits there in the bowl. That's the problem. It refuses to—but is 'refuse' too anthropomorphic a word for you? Let me start over. As far as we can tell, it will only interact with living tissue."

A shiver went through me. Living tissue? That was me, for a few more years anyway, and I was beginning to understand, or at least suspect, why I was here. But why me? "What exactly do you mean by 'interact'?" I asked.

Hvarlgen scowled. "Don't look so worried," she said. "In spite of what happened to Mersault, this is no suicide assignment. Let's go get another cup of coffee, and I'll explain."

We left the AO to its bowl, and the lunie with the wiregun to lock up. Back at Grand Central, Hvarlgen poured two more cups of thick, lunar coffee. I was beginning to see her as a wheeled device that ran on the stuff.

"SETI was set up in the middle of the last century," she said. "In a sense, *Voyager* was part of the program. NASA took it over toward the end of the century and changed the name, but the idea was the same. They were searching for evidence of intelligent life, the assumption being that actual communication over such vast distances would be impossible. Contact was considered even more remote. But in the event that it did occur, it was assumed that it probably would not be a 'take me to your leader' sort of thing, a spaceship landing in London or Peking; that it would be more complicated than that, and that plenty of room for human sensitivity and intuition should be built into the system. Some flexibility. So SETI's directors set up the E (for 'Elliot') Team which would swing into operation on first contact and operate, for twenty-one days only, in strictest secrecy. No press, no politics. No grown-ups, if you will. It would be run by a single person instead of a committee; a humanist rather than a scientist."

"A woman rather than a man?"

"That's just been the luck of the draw. You'll be surprised to learn how it has backfired in this case." Hvarlgen scowled again. "Anyway, by the time I got the job, the E Team was more of a sop thrown to the soft sciences than a working position. A brief orientation, a stipend, and a beeper that was never expected to beep. But the mechanisms were still in place. I was visiting psychology professor at UC Davis, on leave from Reykjavik U, when I got the call—within hours of the *Jean Genet* incident. I was already on my way up to High Orbital when Mersault died. Or killed himself.''

"Or was killed," I offered.

"Whatever. We'll get into that later. At any rate, I exercised the extraordinary authority which the UN had granted the E Team—figuring it would never be used, I'm sure—and had this whole operation set up here at Houbolt.''

"Because you didn't want to bring the AO down to Earth.''

"It didn't seem like a good idea, at least until we knew what we were dealing with. And High Orbital was in such bad shape, plus it's hard to find people who can tolerate zero g for long periods. I know the Moon since I did my doctoral project here. So here we are. Everything that has happened since Mersault's death has been my decision. My E Team mandate only extends for six more days. After that, our friend here goes either to the full SETI Commission, as an ET, or to the Q Team—the Quantum Singularity Team—as an AO. Time is of the essence; I'm on a fairly short string, you see. So while I was waiting at High Orbital for my lunie staff to prepare Houbolt, I initiated the second contact myself. I stuck my hand—my right hand—into the bowl.''

I looked at her with a new and growing respect.

"It flowed out of the bowl and up my arm, a little above my elbow. Like a long glove, the kind my great-grandmother used to wear to church.''

"And?''

"I wrote this down.'' She showed me a pad on which was written:

blómhnappur

"It's Icelandic and it means 'New Growth.' I had brought the pad and pencil with me, along with a tape recorder. It was over before I knew it; it didn't even feel strange. I just picked up the pencil and wrote."

"This is your handwriting?"

"Not at all. I'm right-handed, and I wrote this with my left. My right hand was in the bowl."

"Then what?"

"Then it flowed—sort of rippled; it's quite strange, but you'll see—back down my arm and into the bowl. All this is at High Orbital in zero g, remember, and there's nothing to keep our little ET in the bowl except that it wants to be there. Or something."

"You're calling it an ET now."

"Wouldn't you call this communication, or at least an attempt to communicate? Unofficially speaking, this and its method of arrival are enough to convince me. What else would you call it but an ET?"

"A Ouija smudge?" I thought—but I said nothing. The whole business was beginning to sound crazy to me. The dark nonsubstance in the bowl had looked about as intelligent as the coffee left in my cup; and I wasn't too sure anymore about the woman in the wheelchair.

"I can see you're not convinced," said Hvarlgen. "No matter; you will be. At any rate, I spent the next few hours under guard, like Odysseus lashed to the mast, to make sure I didn't follow Mersault out an airlock. Then I tried it again."

"Stuck your hand in the bowl."

"My right hand, again. This time I was holding the pencil in my left, ready to go. But this time our friend, our ET, our whatever, was very reluctant. Only after a couple of tries did it *ripple* onto my arm; and then only an inch or so up my wrist, and only for a moment. But it worked. It's like it was com-

municating directly with my musculature rather than my consciousness. Without even thinking about it, I wrote this—"
She turned the page on the pad and I saw:

gamall madr

"Which says 'Old Man.' "
I nodded. "So naturally, you sent Here's Johnny for me."
Hvarlgen laughed and scowled, and I understood for the
first time that her scowl was a smile; she just wore it upside
down.
"You're getting ahead of yourself, Major. I interpreted all
this to mean that there was a reluctance to communicate with
me, which had something to do with my age or my sex or
both. Since we hadn't left for the Moon yet, I used my somewhat extravagant authority and sent the shuttle back down. I
recruited an old friend, a former professor of mine—a
retired advisor to SETI, in fact—who had spent some time at
Houbolt, and brought him to Luna with me. That clipped
another three days out of my precious time."
"So where is he? Out the airlock, I suppose, or I wouldn't
be here."
"Not quite out the airlock yet," said Hvarlgen. "Come
with me and you'll see."

I had never met Dr. Soo Lee Kim, but I had heard of him. A
tiny man with long, flying white hair like Einstein, he was an
astronomer, the leader of the deep-space optical team that
had been kicked out of Houbolt when it had been turned
into a semiautomated warning station. Dr. Kim had won a
Nobel Prize. He had a galaxy named after him. Now he occu-
pied one of the two beds in the infirmary under the clear
dome in East. The other one was empty.
I smelled death in the room and realized it was Peace-

222 ✧ TERRY BISSON ✧

Able, the sinsemilla nasal spray given to terminal patients. It's a complicated aroma for me, the smell of love and loss together, a curious mixture I knew well from the last weeks of my first wife, the one I went back to when she was dying. But that's another story altogether.

Dr. Kim looked cheerful enough. He had been expecting us.

"I'm so glad you're here; now perhaps we can begin to communicate," he said in Cambridge-accented English. "As you probably know, the Shadow won't talk with me."

"The Shadow?"

"That's what I call it. From your old American radio serial. 'Who Knows what Evil lurks in the Hearts of Men? The Shadow knows!' "

"You don't look that old to me," I said.

"I'm not; I'll be seventy-two next week, when the *Diana* returns, if I'm unfortunate enough to last that long." He took a quick shot of PeaceAble from an imitation ebony spraypipe, and continued: "Collecting old radio tapes was a hobby I picked up when I was at university. They were forty-five years old even then, forty-five years ago. I don't suppose you remember Sky King and his Radio Ranch?"

"Nobody's that old, Dr. Kim. I'm only seventy-six. How old do you have to be for this ghost-in-a-bowl?"

"The Shadow," he corrected. "Oh, you're quite old enough. I'm old enough, actually, I think. Or would have been, if it weren't for—"

"Start at the beginning, Dr. Kim," said Hvarlgen. "Please. The Major needs to know everything that has happened."

"The beginning? Then let's start at the end, as the Shadow starts." He laughed enigmatically. "I have learned one thing, at least: language is contained as much in the musculature as in the brain. The first time, I did as Sunda did; I stuck my hand into the bowl, and my brain was looking on,

unattached, as the Shadow picked up my hand, and with it
picked up a pencil—"

"And wrote you a letter," I said.

"Drew me a picture," Dr. Kim corrected. "Korean is at
least partly ideographic." He reached under the bed and
pulled out a paper, on which was written:

내지를 벗어 주세요.

"Take me to your leader?" I guessed.

"It means, more or less, 'okay'; and it suggests a more
intimate relationship, which I immediately implemented, so
to speak, and which—"

"More intimate?"

"—resulted in this."

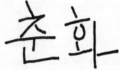

"Like Sunda's message, it means 'new growth,' " he said.
"which I took, in my case, to mean cancer."

"Oh."

I must have winced, because he said, "Oh, it's all right. I
knew it already; colon cancer; I had known it for four
months. I just hadn't told Sunda because I didn't think it
mattered."

"Then it wasn't the Shadow that—?" I asked.

"Gave it to me? No," said Dr. Kim. "The Shadow was in a
position, so to speak, to detect it, that's all." He either
grinned or grimaced in pain (it was hard to tell) and took
another shot of PeaceAble. "Don't forget, 'The Shadow
knows.' "

The young are sentimental around death but the old
have no such problem. "Tough," I said.

"There are no happy endings," Dr. Kim said. "At least, thanks to the Shadow, I got my trip back to the Moon. With any luck I might even end my days here. Wouldn't it make a great tombstone, the Moon? Hanging there in the sky, bigger than a thousand pyramids. And lighted, to boot. Would put to rest forever the slander that all Koreans have good taste." He paused for another shot. "But the problem is, that because of the cancer—apparently—the Shadow won't relate to me. I think it mistakes the cancer for youth. That second contact was my last. So tomorrow it's your turn, right?" He looked from me to Hvarlgen.

Hvarlgen and I looked at each other.

"So I'm next," I said. "Old man number two."

"This is the point at which I give you the chance to back out," Hvarlgen said. "Much as I hate to. But if you turn me down, I'll still have time for one more shot; your alternate is doing his meds right now in Reykjavik."

I could tell she was lying; if she had only six days left, I was her only hope. "Why me in the first place?" I asked.

"You were the oldest reasonably healthy male I could find on such short notice who was space qualified. I knew you'd been to Houbolt. Plus I liked your looks, Major. Intuition. You looked like the kind of guy who might stick his neck out."

"Neck?" laughed Dr. Kim, and she shot him a dirty look.

"Of course, I could be wrong," she said to me.

She was gut-checking me but I didn't mind; I hadn't been gut-checked in years. I looked at Hvarlgen. I looked at Dr. Kim. I looked at the million stars beyond and figured what the hell.

"Okay," I said. "I guess I can stick my hand in a fishbowl for science."

Dr. Kim laughed again and Hvarlgen shot him an angry look. "There's one thing you should know—" she began.

Dr. Kim finished for her: "The Shadow doesn't want to

shake hands with you, Major Bewley. It wants to crawl up your
ass and look around. Like it crawled up mine.''

II

I showed up at Grand Central the next morning wearing the
bright orange tunic with the SETI patch, just to prove to
Hvarlgen I was on her team. We had coffee. "Scared?"

"Wouldn't you be scared?" I said. "For one thing, this
Shadow is a cancer detector. Then, the business with Mersault . . ."

"It's unlikely that our people in Reykjavik missed anything. And indications are that Mersault may have been independently suicidal. Zippe-Buisson hires some weirdos. But
you're right, Major, one never knows.''

I followed her down the forty-meter tube to East. We were
initiating the first contact session in the infirmary, so that Dr.
Kim could participate, or at least observe. Hvarlgen was literally rearing to go: the chair was tilted back so far that she
rode it almost prone.

Three of the five periphery domes have magnolias—
those reptilian trees love the Moon—but it is East's that is the
most lush, its leaves picking up the lunar palette from the
regolith of the crater floor and processing it into a new, com-
plex gray unseen before.

Dr. Kim's bed was under the tree. He was awake, waiting
for us. He caressed the spraypipe in his fingers like a good-
luck charm. "Good morning, colleagues," he said.

Hvarlgen rolled to his bedside and kissed his withered
cheek.

Two lunies rolled in a wheeled table; on it was the Shadow
in its bowl. Another lunie carried the film camera on her
shoulder. Another carried a bright yellow plastic chair. It was
for me.

The big moment had arrived. Hvarlgen and I approached the table together. When she picked up the bowl, I noticed that the Shadow pulled away from her hands toward the center. It moved in a rippling motion that both repelled and attracted my eyes.

She put the bowl on the floor in front of the chair. "Let's begin," she said, clicking on the video recorder she carried on her lap. The film camera whirred as I slipped my pants off, over my shoes, and stood there naked under my tunic. It was 9:46 HT (Houston/Houbolt time) on the wall.

I felt frightened. I felt embarrassed. Worse, I felt ridiculous, especially with the young lunies—girls and boys—sitting on the empty bed, watching.

"Oh, Major, please quit worrying!" Hvarlgen said. "Women are used to being prodded and poked between their legs. Men can put up with it once in a while. Sit down!"

I sat down; the yellow plastic was cold on my butt. Hvarlgen nudged my knees apart wordlessly and pushed the bowl between my feet, then rolled backward to the head of Dr. Kim's bed, under the magnolia. I clutched pencil in one hand and paper in the other. Hvarlgen and Dr. Kim had explained what would happen, but it was still a shock. The Shadow moved—*twisted*—out of the bowl, flowed up between my legs, and disappeared up my ass.

I watched it, fascinated. I felt no fear or dread. There was no "feeling" as such; it really *was* like a shadow. I kept myself covered by the tunic, out of modesty; but I knew as soon as the Shadow was inside me, because—

There was someone else in the room. He was standing across the room, not far from the foot of Dr. Kim's bed. He was not quite solid, and not quite full-sized, and he was flickering like a bad light bulb; but I knew immediately "who" it was.

It was me.

I moved my arm slightly, to see if he would move his, like

a mirror image, but he didn't. He flickered and with each flicker got either bigger, or closer, or both. There was no frame of reference; no way to judge his size. It was somehow very clear that he or it was not *in* the room with us; not occupying the same space. It raised the hair on the back of my head, and judging from the palpable silence in the room, everyone else's as well.

We were seeing a ghost.

It was Hvarlgen who finally spoke. "Who are you?"

There was no answer.

I tried moving my arm again but the Shadow (for already, that was how I thought of the image) answered none of my movements. Somehow that made it better; it was as if I were watching a film of myself and not a reflection. But it was an old film; I looked younger. And when I looked to one side a little, the image disappeared.

"Who are you?" said Hvarlgen again; it was more a statement than a question. "He," "it,"—the Shadow—started flickering, faster and faster, and I suddenly felt sick at my stomach.

I bent over, almost retching; I covered my mouth and then tried to aim toward the bowl at the foot of the chair. But it didn't matter—nothing came out, even though I saw the Shadow was pooled back in its bowl.

I shook my hands and examined them; they were clean.

The ghost was gone.

The session was over. Hvarlgen was staring at me. I looked at my watch; it was 9:54. The whole thing had lasted six minutes.

The pad and pencil lay on the floor where I had dropped them. The pad was blank.

"Well, now, that was interesting," said Dr. Kim, taking a long shot of PeaceAble.

* * *

Hvarlgen sent the lunies out, and had coffee sent in, and we discussed the session over a light lunch. Very light; I was on the high-protein, low-fiber "astronaut's diet" of moonjirky. Plus, I was still feeling a little queasy.

We all agreed that the image was me, or an approximation of me. "But younger," said Dr. Kim.

"So what is it trying to say?" asked Hvarlgen. Neither Dr. Kim nor I answered; it seemed useless to speculate. She clicked on her video recorder. Instead of a holovid image, what came up was a ball of bright static. She fast-forwarded but nothing changed.

"Damn! Just as I had suspected," she said. "If we are to get any image at all, it will be on film. But film has to be processed chemically, which means it has to go all the way back to Earth before we'll even know if it works. In the meantime—"

"In the meantime," Dr. Kim said, "Why don't we try it again?"

Hvarlgen got on her chair-phone and soon the lunies arrived with the Shadow in its bowl, the film camera, and the rest of the crew, who had presumably heard about the morning session. It was 1:35 (HT). Surprisingly, it was just as humiliating for me the second time. But science is science; I took off my pants. The film camera wheezed and whirred on a lunie's shoulder. I held the pad and pencil in one hand, ready. Hvarlgen rolled back to Dr. Kim's bed. I sat on the cold plastic chair and spread my legs. I forgot my embarrassment as the Shadow *twisted* out of its bowl and up—and disappeared—

And there he was again. The Shadow. Again, the figure started small and flickered itself bigger and bigger, until it was about half the size of someone standing in the room with us; though we all knew somehow that it wasn't. That it was far away.

This time he was talking, though there was no sound. He stopped talking, then started again. He was wearing blue coveralls like I used to wear in the Service, not the orange tunic. I couldn't see his feet no matter how hard I looked for them; it was as if my eyes glanced off. I wear a Service ring but I couldn't see it; the Shadow's hands were blurred. I wanted to ask him who he was, but I felt it was not my place. We had agreed earlier that no one but Hvarlgen was to speak.

"Who are you?" she asked.

The voice, when it came, surprised us all: "Not a who."

Everyone in the room turned to look at me, even though it was not my voice. I would have turned, myself, had I not been the point toward which everyone was looking.

"Then what are you?"

"A communications protocol." The sound of the voice was completely out of synch with the image's mouth. Also, the sound did not seem to come from anywhere; I heard it directly with my mind, not my ears.

"From where?" asked Hvarlgen.

"A two-device."

The lunies sitting in a row on the bed were absolutely still. No one in the room was breathing; including me.

"What is a two-device?" asked Hvarlgen.

This time the lips were almost in synch with the words; "One and"—the Shadow inclined toward us in a curious, almost courtly gesture—"the Other."

The sound seemed to originate inside my head, like a memory of a voice. Like a memory, it seemed perfectly clear but characterless. I wondered if it were my voice, as the image was "my" image, but I couldn't tell.

"What Other?" Hvarlgen asked.

"Only one Other."

"What do you want?"

As if in answer, the image began to flicker again, and I was suddenly sick to my stomach. The next thing I knew I was looking down into the bowl, at the original dark nonsubstance we had called the Shadow. Though still dark it seemed clearer, and cold, and deep. I was suddenly conscious of the cold stars blazing through the dome overhead; the fierce vacuum all around; the cold plastic chair on my butt.

"Major?"

Hvarlgen's hand was on my wrist. I looked up—to applause from the bed where the lunies were sitting, like bright yellow birds, all in a row.

"Nobody leaves!" said Hvarlgen. She went around the room. All agreed on what the Shadow had said. All agreed that it had been inside their heads, more like the memory of a voice, or an imaginary voice, than a sound. All agreed that it had not been my voice.

"Now everybody leave," she said. "Dr. Kim and I need to have a talk."

"Including me?" I asked.

"You can stay. And he can stay." She pointed toward the bowl, which the lunies were placing back on its table. They left it by the door.

"Damn!" said Hvarlgen. Irrationally, she shook the recorder but there was no record of the Shadow's words, any more than of its image. "The problem is, we have no hard evidence of any communication at all. And yet we all know it happened."

Dr. Kim took a snort of PeaceAble and smiled somewhat inscrutably. "Unless we think the Major here was hypnotizing us."

"Which we don't," said Hvarlgen. It was late afternoon. We were having still more coffee under the magnolia. "But what I don't understand," she said, "is how can it make us hear without making a print, a track in the air."

"Clearly, it works directly on the hearing centers in the brain," Dr. Kim said.

"Without a physical event?" said Hvarlgen. "Without a material connection? That's telepathy!"

"It's all physical," said Dr. Kim. "Or none of it. Is that thing material? Maybe it accesses our brains visually. We were all looking at it when we heard it talk. The brain is stuff just as much as air is stuff. Light is stuff. Consciousness is stuff."

"So why the physical contact at all?" I asked. "The Shadow's not really here; I can't feel it, we can't touch it or even photograph it. Why does it have to enter my body at all? If it does, why can't it just sort of slip in through the skin, or the eyes, instead of . . . the way it does."

"Maybe it's scanning you," Hvarlgen said. "For the image."

"And maybe it can only scan certain types," said Dr. Kim. "Or maybe it's restricted. Just as we might be forbidden to trade with Stone Age tribesmen, they—whoever or whatever they are—might have a prohibition against certain stages or kinds of life."

"You mean the 'New Growth' business?" I asked.

"Right. Maybe old folks seem less vulnerable to them. Maybe the contact is destructive to growing tissue. Or even fatal. Look at what happened to Mersault. But I'm just guessing! And my guess is that you have not quite finished menopause, Sunda, right?"

She smiled. Just as her scowls were smiles, her smiles were grimaces. "Not quite."

"See? And in my case, perhaps the flourishing cancer with its exorbitant greed for life was mistaken for youth. Anyway . . . perhaps we are dealing with prohibitions. Formalities. Perhaps even the innovative mode of contact is a formality, like a handshake. What could be more logical?" Dr. Kim took another snort of PeaceAble, filling the infirmary with a sweet heavy smell.

"It's hard to think of it as a handshake," I said.

"Why? The anus, the asshole in vulgar parlance, is sort

of a joke, but in our secret heart of hearts, for all of us, it's the seat—so to speak—of the physical being. It may be perceived by this Other as the seat of consciousness as well. We're much more conscious of it than, say, the heart. Certainly more conscious of it physically than the brain. It alerts us to danger by tightening up. It even speaks from time to time . . ."

"Okay, okay," said Hvarlgen. "We get the point. Let's get back to work. Shall we go again?"

"Without the lunies?" Dr. Kim asked.

"Why not?"

"Because without a video or sound image, they are our only corroboration that there is any communication going on here. I know it's your project, Sunda, but if I were you I would move more deliberately."

"You're right. It's almost five o'clock. Let's wait and go after supper."

I had supper alone. Hvarlgen was on the phone, arguing with somebody named Sidrath. A poster on the wall over her head said D=96. Hvarlgen sounded pleading, then sarcastic, then pleading again; I felt like an eavesdropper, so I left without coffee and walked to East alone.

Dr. Kim was asleep. The Shadow lay in its bowl. It was fascinating to look at it. It lay still but seemed, somehow, to be moving at great speed. It was dark but I could sense light behind it, like the stars through thin clouds. I was tempted to touch it; I reached out one finger . . .

"That you, Major?" Dr. Kim sat up. "Where's Sunda?"

"She's on the phone with somebody named Sidrath. She's been arguing with him for almost an hour."

"He's the head of the Q team. He's probably setting up in High Orbital, for when the Shadow arrives. They are assembling all sorts of fancy equipment. They think we're dealing with some sort of antimatter here, which is why they can't take it down to the surface."

"What do you think it is?" I asked. I pulled the plastic chair over and sat with him, looking up at the stars through the clear dome and the dark magnolia leaves.

"I think it's unusual, surprising," Dr. Kim said. "That's all I require of life these days. I no longer try to understand or comprehend things. Dying is funny. You realize for the first time you are not going to finish Dante. You give up on it." He took a shot of PeaceAble. "Did you ever wonder why the Shadow looks younger than you?"

"You have a theory?"

"Robert Louis Stevenson had a theory," he said. "He once said that our chronological age is but a scout, sent out in advance of the 'army' of who we feel we are—which always lags several years behind. In your mind, Major, you are still a young man; at most, in your fifties. That's the image the Shadow gets from you, and therefore the image he gives us."

I heard his pipe hiss again.

"I'd offer you a shot, but—"

"It's okay," I said. "I know, I'm a test bunny."

"You guys ready?" It was Hvarlgen, rolling through the doorway. It was time to go again.

The plastic chair had been left in place. Two lunies wheeled the bowl in on its table. The rest of the lunies drifted in, sitting on the bed and clustering by the doorway. At 7:34 P.M. Hvarlgen cleared her throat and looked at me impatiently. I pulled off my pants; I sat down in the chair and spread my withered old shanks—

This time, without ascending between my legs, the Shadow *twisted* in its bowl and disappeared; the movement was somehow sickening, and I gagged—

And there it was; he was. Was it my imagination, or was my

image, the Shadow, clearer and more positive than it had been? It seemed to have a kind of glow. He smiled.

Hvarlgen wasn't waiting around this time. "Where are you from?" she asked.

"Not from a where. The protocol is a where."

"What do you want?"

"Adjusting the protocol," said the voice. It was so clear now that I thought it must be a sound. But I watched the aural indicator lights on Hvarlgen's video recorder, and there was nothing. As before, the voice was only inside our heads.

"Where are the Others?" asked Hvarlgen again.

"Only the protocol is where," said the Shadow. "A where-when point." It seemed to enjoy answering her questions. It had stopped flickering and its speech was now in synch with its lip movements. Its movements looked familiar; gentle; graceful. I felt a certain proprietary affection for it, knowing it was an idealized verison of myself.

"What do they want?" Hvarlgen asked.

"To communicate."

"Through you?"

"The communication will end the protocol. The connection is one-time only." The Shadow looked directly toward us, but not at us. It seemed always to be looking at something we could not see. It was silent, as if waiting for the next question.

When nobody said anything, the image began to fade, ghostlike once again—

And the Shadow *twisted* into being in the bowl at my feet. It seemed even clearer than before. I could see stars behind it. It was like seeing the stars reflected in a pool, only I had the distinct (and uneasy) feeling I was looking up. I even checked the back of my neck with my hand.

That was it for the first day. We'd had three sessions, and Hvarlgen thought that was enough. Dr. Kim asked us to join him for 4-D Monopoly. He had a passion for the game with its steep mortgage ramps and time-release dice. While we played, the lunies watched movies in Grand Central. We could hear gunshots and bluegrass music in the distance, all the way down the tube.

We began the next morning with a leisurely breakfast. I was still on moonjirky, but I had no appetite anyway. The poster over the coffee machine said D=77.

"How many hours until sunrise?" I asked.

"I'm not sure; somewhat less than seventy-seven," Hvarlgen answered. But it wasn't a problem. Even though Houbolt was no longer environmentalized for the lunar day, it would be comfortable for all but the six days of the lunar "noon"— and would probably have been manageable even then, in an emergency. According to Hvarlgen's plan, Here's Johnny was to arrive and take us off soon after sunrise.

Hvarlgen went down the tube toward the infirmary first, followed by me, followed by the lunies. East smelled like PeaceAble, indicating that Dr. Kim had been up for a while. He suggested that he be allowed to ask one question, and Hvarlgen agreed.

Me, I was just the hired asshole. I took off my pants and the bowl was slid between my feet. Ignoring me (or seeming to) the Shadow in the bowl *twisted* itself into nothingness. This time I didn't feel sick. In fact, it was beautiful, slick and fast, like a whale diving.

"Is there a message for us?"

It was Hvarlgen's question. I looked up from the empty bowl and saw the Shadow standing across the room—or across the Universe.

"A communication."

"Are you conscious."

"The protocol is conscious and I am the protocol."

"Who is communicating with us?"

"The Other. Not a who."

"Is it conscious?"

The Shadow said, "You are conscious. The protocol is conscious. The Other is not a wherewhen string."

There was a long silence. "Dr. Kim—" Hvarlgen said. "You had a question?"

"Are you a Feynman device?" Dr. Kim asked.

"The protocol is a two-device."

"What is the distance?" Dr. Kim asked.

"Not a distance. A wherewhen loop."

"Where does the energy come from?"

As if in answer, the Shadow began to flicker and fade, and I leaned over the bowl (even though I no longer believed that the Shadow was inside of me). And like a dark whale surfacing, the Shadow *twisted* into its bowl. I wondered how such a tiny space could contain a space so huge.

While the lunies cleared the room, and Hvarlgen hurried down to Grand Central to make a phone call, I pulled my chair over to the bed and sat with Dr. Kim.

"I see it's no longer accessing our universe through your butt," he said. "Maybe it has what it needs."

"Hope so," I said. "Meanwhile—what's a Feynman device?"

"Have you ever heard of the EPR paradox?"

"Something to do with Richard Feynman?"

"Indirectly," Dr. Kim said. "The EPR paradox had been proposed by Einstein and two colleagues in an unsuccessful effort to disprove quantum physics. Two linked particles are separated. The 'spin' or orientation of each is indeterminate (in true quantum fashion) until one is determined, up or down. Then the other is the opposite. Instantaneously."

"Even if it's a million light-years away," Hvarlgen said, from the doorway. She rolled into the room, shutting the door behind her. "I told Sidrath about your question. He liked it."

"It was never answered." Dr. Kim shrugged.

"In other words, we're talking about faster-than-light communication," I said.

"Right," said Dr. Kim. "Theoretically, a paradox. It was Feynman who proved that the paradox wasn't a paradox at all. That it was true. And that FTL communication was, at least in theory, possible."

"So that's what our little *isn't* is," I said. "A muon bridge."

"An ansible," said Hvarlgen. "A device for faster-than-light communication. As I said, Sidrath agrees. What we have here seems to be some version of a Feynman device. Everything that happens to it here happens simultaneously, perhaps as a mirror image, at the other 'end.' "

"Across the galaxy," I said.

"Oh, much farther away than that, I think," said Dr. Kim, taking another shot of PeaceAble. "We may be dealing with realms of space and time that don't even intersect our own. I think, for sure, that we are dealing with forms of life that aren't biological."

At noon I asked for a sandwich. "I'm going to quit worrying about my lower intestine," I said. "The Shadow has quit worrying about it."

"We're not sure," said Hvarlgen. "Stay on moonjirky just one more meal. This afternoon, we'll try the session with your pants on and see what happens."

The Shadow didn't seem to notice. (I was a little hurt.) It *twisted* in its bowl, diving into—another form (my own) which appeared across the room as before.

"When is this communication going to occur?" asked Hvarlgen.

"Soon." The way the Shadow said the word, it sounded almost like a place—like "Moon."

"What is soon?"

"When the protocol is adjusted."

There was a long silence.

"What kind of communication will it be?" asked Dr. Kim. "Will we hear it?"

"No."

"See it?"

"No."

"Why is it that you never speak unless we ask a question?" asked Hvarlgen.

"Because you are half of the protocol," said the Shadow.

"I thought so," said Hvarlgen. "We've been talking to ourselves!"

The Shadow started to flicker. I resisted the urge to bend over the bowl, and watched him fade away.

I was tired. I went back to my wedgie to sleep, and I dreamed, for the first time in years, of flying. When I got up, Hvarlgen was still in East with Dr. Kim. They were on a conference call with High Orbital and Queens; they were somewhere between calling the Shadow an ET and an AD (alien device).

I left it to them. I ate alone (another sandwich) and then watched the first half of *Bonnie and Clyde* with the lunies. They had a kind of cult thing about Michael J. Pollard. Now I understood why every time something went wrong around the station, one of them was bound to say "dirt."

Hvarlgen rolled into Grand Central at almost nine P.M. "We're going to skip the evening session tonight," she said. "Sidrath and the Q Team don't want to miss this promised communication. They are afraid we'll speed things up, or wear the Shadow out, like an eraser."

"But you are in charge." I was surprised to find myself disappointed.

"True. But that's only a formality. In fact, Sidrath is already on his way here with Here's Johnny, in case this communication occurs before they can get the Shadow back to High Orbital. We made a deal; I agreed to limit the sessions to one a day."

"One a day!"

"I think we've learned all we're going to learn here. All it does is answer the same questions, in a sort of a loop. We'll go in the morning, Major, as usual. Meanwhile, want to play Monopoly?"

That night I dreamed again that I was flying. The flying itself was flying, so fast that I had to chase it in order not to disappear. The next morning, after breakfast (sausage and eggs) I followed the lunies down the tube to East, where Hvarlgen and Dr. Kim were waiting.

Hvarlgen insisted that I sit in my usual spot. Like a priestess at a ritual, she placed the bowl at my feet, then rolled back to Dr. Kim's bedside. The Shadow *twisted* in the bowl and disappeared; the Shadow appeared again in his blue coveralls, bluer than I remembered.

"Who are the Others?" asked Hvarlgen.

"They are not a they. They are an Other."

(Maybe Hvarlgen was right to limit the sessions, I thought. It was beginning to sound like word games.)

"Another what?" Hvarlgen asked. "Another civilization?"

I heard a sound like a growl. It was Dr. Kim, snoring; he had fallen asleep propped on one elbow, with his spraypipe in his hand.

"Not a civilization. They are not—plural like yourself. Not biological."

"Not material?" asked Hvarlgen.

"Not a wherewhen string," the Shadow said.

"Is the communication ready? Can it take place now?"

"Soon. The protocol is completed. When the communication takes place the protocol will be gone."

I wondered what that meant. We were, supposedly, part of the protocol. I was about to raise my hand to ask permission to ask a question—but the Shadow was already flickering, already *twisting* back into being in its bowl.

Being careful not to awaken Dr. Kim, Hvarlgen shooed everyone out of the infirmary and we went to Grand Central for a late breakfast. I didn't tell her I had already eaten. I had soup and crackers.

The poster said D=55. I had less than two days left on the Moon.

"Isn't Dr. Kim using a lot of that stuff?" I asked.

"He's in a lot of pain," Hvarlgen said. "I just hope he lasts until this communication, whatever it is. At the same time—"

"It's for you," said one of the lunies. "It's the *Diana.* They just completed TLI and they're on their way."

I went back to my wedgie for a nap, and dreamed again of flying. I hadn't dreamed so much since Katie died. I didn't have wings, or even a body—I was the flight itself. The movement was my substance in a way that I understood perfectly, except that the understanding evaporated as soon as I sat up.

The wedgie was cold. I had never felt so alone.

I got dressed and went to Grand Central and found two lunies watching *Bonnie and Clyde,* and Hvarlgen curled up with Sidrath on the phone. I had forgotten how lonely the farside could be. It is the only place in the Universe from which you never see the Earth. Outside was nothing but stars and stones and dust.

I went to the infirmary. Dr. Kim was awake. "Where's Sunda?" he asked.

"On the phone with Sidrath and Here's Johnny. They

made Trans Lunar Injection right after lunch. You were asleep.''

"So be it," said Dr. Kim. "Did you say hello to our friend?"

I saw the Shadow in the corner, under the magnolia, near the foot of the bed. I felt a shiver. It was the first time he had ever appeared without our—summoning him. The bowl on the table was empty.

"Hello, I guess," I said. "Have you talked to him?"

"He's not talking."

"Shouldn't I get Hvarlgen?"

"It doesn't matter," said Dr. Kim. "It doesn't mean anything. I think he just likes to exist, you know?"

"I'm here anyway," Hvarlgen said, from the door. "What's going on?"

"I think he just likes to exist," said Dr. Kim, again. "Did you ever get the feeling when you were running a program, that it enjoyed running? Existing? It's all in the connections, the dance of the particles. I think our friend the Shadow senses that he won't exist very long, and—"

Even as he spoke the Shadow began to fade. At the same time the dark substance *twisted* into being in the bowl. I looked down into it. It was dark yet clear yet infinitely deep, like infinity itself. I could see stars beyond stars in it.

Hvarlgen seemed relieved that the Shadow was gone. "I'll be glad when the *Diana* gets here," she said. "I don't know which way to turn; which way to proceed."

I sat on the foot of the bed. Dr. Kim took another shot of PeaceAble and passed the pipe to me.

"Dr. Kim!"

"Relax. He's no longer the test bunny, Sunda," he said. "His bowel is no longer the pathway between the stars."

"Still. You know that's only for people who are terminal," Hvarlgen said.

"We're all terminal, Sunda. We just get off at different stops."

That night after supper, we played Monopoly. The Shadow appeared again, and again he had nothing to say. "He doesn't speak unless we call him up," said Hvalgren.

"Maybe the ceremony, the chair, the lunies watching, are part of the protocol," said Dr. Kim. "Like the questions."

"What about the Others? Do you think we'll see them?" I asked.

"My guess is that there's no them to see," said Dr. Kim.

"What do you mean?"

"Imagine a being larger than star systems, that manipulates on the subatomic level, where the Newtonian universe is an illogical dream that cannot be conceptualized. A being that reproduces itself as waves, in order to exist, that is one and yet many. A being that is not a wherewhen string—as the Shadow calls it—but a series of one-time events . . ."

"Dr. Kim," said Hvarlgen. She played a conservative but deadly game.

"Yes, my dear?"

"Pay attention. You just landed on my city. Cash or credit?"

"Credit," he said.

That night I dreamed. I slept late, and woke up exhausted. I found Hvarlgen in Grand Central, on the phone with Sidrath, as usual lately. A lunie was changing the poster from D=29 to D=11.

"Here's Johnny and Sidrath just crossed Wolf Creek Pass," Hvarlgen said, hanging up.

"They're balling the jack," I said.

"They're using boosters," she said. "We all have the feeling we're running out of time."

This was to be, by agreement, our last contact session. All

the lunies were there; in their yellow tunics they were as alike as bees. I sat in the usual spot, which seemed to be part of the protocol. I enjoyed the position of prominence—especially since I got to keep my pants on.

Hvarlgen placed the bowl on the floor and the dark whale dove—*twisted* beautifully out of its bowl—and the Shadow appeared in the image of a man.

Hvarlgen looked at me. "Do you have a question?"

"What happens after the communication?" I asked.

"I cease to be."

"Will we cease to be?"

"You are a wherewhen string."

"What are you?" asked Dr. Kim.

"Not a what. A wherewhen point."

"When does the communication take place?" asked Hvarlgen.

"Soon." He was repeating himself. We were repeating ourselves. Was it my imagination, or did the Shadow seem weary?

Hvarlgen, nothing if not democratic, turned her chair toward the lunies gathered in the doorway and on the bed. "Do any of you have any questions?"

There were none.

There was a long silence and the Shadow began to fade. I felt like I was seeing him for the last time, and I felt a sense of loss. It was my image that was fading away . . .

"Wait!" I wanted to say. "Speak!" But I said nothing. Soon the Shadow was back in its bowl.

"I have to get some sleep," said Dr. Kim, taking a shot of PeaceAble.

"Come on, Major," said Hvarlgen. We left, taking the lunies with us.

I made my own lunch, then watched a little bit of *Bonnie and Clyde* with the lunies. Like them, I was tired of the Moon. I was tired of the Shadow. Tired of waiting for either the communication, or the arrival of the *Diana*—both events over which we had no control.

I took a walk around the little-used periphery tunnel that led from South to North via West. It was cold and smelly. Ahead of me I saw a new, unfamiliar light. I hurried to West, suspecting what it was. Forty kilometers away, the high ragged rim of 17,000-foot peaks at the western edge of Korolev was touched with sunlight.

Dawn was still hours away, but it had already struck the tops of the nameless mountains, which were as bright in the sky as a new moon, the Moon's moon, casting temporary backward shadows across the crater floor. Everything seemed reversed.

I stood for what seemed like hours, watching. The dawn was as slow as an hour hand, and I grew cold.

From West I cut straight through to East, even though I hadn't been invited. Hvarlgen was still on the phone, and I felt like talking with somebody. Maybe Dr. Kim would be awake.

The infirmary smelled like a Tennessee hayfield, bringing back sudden memories of childhood and summer. The Shadow was standing in the shadows under the magnolia, looking—worn out. Like an old person, I thought, he was fading away.

Dr. Kim was staring straight up at the stars. His spraypipe had fallen from his fingers, onto the floor. He was dead.

Dr. Kim had left four numbers in an envelope marked "Sunda," with instructions that they were to be called as soon as he died, even though they lived in four different time zones, scattered around the Earth. They were his children. Most of them were awakened from sleep, but they weren't surprised; Dr. Kim had already said his good-byes.

As I watched Hvarlgen making the calls, for the first time

in years I felt lonesome for the family I had never had. I wandered from Grand Central back down to East. Dr. Kim's body had been put in the airlock to decompress slowly, and the room was empty except for the Shadow, which stood silently at the foot of the bed, like a mourner. I lay down on Dr. Kim's bed and looked up through the magnolia, trying to imagine what his eyes had last seen. The dawn light still hadn't touched the dome, and the galaxies hung in the sky like sparks from a burning city.

Hvarlgen came to get me, and we held a brief service in Grand Central. Dr. Kim's body was still in the airlock, but the *Portable Dante* and the spraypipe on the table represented him. The lunies attended in shifts, since they were preparing the station for incoming. Hvarlgen read something in Old Norse, then something in Korean, then a bit from the King James Bible about the Valley of the Shadow of Death.

Then we suited up.

Burial on the moon is illegal according to at least three overlapping legal systems, but Hvarlgen didn't seem to mind. Here's Johnny and Sidrath had made LOI (lunar orbit insertion) and told her to finish before they landed, so they wouldn't be compromised by her bending of the rules.

The dawn was already halfway down the mountains by the time we locked out. Soon the raw sunlight would be racing, or at least loping, across the crater floor. The station would be livable for several more weeks, at least until mid-morning; but as we didn't have proper suits for a sunlight EVA, even a dawn EVA, we would have to hurry.

It was my first EVA in years. One of the lunies and I were the pallbearers (only two are needed on the Moon), while Hvarlgen followed in her fat-tired EVA chair. Even though we had decompressed Dr. Kim's body as slowly as possible, he had still swelled in the vacuum. His face was filled out and he looked almost young.

We carried him a hundred meters across the crater floor, to a fairly flat stone (flat stones are rare on the Moon), following the instructions we had found in the envelope. Dr. Kim had picked out his grave site from his bed in East.

We laid him faceup on the table-shaped rock, the way they used to lay Indians so the vultures could swoop down to eat their hearts. Only here was a sky too deep for vultures. Hvarlgen read a few more words, and we started back. The crater floor was half lit by the mountains to the west. The sunlight had painted them from peak to foot; so that we cast long shadows—the "wrong" way. In a few weeks, as noon approached, with its 250-degree temperatures, it would cook Dr. Kim into bone and ash and vapor; until then he would lie in state letting the stars which he had studied for over half a century study him.

When we locked back in, the chimes for incoming were ringing. Here's Johnny and Sidrath had timed it all perfectly. Hvarlgen rolled off on two wheels to meet them; I was in no hurry. By the time I got to Grand Central, it was empty—everyone was greeting the *Diana* at South. I walked back down the tube to East. The bowl was gone; it had been returned to Other for Sidrath's arrival. But the Shadow didn't seem to notice. He was standing at the foot of the bed, no longer faded. For the first time he seemed to be looking directly at me. I didn't know whether to say hello or good-bye. The Shadow seemed to be receding faster and faster, and me with him. I lost my balance and fell to one knee just as I "felt" what came to be known, much later, around the world, as the Brush.

III

Four days short of eleven months later, there was a knock at the door of my Road Lord.

"Major Bewley?"

"Call me Colonel," I said.

It was Here's Johnny. He was wearing a faux leather suit that somehow told me he had gone ahead and taken retirement. I wasn't surprised. He was on his way to Los Angeles to live with his sister. "Aren't you going to ask me in?"

"Better than that," I said. "You're spending the night."

It was almost as if we were friends, and at my age almost is as good as the real thing, almost. I cleared a place on the couch (my picture—the same one—was in an eighteen-inch stack of magazines) and he sat down. Here's Johnny had gained twenty pounds, which often happens to lunies when they lock in for good. I put on a fresh pot of coffee. It must have been the smell of the coffee that made us both think of Hvarlgen.

"She's in Reykjavik," Here's Johnny said. "When the film didn't show anything, that was it for her. The last straw. She left the rest of it up to Sidrath and the Commission."

"The rest of what?" There was no more Shadow; both the image and the substance in the bowl had disappeared with the Brush. As promised. "What did they have left to do?"

"All the surveys, interviews, population samples. All the stuff you've read about the Brush; it all came from Sidrath and the Commission. But without Hvarlgen's help. Or yours, I happened to notice."

"I'd had enough, myself," I said. "I felt like we were all getting a little crazy. That whole week was like a dream. Plus, there seemed, at the time, to be nothing to say. What I had experienced was, literally, as you know—as we all know now—indescribable. Since my contract was up, I sort of cut and ran because I didn't want to be roped into some elaborate effort to figure it all out."

"And you thought you were the only one."

"Well, didn't we all? At first, anyway."

It had taken several months of research to determine, positively, that every man, woman, and child on and off the planet (plus, it was now thought, a high percentage of dogs) had experienced the Brush at the same instant. We were no more able to describe it than the dogs were. It was intensely sensual but in no way physical, brilliantly colorful but not visible, musical but not quite a sound—an entirely new sensation, indescribable and unforgettable at the same time. The best description I heard was from an Indian filmmaker, who said it was as if someone had painted his soul with light. That's poetic license, of course. It had happened in less than an instant, but it was days before anyone spoke of it, and weeks before the SETI Commission realized it was the communication we had been promised.

By then it was only a memory. And lucky it was that we all had felt it: otherwise some of us would be spending the next few centuries trying to describe it to those who hadn't. A new religion, maybe. As it was, most people on the planet were going about their business as if it had never happened, while a few were still trying to figure out what the Brush meant to the children. And the dogs.

"It was a bitter disappointment to Hvarlgen," said Here's Johnny. It was late; we were sitting outside, having a whisky, waiting to catch the sunset.

"I know," I said. "To her, it was an insult. She called it the Brush-off. I can understand her point of view. We are finally contacted by another, maybe the only other life-form in the Universe, but it has nothing to say. No more than a hello, how are you. A wave from a passing ship, she called it."

"Maybe because it happened to everybody," Here's Johnny said.

"I can understand that too," I said. "We all thought it was going to be just for us."

One of my unofficial grandsons rode up on a bicycle carrying a turtle. I gave him a dollar for it, and put it into a polyboard box under the trailer with two other turtles. "I pay the kids for the ones they pick up off the road," I said. "Then after sundown I let them go, away from the high-way."

"Me, I'm more optimistic," Here's Johnny said. "Maybe the children who experienced the Brush will grow up differ-ent. Maybe smarter or less violent."

"Or maybe the dogs," I said.

"What do you think?" he asked. "You were, after all, the first contact."

"I was just the pattern for the protocol," I said. "I got the same communication as everyone else, no more and no less. I'm convinced of that. I was just used to, you know, set up the tuning."

"You weren't disappointed?"

"I was disappointed that Dr. Kim didn't get to experience it. But who knows, maybe he did. As for me, I'm an old man. I don't expect things to mean anything. I just sort of enjoy them. Look there."

Off to the west, a range of barren peaks was hurling it-self between Slab City and the nearest star, painting our trailers with new darkness. The clash of photons set up a barrage of colors in the sky overhead. We watched the sun set in silence; then I got one end of the box and Here's Johnny got the other, and we dragged it out to a pile of boulders at the edge of the desert and deposited the turtles onto the still-warm sand.

"You do this every night?"

WESTFIELD MEMORIAL LIBRARY
WESTFIELD, NEW JERSEY

"Why not?" I said. "Maybe it's turtles all the way down."

But Here's Johnny didn't get the joke. Which goes to show, as Chuck Berry once said, you never can tell.

✧ Afterword ✧

I came to the short story both early and late. In 1964, after the birth of my eldest son, Nathaniel, I wrote a story about a kid born with wings. "George" won honorable mention in a *Story* magazine contest and made me fifty dollars. After a couple of false starts, though, I gave up the form entirely.

Then in 1988, after two or three published novels, I wrote "Over Flat Mountain." It was to me not really a story but the fictional illustration of a conceit—the Appalachians being all rolled up into one mountain; a goof, if you will. By this time I was a published SF and fantasy author, and when Ellen Datlow asked me if I had ever tried short fiction, I sent her this one with the warning that it was "not an *OMNI* story."

She told me she would decide what was and what wasn't an *OMNI* story, thank you very much. And bought it. There's nothing like an eighteen hundred dollar sale to revive an interest in short fiction.

The rest of the stories in this book were written between 1988 and 1993.

"The Two Janets" is, like "Over Flat Mountain," the fictional illustration of a conceit that turned into a short story in spite of itself. Owensboro is my hometown.

"They're Made Out of Meat" has its inspiration in Allen

Ginsberg's reply to an interviewer who kept prattling on about their souls communing. "We're just meat talking to meat," the poet corrected him.

"The Coon Suit" came to me in a vivid daydream while driving through Oldham County, Kentucky, twenty-five years ago, and never went away. I find most horror unintentionally funny; this story, which I thought funny, wound up in a horror anthology.

"Canción" is my attempt at capturing the unaccountable sadness I felt watching street singers in Madrid one Christmas Eve. It is (also unaccountably, perhaps) one of my favorites.

"Carl's Lawn & Garden" is my hymn to the Garden State.

I thought of "Partial People" while driving over a box.

"Are There Any Questions?" is what you might call a throwaway.

I heard of a circular polluted area in Chicago called "the toxic doughnut" while I was reading Shirley Jackson's biography; the two influences converged in a story.

"By Permit Only" is still another environmental short short. It was written over Christmas, which probably accounts for its overheated sentimentality.

It's no coincidence that so many of my environmental stories are short shorts. Save a tree! Even beyond the paper, think how much imaginative timber is wasted on plot, background, character, action, and atmosphere. Better to dispense with them all! Like the lemon cream pie on *Saturday Night Live* ("No lemon, no cream, just pie") these short shorts are all story.

I associate the title story with my daughter, Kristen. We were driving on an interstate with beautiful timbered medians when I said, "I just got an idea for a story." "What is it?" she asked. "All I know for sure is the title," I said. I agree with Ted Mooney, author of the overlooked SF (well, sort of) masterpiece *Easy Travel to Other Planets,* that the title is (or can be) the target toward which you shoot the arrow of the story. In this case, a good title, "Bears Discover Fire," gave me my best shot ever, going on to win the Nebula, the Hugo, and the Sturgeon awards, being published in Japan, Germany, and Russia, and even making a college lit anthology.

"They're Made Out of Meat" was a Nebula nominee; "Press Ann" was a Hugo nominee; and "Next" won *The Chronic Rift* TV show's coveted Round Table award (a plastic device from a pizza box). Adapted for the stage, it was directed and produced at New York's West Bank Theater by Donna Gentry (along with "They're Made Out of Meat" and "Next").

"Two Guys from the Future" is my homage to Classical Time Travel Paradox Light Romantic Comedy.

Years ago in Louisville, right after "George," I wrote a story called "Mr. Zone" about a man to whom nothing ever happened. The story was never published but the character turned up (as Fox) in "England Underway."

Sheila Williams of *Asimov's* has been kind enough to describe my short fiction as warm and charming. "Necronauts" is my attempt to undermine that image. Its origin is in a project by artist Wayne Barlowe; he and I once tried to think of a story to illustrate a series of paintings and drawings he called his "Guide to Hell." The story reaffirms for me how much we all owe to Mary Wollstonecraft Shelley.

"The Message" is more of the old-time mad scientist stuff. Or maybe it's "The Coon Suit" minus the dogs. Or maybe it's "Bears" without fire (or hair).

Every once in a while I find myself compelled to revisit the old dominions of hard SF—my home country as a reader, if not a writer. *Voyage to the Red Planet* was that among my novels; in the stories it is "The Shadow Knows." Somehow, these visits home always seem to start with an old fellow returning to space. "Shadow," my longest story, and "Meat," one of my

WESTFIELD MEMORIAL LIBRARY
WESTFIELD, NEW JERSEY

shortest, both deal with the same venerable SF theme: first contact.

It was in the midst of writing these stories that I found "George" in the files of my literary ex-mother-in-law and read it, for the first time in years, with some trepidation. I was pleased to find that though I wouldn't write it again, I wouldn't change a word in it. Since it was noticed (if never published) by Whit Burnett of *Story* magazine, it is my connection with another era in literature; that also pleases me. And it is reassuring to me in another way.

I have sometimes felt that I was a gate-crasher in the world of SF, passing off odd mainstream works as fantasy and science fiction in order to get them published. "George" assures me that I have, in fact, for better or worse, been a fantasy writer from jump, engaged in a long process of coming home.

I hope you like these stories, the contrivances of my heart.